"You're going to go through with this, aren't you? On your own?"

Ellie shrugged and turned to walk on. "I don't know. Maybe. If I have to."

McCall caught her arm and held on to it when she would have jerked away. "I can't let you do that."

She gave a small, incensed gasp. "You mean you think you can stop me?"

"No," McCall said with a weary sigh. "I mean I'm going with you."

There were a lot of reactions he could have anticipated from her, and he got none of those. What she did instead was look at him for a long time without saying a word, a long enough time for him to start to have second—and third—thoughts.

Then she put her palms flat against his chest, stood up on her toes and kissed him. And he stopped thinking altogether.

Dear Reader,

Welcome to another month of hot—in every sense of the word—reading, books just made to match the weather. I hardly even have to mention Suzanne Brockmann and her TALL, DARK & DANGEROUS miniseries, because you all know that this author and these books are utterly irresistible. *Taylor's Temptation* features the latest of her to-die-for Navy SEALs, so rush right down to your bookstore and pick up your own copy, because this book is going to be flying off shelves everywhere.

To add to the excitement this month, we're introducing a new six-book continuity called FIRSTBORN SONS. Award-winning writer Paula Detmer Riggs kicks things off with *Born a Hero*. Learn how these six heroes share a legacy of protecting the weak and standing up for what's right—and watch as all six find women who belong in their arms and their lives.

Don't miss the rest of our wonderful books, either: *The Seduction of Goody Two-Shoes,* by award-winning Kathleen Creighton; *Out of Nowhere,* by one of our launch authors, Beverly Bird; *Protector with a Past*, by Harper Allen; and *Twice Upon a Time,* by Jennifer Wagner.

Finally, check out the back pages for information on our "Silhouette Makes You A Star" contest. Someone's going to win—why not you?

Enjoy!

Leslie J. Wainger
Executive Senior Editor

Please address questions and book requests to:
Silhouette Reader Service
U.S.: 3010 Walden Ave., P.O. Box 1325, Buffalo, NY 14269
Canadian: P.O. Box 609, Fort Erie, Ont. L2A 5X3

The Seduction of Goody Two-Shoes

KATHLEEN CREIGHTON

INTIMATE MOMENTS™

Published by Silhouette Books

America's Publisher of Contemporary Romance

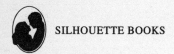 SILHOUETTE BOOKS

ISBN 0-373-27159-X

THE SEDUCTION OF GOODY TWO-SHOES

Copyright © 2001 by Kathleen Creighton-Fuchs

Books by Kathleen Creighton

Silhouette Intimate Moments

Demon Lover #84
Double Dealings #157
Gypsy Dancer #196
In Defense of Love #216
Rogue's Valley #240
Tiger Dawn #289
Love and Other Surprises #322
Wolf and the Angel #417
*A Wanted Man #547
Eyewitness #616
*One Good Man #639
*Man of Steel #677
Never Trust a Lady #800
†One Christmas Knight #825
One More Knight #890
†One Summer's Knight #944
†Eve's Wedding Knight #963
*The Cowboy's Hidden Agenda #1004
*The Awakening of Dr. Brown #1057
*The Seduction of Goody Two-Shoes #1089

*Into the Heartland
†The Sisters Waskowitz

Silhouette Desire

The Heart Mender #584
In from the Cold #654

Silhouette Books

Silhouette Christmas Stories 1990
"The Mysterious Gift"

KATHLEEN CREIGHTON

has roots deep in the California soil but has relocated to South Carolina. As a child, she enjoyed listening to old timers' tales, and her fascination with the past only deepened as she grew older. Today, she says she is interested in everything—art, music, gardening, zoology, anthropology and history—but people are at the top of her list. She also has a lifelong passion for writing, and now combines her two loves in romance novels.

SILHOUETTE MAKES YOU A STAR!

Feel like a star with Silhouette.
Look for the exciting details of our new contest
inside all of these fabulous Silhouette novels:

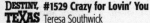

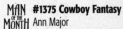

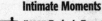

Prologue

"This one's alive," the customs inspector said, "but barely."

U.S. Fish and Wildlife Service biologist Rose Ellen Lanagan—Ellie to family, friends and a few select co-workers—took the limp body in her hands, her heart thumping a slow and steady dirge. One hooded yellow-ringed eye glared listlessly at her as her fingers stroked the satiny blue feathers...such an incredible shade of blue. Hyacinth blue.

"Sure got a full crop for being packed so long in that crate," she remarked in a soft and even tone that would have been a warning to anyone who knew her well. Ellie Lanagan was angry. Angry with a cold intensity that shocked even her. Deep inside where no one could see, she was shaking with it.

Her eyes went to the rows of brightly colored bodies laid out on a sheet that had been spread on the warehouse floor. The customs inspector was already bending over them, his fingers gingerly probing, careful not to disturb the bodies more than necessary lest some vital clue as to their point of origin be lost to the experts waiting to examine them in the department's forensics labs.

"These, too," he said on an exhalation. Squatting on his heels, he drew a pair of tweezers from his shirt pocket. A moment later he held up a small plastic bag filled with white powder. Carefully, he opened the bag, dipped the tip of a pinky finger in the powder, tasted, then spat. He shook his head, swearing softly.

"Two for the price of one," Ellie muttered, as she felt the body in her hands suddenly go limp. She had to swallow hard before she could choke out the words, "I'd give anything to get these people."

The third person in the warehouse had been standing well back from the evidence in the spread-legged, crossed-arms stance that screamed "law enforcement" even without the shoulder holster that criss-crossed beneath an immaculate gray suit. Now he moved forward and spoke in a quiet drawl. "Anything?"

"*Anything,*" Ellie grimly—perhaps recklessly—confirmed.

USFWS Special Agent Kenneth Burnside's eyes narrowed and his cheeks broadened with his smile, so that he looked—deceptively—like a good-natured baby. "Glad to hear you say that, darlin'," the Savannah native drawled. "And I believe I know a way you might do that."

Ellie glared up at him, frustrated and torn; it wasn't the first time Agent Burnside had tried to recruit her, and quite frankly, she'd sometimes been inclined to distrust his motives. "I'm a biologist, not a cop."

"You'd be fully trained." Burnside's voice was persuasive, in the soft and lilting way of the South. "Come on, Doc...we need you. Together we can get these guys."

Ellie stared down at the now-inert body in her hands, picturing it instead in the rare and heart-stopping flash of blue against the unremitting green of a Brazilian rain forest. She felt the helpless anger drain out of her and a cold resolve come to take its place.

"All right," she said at last, in the snappy, rough-edged, almost angry-sounding way that was her norm. "You got me. I'm there. Just tell me where I have to go to sign up."

Burnside chuckled and held out his hand. "You just did. Welcome to the team, darlin'."

Chapter 1

Quinn McCall applied one more daub of electric-blue paint to his newest masterpiece and stood back to admire the result. With one eye squinted against the glare of the late-morning sun, as well as the trickle of smoke that curled lazily skyward from a dangling cigarette, he considered the grouping of three parrots—one in each of the primary colors—pleasingly arranged amidst a riot of green foliage and orange hibiscus blossoms. Yep, he thought, he'd been right to stick to just the three; throwing in that cockatoo would have been a bit much. Even for a McCall.

Alerted by the baritone bellow of a boat's whistle, he glanced at the cheap watch nestled amongst the sun-bleached hairs on his left wrist. Praises be, in spite of the sinister presence of Tropical Storm Paulette, still lurking somewhere out there in the Caribbean, the launch from the weekly cruise ship was right on time. At this very moment, in fact, it was opening its gates to disgorge the latest wave of tourists eager to fork over their money on "authentic" local souvenirs. And he, Quinn McCall, was ready and waiting to take it from them. As, of course, were the hordes of street vendors, con artists, beggars and pickpockets that regularly plied their trades in the main plaza and adjoining market streets of Puerta Marialena.

McCall had staked out his favorite spot, near the main traffic flow from the harbor but commanding a view of the entire plaza, so that his was very nearly the first and the last shopping opportunity a tourist would encounter on his way to and from the pier. And, with the island of tropical landscaping, including some picturesque palm trees, behind him, he'd have shade before midday, not to mention banks of bougainvillea to provide an appropriately gaudy backdrop against which to display his wares. Yes, it was a good spot; he usually did well here.

He always did well, actually. Well enough. It seemed the only thing more popular with the tourists than the genuine native stuff was an honest-to-God exiled gringo wasting away in Margaritaville. There was an element of envy in their stares, he'd always thought, especially the men's. A touch of *there but for a wife, a mortgage and a lack of* cojones *go I.*

And from the women…well, call it a sort of subdued nervous excitement, as if they felt they might be in the presence of some wild, exotic and possibly dangerous creature. Someone not quite civilized, more Hemingway than Jimmy Buffet.

And he took pains to look the part, in his standard uniform of cutoff jeans, sandals and a tropical print shirt—worn hanging open if the day was particularly hot, which it almost always was on the Caribbean shores of the Yucatan—accessorized with the dangling cigarette and several days' growth of beard. No sunglasses: that would make him look too much like one of "them." He preferred a Panama hat to keep the sun out of his eyes, but only when absolutely necessary. Actually, he rather liked the crow's feet the Mexican sun had etched at their corners. More important, so did his female customers.

Of which there were bunches heading his way at that very moment. Mentally rubbing his hands in anticipation, McCall turned the just-finished painting ever so slightly on the easel and made a show of adding a tiny daub of paint to the blue parrot's feathers. Out of the corner of his eye he monitored the progress of the latest wave—the usual assortment of pasty middle-aged *norteamericanos,* in pairs, mostly—anniversary couples or the odd honeymooners—or noisy, boisterous groups of women from places like Dallas, Atlanta and Hoboken. Young, single women were a rarer commodity, which he thought was maybe why he noticed that particular lady right away. Then again, the fact that she was cute as a pup might have had something to do with it.

Either way, once he'd spotted her, it was hard to pull his eyes or his attention away from her. Not that she was such a knockout—*cute* really was the best word to describe her—but there was something about the way she moved, with a seemingly contradictory blend of self-confidence and a beguiling naïveté. Pert, he thought, mildly surprised to realize he even knew a word like *pert.* She was short, petite without appearing fragile, with the kind of trim and tidy little body that had always appealed to him. Hair the color of cinnamon, worn short and with a bit of curl that looked natural. Too far away to tell about her eyes.

He could feel his awareness of her creep along the back of his neck as the wave of newcomers swept into the plaza. Would she stop? Or, as anyone with a lick of artistic taste ought to do, wrinkle her nose fastidiously and move on.

"Good grief."

The exclamation was muttered, barely audible, but McCall heard it, felt it almost, like warm breath across his skin. He glanced around and there she was right beside him, her head barely topping his shoulder.

He turned toward her, eyebrows raised in pretended surprise, teeth bared in a wolfish but welcoming smile around the stump of his cigarette. "*Yes,* ma'am," he said, expansive, inviting. "How's about a nice little souvenir of old Mexico—every single one hand-painted and hand-signed."

She jerked her fascinated gaze from the painting to throw him a startled glance. "You're American." Her voice was husky with what he thought was probably embarrassment, realizing he'd have understood that little comment of hers.

Still smiling, McCall plucked the cigarette from his teeth with a sweeping gesture. "Guilty." He pointed the butt at the three parrots. "You like that one? Sorry, can't let you have it, it's still wet. But hey, I can ship it to you later, if you—"

She shook her head, and he saw her turn slightly pink. "No! I mean, it's…uh, they're very…colorful." He could see honesty arm-wrestling with politeness. Honesty won. Impatience gave her voice an edge as she added, "It's just…way too big." The edge wasn't unpleasant, he decided, just sort of like an itch between his shoulder blades he couldn't reach to scratch.

"You think so?" McCall considered his work in progress, frowning. "I try to make 'em small enough so people can take 'em home in a shopping bag. I'll ship if I have to, but I'd rather not."

"No, I mean the conyer—the yellow one," she earnestly explained, seeing his blank look. "It should be only half the size of the two macaws."

Oh brother. Everybody was an art critic. Mentally rolling his eyes, McCall snatched the remnants of the cigarette from his mouth in mock amazement. "*No.* Is that right?"

"I own a pet shop," she explained, and her flush deepened slightly as she shrugged. He wondered why.

"Hmm." McCall's fingers rasped on his beard-stubbled chin as he thoughtfully regarded the painting. He looked sideways at his critic. "You ever hear of perspective?"

She shook her head. "The conyer's *behind* the macaws—that would make it even smaller." She gazed steadily at him, not giving an inch.

He could see now that her eyes were hazel, almost golden in this light. And that the sprinkle of freckles scattered across her nose and cheeks exactly matched her hair. And that she was wearing a gold wedding band on the appropriate finger of her left hand.

"*Damn,*" he muttered for more than one reason, snapping his fingers, and was rewarded with the sudden and unexpected brilliance of her smile.

To his regret, before he'd even had time to absorb the wonder of that smile she'd moved away from him to stroll among the rest of his stock—a riotous mix of tropical flora and fauna, hung without regard for color compatibility on their racks against the garish backdrop of bougainvillea— with lips slightly parted, as if in awe. Having reached the end of the display, she gave her head a little shake and turned it toward him to inquire in a tone of disbelief, "You actually *sell* these?"

He was amused rather than insulted—even, in some remote part of himself, pleased to discover that she seemed to possess both taste and intelligence. But he hid it from her, instead scowling around his cupped hands as he lit a new cigarette. "Like hotcakes, sister."

Undaunted, her eyes held his, and he saw laughter in them as she persisted in a cracking voice, "Where do you suppose they hang them?"

Oh hell. He threw back his head and laughed. How could he help it? When he looked again, she'd moved on to the next booth and was idly fingering through a pinwheel of embroidered shawls. He felt a pang of genuine regret at her going, but the laughter stayed with him for a while, quivering just beneath his ribs as he turned his attention to more likely customers.

Ellie was still smiling as she wandered among the stalls in the sun-baked plaza, touching an embroidered blouse here, a painted clay pottery pig there. For some reason the exchange with that scruffy American *artist*—using that term extremely loosely—had lifted her spirits. She hadn't any idea why—the paintings were almost wonderfully dreadful, and the artist himself the very image of the sort of man conscientious mamas once warned their innocent little girls about. Perhaps she'd just so badly needed her spirits lifted.

It took only that thought to make them plummet again. How could Ken... *No*. Firmly, and not for the first time, she squelched the desire to blame her partner for a circumstance that truly was not his fault. Probably it was so tempting—it felt so *good* to blame Burnside for every little thing that happened to annoy her—simply because *he* annoyed her so. Which she judiciously admitted wasn't his fault, either. He couldn't help being the kind of overly macho, arrogant know-it-all type of male for whom she'd always had zero tolerance. Most likely he'd been born that way, and being raised in the male-chauvinist bastions of the Old South hadn't helped his personality development any. Certainly, he was never going to change.

And, in spite of that character flaw—perhaps, she secretly admitted, even because of it—he *was* a very good agent. He was cautious, a meticulous planner, which Ellie liked and wholeheartedly approved of. Like her, he left nothing to chance. But not even they could have foreseen food poisoning.

Food poisoning! Because of it—or a twenty-four-hour-flu bug or *turista* or whatever you wanted to call it—at this very moment her erstwhile partner in an undercover operation it had taken two years to lay the groundwork for and countless hours of tricky and dangerous negotiations to set up, was back on the ship, flat on his back in his stateroom, groaning in helpless agony. *Now,* at the most critical stage of the operation, when the trap had been baited and the quarry was circling, the culmination of all they'd worked for actually in sight!

No, it wasn't his fault.

But dammit, *how could he have let this happen?*

The impotence of her anger penetrated even into her muscles, it seemed, and she drifted to a halt, frowning and lost in thought, amidst the sluggish river of tourists.

"Oof!" she gasped suddenly, as a small, wiry body collided with hers, hard enough to knock her breathless.

Off-balance, she struggled to stay upright, only to feel the strap of her handbag slipping off her shoulder. She felt a tug and snatched at her purse—and grabbed thin air.

"Hey!" she yelled in futile outrage, as a child wearing only a pair of ragged jeans darted and squirmed his way beyond her reach with her brand-new straw handbag clutched to his scrawny chest.

Around her, pudgy people with sun visors on their

heads and cameras dangling from their necks turned to stare in the dazed and clueless way of those witnessing the unexpected and out-of-the-ordinary.

"Come back here!" Ellie bellowed, incensed. Knowing it was useless, she took off in pursuit anyway, gasping, "Somebody stop him! He took my purse!"

My purse. Just that quickly, panic replaced anger. Not that there was so much money in the handbag—this was, after all, a government operation, and *she* certainly wasn't rich—but the instructions, the procedure for setting up a meeting with their contacts—*that* was something that could not be replaced.

Oh God, what would she do if she lost it? Compared to this disaster, Agent Burnside's case of food poisoning was a mere blip. A hiccup.

Trying to make headway through the knot of tourists, most of whom had now stopped dead in confusion, was like trying to walk uphill in a mudslide. Still, she was sure she'd have had a chance if it hadn't been for the sandals. Ellie wasn't used to sandals, which, like the Hawaiian print shorts and tank top she wore, were part of her "tourist" disguise. Give her a nice solid pair of Nikes and she could outrun just about anybody; in spite of—maybe because of—her size, she had always been quick. In these cursed hard-soled sandals, though, all she could do was flail her way among the frozen spectators, slipping and stumbling on the uneven adobe brick pavers, while far ahead through a shimmer of frustrated tears she could see the purse-snatcher darting through the crowd, making for the entrance to the plaza. If he got beyond the plaza, Ellie knew, he'd vanish into the maze of narrow, dusty streets, the warren of scrap wood and tin shacks, the tangle of fishing boats...the part of this tourist town the tourists never saw. She'd never see him or her purse again, of that she was certain.

A moment later she wasn't certain of anything, even the evidence of her own eyes.

One second the boy was there, shaggy dark head and narrow sun-bronzed back plainly visible, all but branded on her retinas. The next second he'd disappeared—vanished—and her purse...*her precious purse!* was flying... flying in seeming slow motion, tumbling lazy as a butterfly through the shimmering sunlight, shoulder strap like a looping lariat against the sky. And then an arm, lean and tanned as leather, reached up and fingers stained with electric blue snatched the purse right out of the air.

Breath gusted from Ellie's lungs as she halted, openmouthed, rendered speechless by overwhelming relief coupled with wonder. Not that miracles, and the silent, breathless awe that accompany them, were unknown to Ellie; in her lifetime so far she'd been privileged to witness quite a few: Orcas breeching in the Alaskan Straits; the birth of a dolphin; a loggerhead turtle struggling up a sandy Georgia beach on an inky-black night. Not to mention a thousand smaller miracles, the kind that happen every single day and so few people even notice. But this was different. This was the first miracle she could recall that involved another human being. And a male human being at that.

The crowd parted almost magically, and even that seemed only part of the miracle. Still stunned, Ellie watched the culprit shuffle toward her, now sniffling piteously, tears making shiny tracks on his dusty cheeks. His skinny ribs were heaving, and there were fresh, quartersized abrasions on his knees—a matched set. The paintsmudged hand clamped on the back of his neck looked large against its vulnerability, and strong enough to snap it.

"This belong to you?" The owner of the hand, only slightly less scruffy than his captive, was holding out her handbag, dangling by its strap from one hooked finger. Under the brim of his Panama hat his eyes were squinted and his teeth were showing, but it didn't look to Ellie like a smile. More like Clint Eastwood in one of those old westerns where he always seemed to be wearing a serape.

It suddenly seemed necessary to lubricate her voicebox before she spoke, although when she tried to swallow it didn't help much. The scratchy sound that came out was just pretty much Ellie's normal speaking voice. And she couldn't do much about that, since she'd inherited it approximately twenty-eight years ago from her mother.

"I...I don't know how to thank you." It was no more than the truth; having always prided herself on being an uncommonly independent and resourceful person, she'd never been in such debt to a man before.

The artist—her benefactor—snorted and made a jerking motion with his head, aiming it over his shoulder in the general direction of his display. "You want to thank me, you can pay me for that picture I brought him down with."

That was when Ellie first noticed that the boy's bare feet and shins bore smears of the same blue paint that decorated the artist's hands. Her mouth dropped open and she smothered a gasp of dismay with her hand. "*Oh.* Oh, I'm so sorry. Well, I—of course I'll..." And she was rummaging through her purse, fumbling for her wallet. "How much do I—"

He waved her off, like someone swatting at a fly. "Forget it. Water over the bridge." Bestowing a look of annoyance upon his captive's dusty bowed head, he growled, "What do you want to do with him?"

"Me! *Do* with him?" She clapped a hand to her forehead and looked around at the gathering of tourists, perhaps in hopes of some sort of advice. Though officially a member of law enforcement, she'd had no experience in dealing with juvenile delinquents, or juveniles of any kind, for that matter.

Plus, beneath her crusty exterior there lurked a guilty secret: a heart like a half-melted marshmallow. This was a little boy, for God's sake! One who didn't appear to have been eating regularly lately, if not for most of his life so far. And at that, panic of a new sort seized her. She knew herself very well. She had her wallet in her hand; in another moment she was afraid she was going to give the kid every dime she had with her.

"Do with him?" she repeated in a hissed undertone, sidling closer to the boy's captor. "What am I supposed to do with him? He's just a little boy."

"A little *thief*," someone in the crowd muttered. There were rumblings of agreement. Someone else added something that included the word *police.*

"Look, I've got my purse back," Ellie said to placate the gathering at large, and then, to the keeper of the captive, trying to keep a pleading note out of her voice, "There's no harm done, can't you just let him go?"

The "artist" shrugged.

Just then the purse-snatcher, seizing the moment—and taking no chances on anyone changing his mind or being outvoted—squirmed out from under his captor's hand and vanished into the crowd.

There were a few cries of mild protest and dismay. Someone—a man—said loudly, "What'd you let him go for? Kid's nothin' but a thief. Shoulda handed him over to the police before he hits on somebody else.''

''Not my problem,'' the artist mumbled around the revolting stump of his cigarette. With that he turned and shambled back toward his stall, sandals slapping on the baked adobe bricks.

For a moment or two Ellie just stood and watched him go, frowning and chewing on her lip while around her the crowd slowly dispersed, talking in breathless, gossipy undertones to one another as people do when they've been privileged to witness some untoward, possibly violent event. Presently, she drew a quick, decisive breath. No way around it—at the very least she owed the man a thank-you.

She couldn't have said why she should feel such inner resistance to doing something simple good upbringing demanded. Such a peculiar tightening in her belly. A quickening of her pulse. It made no sense to her. Certainly it wasn't his surly manner that put her off. Rose Ellen Lanagan didn't know the meaning of the word *intimidation.*

Besides, she'd seen the twinkle in those cool blue eyes of his. Heard the warm, contagious peal of his laughter. That crustiness was ninety percent show, she was sure of it, though what purpose he thought it served she couldn't imagine.

The artist had retrieved the painting he'd sacrificed in the interests of justice and was regarding it stoically, held at arm's length in front of him. He must have sailed it, Ellie now surmised, into the path of the fleeing purse-snatcher, rather like an oversized Frisbee.

''That was quick thinking,'' she said, coming up behind him.

The artist grunted without looking away from his masterpiece, which, smeared and smudged almost beyond recognition, in Ellie's opinion now had actually attained a certain surrealistic charm. Personally, she considered it a vast improvement over the original.

With "thank you" hovering on the tip of her tongue, she hesitated; once again, the words seemed meager, hopelessly inadequate, not to mention alien to her nature. They came out sounding more prissy than anything.

"I really would like to pay you—for the painting," she briskly added as the artist shot her a sharp, almost hostile look. His eyes weren't cool at all, she realized, but a clear, almost transparent blue, like midsummer skies, with whites as soft and clean as cotton clouds. All at once her voice seemed to stick in her throat, and when she forced it through anyway it emerged sounding even more raggedy than usual. "It's the least I can do."

The moment stretched while he stared at her with that keen and piercing glare. While she noticed for the first time that his lips, without that awful cigarette clamped between them, seemed finely chiseled, almost sensitive—unusual for a man's lips. For some reason her own suddenly felt swollen and hot, giving her a wholly alien urge to cool them with her tongue. And then…

"Keep it," he said, thrusting the canvas at her so abruptly that she actually gasped. "Maybe it'll remind you to be more careful next time."

He turned away from her and was almost immediately swallowed up by a crowd of lady tourists, all cooing and chirping their appreciation for his heroism and his compassion, and eager to take home a souvenir of the Purse Snatching Incident.

Feeling somehow dismissed, Ellie left him posing for photographs with a group of middle-aged belles from Atlanta. And as she made her way back to the pier she was wondering, with a cynicism that was also foreign to her nature, if he might have paid that boy to snatch her purse, just to drum up business.

Ellie dropped the painting of three drunken-looking parrots onto one of the two single beds in the stateroom she shared—platonically—with her partner and fellow agent with the U.S. Fish and Wildlife Service.

"Don't ask," she said, plucking a Hershey's Kiss from the bag on her bedside table, even though the muffled groan that was her supposed husband's only response made it clear he'd no interest in doing anything of the kind. Concern and guilt quickly banished the grumpy mood she'd come in with. "Still feeling lousy?"

The question was wholly unnecessary; Ken Burnside looked, to quote one of her mom's favorite clichés, like something the cat dragged in—and given the sorts of things the cats were prone to dragging into her mom's barn back in Iowa, that was saying something.

"I think I've got a fever," Ken said in a hushed and pitiful voice.

He looked it, too, but Ellie squelched an instinctive urge to step closer and lay a ministering hand on his brow. She'd had to fight off the man's attentions often enough in the early days of their working relationship so that, even though the ground rules between them had been firmly established long ago, she still didn't quite trust him. Not even now, when he was laid out in his bed with his eyes closed, skin sweaty and roughly the color of old library paste.

"Maybe you should see a doctor," she offered by way of compensation, peeling the last of the foil off the chocolate and popping it into her mouth.

"It's just the stomach flu." Rousing himself enough to

open both eyes, he inquired blearily, "How'd it go in town?"

"Umm. Great." Feeling calmer, she helped herself to a couple more Kisses and settled herself cross-legged on her own bed, carefully avoiding the still-gooey canvas. "I think I've pretty well established myself as your typical dopey tourist," she said as she pulled off her sun visor. "Got my purse snatched." Burnside made a strangled sound that may have been a snort. "Don't worry," she assured him, "I got it back—intact." She didn't think it was necessary to tell him how close she'd come to losing the vital meeting information. She was the rookie on this operation, and suspected her partner was already nervous about how she was going to handle herself when things got tricky.

"No further contact from the smugglers, though, and I gave them plenty of opportunity." She gave the lump of misery in the next bed a dubious glance. "You going to be able to go with me tonight?"

"Don't…think so," Ken said in an airless whisper that alarmed her.

"We have to make that meeting." Ellie's heart rate was beginning to speed up. She hurriedly unwrapped another chocolate. "The instructions were clear on that. They won't contact us to set up a meeting until they're sure it's not a trap. We have to be out there where they can look us over—make sure we're not being followed."

There was some deep, carefully controlled breathing. Then, in a voice tight with pain, "Maybe we should contact General Reyes—let him know what's going on."

"Let him know what? There's nothing to report, and won't be until after that meeting. *If* there's a meeting; we don't even know for sure they'll go for it. It's for sure they won't if we don't show up at—where is it?—José's

Cantina.'' She paused, then said flatly, "If you can't make it, I'll just have to go by myself.''

This time there was no doubt about the snort. "Lanagan,'' Burnside said in a faint but firm voice, "I know these people. They're old May-hee-co—*back-country* Mexico. They won't do business with a woman—especially one that looks like you. They'll chew you up and spit you out...'' He closed his eyes and licked his lips, clearly exhausted by that effort.

Ellie watched him for a long moment, a knot of cold fear taking shape in her stomach in spite of the insulating coating of chocolate. Finally she said in a low voice, "Ken, we can't screw this up—not now.''

Her partner gave a deep, guttural sigh, then mumbled, "I'll be okay. We still have a few hours. Don't worry, I'll make it to José's with you...you'll see.''

It was an important part of McCall's credo that any day could be made better by a shot of tequila washed down with several bottles of *pulque*. Not that today had been all that bad; it had turned out to be a pretty good day, actually, in spite of the loss of "The Three Caballeros'' to the feet of a street thief and a *turista* with golden eyes and hair and freckles the exact color of cinnamon.

As a matter of fact it was the integrity of that personal creed of his, as affected by the street thief and the cinnamon girl, that had him worried, and making for his favorite watering hole for reinforcement at the first soft promise of twilight. *Live and let live.* He'd come way too close to forgetting his favorite motto to suit him. Today a lady's purse, tomorrow...who knew where such a careless act could lead? If he didn't look out, before he knew it he'd be sliding down that long slippery slope toward a social conscience. Uh-uh, no thank you, not for him. No sirree.

That was why he sailed into José's Cantina with a wave and his usual, ''José—*¿Qué pasa?*'' for the guy behind the bar—who also happened to be the owner—and swam his way through the noisy murk to his favorite table without taking much notice of who else was in the place. If he had, he'd have turned around and walked right out again and never looked back. He swore he would have.

As it was, by the time he saw her—Lord help him, the cinnamon girl!—sitting there all alone at the table in the front corner by the glassless window, he was already settled comfortably in his own favorite creaky rattan chair with the tequila, a quarter of lime and a saltshaker and the first of the local brews making wet rings on the table in front of him, and it just seemed like it would be too much of a waste to go off and leave them sitting there. Hell, he thought, might as well drink 'em and see what happened in the meantime.

Maybe nothing would. Maybe none of the regular patrons of the place would notice her. Maybe she'd come to her senses and leave. Maybe the person she was obviously waiting for would show up and McCall wouldn't have to think about how she was going to get herself back to her cruise ship without getting her bones jumped in one of the dark alleys between here and the tourists' part of town.

Maybe it would turn out to be true that the Lord looked out for children, drunks and fools.

Hell, it was none of his business, anyway. *Live and let live.*

But the image of that smile of hers kept crowding into his mind, the way it had burst so suddenly, so wonderously over her grave little face, like...oh, a dozen comparisons he could think of, all of them clichés, none of them quite worthy. So naturally he couldn't help but watch her as he licked lime and salt, slugged the tequila and sat back to enjoy his *pulque,* though he tried to look as if he wasn't—watching her, of course he meant, not enjoying the beer. Noticing the way she kept looking at her watch, frowning.

Noticing the growing ripples of interest from the regulars lounging around the bar, and the helpless looks José—who knew his customers well—kept throwing McCall. The ones that said plainly, *Hey—she's a gringa, you're a gringo, that makes her your responsibility. So do something!*

To which McCall's response was a shrug uniquely Latino in character, but which in any language easily translated to, *She's not my problem, man.*

He'd just about decided to take a chance on ordering a second beer when, Lord help him, he saw the woman get up from her table and head straight for the bar. How could any woman be so stupid, he wondered, even for a *turista?* He'd thought her pretty cute, he remembered, when he'd seen her this morning, but she was seeming less and less cute by the minute. Even her smile was fading from his memory. In fact, he was experiencing a powerful urge to yank her up by the scruff of her neck and haul her home to her mama—or her husband, he amended with a frown, belatedly recalling the gold band he'd seen on the third finger of her left hand.

That memory inspired a new spurt of anger. What was her husband thinking of, to let his wife go off alone to such a dive? Or—a new thought—if he was the one she'd been waiting for, to stand her up like this?

He blamed the anger for making him once again forget his motto as he watched the woman push her way through the massed male bodies at the bar, cinnamon head barely topping burly shoulders—and Mexican men weren't that tall. His muscles tensed and anger sizzled in his belly as he watched those bodies turn to let her through, but just a little, being sneaky about giving way just enough to let her pass but with plenty of contact. Watched her ask José a question, apparently oblivious both to the bodies and to the leers on the faces around her. Watched José shrug and shake his head in reply.

With a sinking feeling in his gut, McCall then watched the woman squeeze back through the pack, and with one final frowning look at her wrist and a sweeping glance around the cantina, go out the door.

A moment later he knew a sense of inevitability—of fate, if you will—as two of the more disreputable-looking bar patrons separated themselves from the wolf pack and slunk out after her, smirking to one another and their comrades in an anticipatory way that made McCall go cold.

Live and let live…live and let live…she's not my problem, he chanted hopelessly to himself, staring into the gloom at the bottom of his *pulque* bottle.

And then, "Ah, the hell with it," he muttered to nobody in particular, tossed a handful of pesos onto the tabletop and followed.

Chapter 2

Outside the cantina, McCall paused to light a cigarette while he checked things out, caution being, in that part of town, always the better part of valor.

A soft breeze—a subtle reminder from Tropical Storm Paulette, like a blown kiss—was whisking away with it the heat of the day and the odors of poverty and inviting in the cool green smell of the sea, and he was savoring that along with his tobacco when the sound of voices drifted to him, carried on the wind. Male voices first, slurred and guttural, speaking Spanish…answered by a lighter one, low and scratchy but definitely female.

And becoming all too familiar.

Following the sound of the voices, McCall was finally able to make out three shapes a little farther down the narrow sandy street, in the shadows just beyond the yellow patch of light from the cantina's open window. He exhaled, tossed his match into the dirt and started reluctantly toward them.

He was still several yards away when he heard a man's laughter abruptly interrupted by a sound rather like, *"Oof."* At the same time, one of the bulkier shapes suddenly and mysteriously doubled over on itself.

A moment later, the taller of the two remaining shapes began to perform a sort of hopping, stumbling dance, like a broken marionette.

Sharp, staccato Spanish rent the velvet night. Cuss words, if McCall was not mistaken. Very angry cuss words.

Seizing the moment, he lunged forward, pushed between the two would-be assailants and their intended victim, grasped her firmly by her upper arms and hustled her rapidly away from the scene of the intended crime.

Naturally, she resisted—silently except for some heavy breathing—until he growled, "Cut it out, you idiot—can't you see I'm trying to help you?"

He felt her body go taut and her face jerk toward him, but she still didn't say anything, not until they'd turned a corner and were out of sight of the cantina and well out of range of the two disgruntled thugs. There McCall halted and let go of her arms.

She stepped away from him then and said breathlessly as she set herself to rights with little brushing, tugging motions, "You're the artist. The American. From the plaza this morning."

McCall snorted. He could see her face, a pale blur in the darkness.

"I didn't need help." She sniffed—a disdainful sound. "Not to handle those two."

McCall made a disgusted sound of his own. "Lady, you don't need help, you need a nanny. All you did was tick them off. What were you going to do when they decided to come after you?"

"Outrun them," she answered promptly, with an arrogant little toss of her head. "I came prepared this time—see?" And she lifted one foot to show him a tidy white running shoe.

"Lord help us," he breathed, exhaling smoke. But in spite of his very best efforts to squelch it, he felt the beginnings of admiration—just a tiny burr of amazement in the center of his chest. Fearing that in another breath he might even laugh out loud, he said instead, "You're way off the tourist path, lady. What the hell were you doing in a dive like that anyway? Much less alone."

"That's none of your business," she said in a surprised and huffy tone.

"Sister, you got that right," McCall shot back. He was thinking dark and sour thoughts about sticking to his motto from now on, no matter what. Live and let live. No doubt about it, that was the way to go.

So what were his feet doing, carrying him along with the foolish *turista,* walking him right beside her as she started off down the now-deserted street? She didn't want his help, she'd told him so. And besides, she was none of his business—she'd told him that, too, and on that subject at least, they were in complete agreement.

"You sure you're headed in the right direction?" he inquired sarcastically after a while, keeping his lips firmly clamped on the filter of his cigarette.

She ignored him and strode confidently on, finding her way as he did, by the light of a rising three-quarter moon and the occasional splashes of pale yellow from an open window or doorway. Voices—snatches of conversations, bits of laughter, a crying baby—made little sparks, tiny explosions of sound in the quiet. Far away McCall could hear the shushing of waves on the *playa,* keeping up a quirky rhythm to their own crunching footsteps.

He said in a pleasant tone, "What'd you do, leave a trail of bread crumbs?"

She threw him a look but didn't reply, and a moment later jerked impatiently, like a balky child, when he took her arm. "The *playa's* this way, ma'am," he said with exaggerated politeness as he steered her oh, so gently in the right direction. "So's the launch that will take you back to your ship. I assume that's where you wanted to go?" He figured with this woman, you never knew.

"Yes. Of course. Thank you." He could hear the prissiness of chagrin in her voice, and feel the stiffness of wounded pride in her arm just before he let go of it.

She didn't say another word, though, not even when they were back on the main tourist drag, safe among oblivious honeymooners strolling beneath strings of lights looped between palm trees, where music swirled and wove through soft voices and bright laughter and white-coated waiters bearing trays of margaritas glided among rattan tables. Instead she kept throwing him questioning, half-puzzled looks.

They were within sight of the pier when she finally said dryly, "I think I can find my way from here, don't you?"

He had no answer for her and his thoughts were too dark and bitter to share, so he just kept on walking beside her in glowering silence, all the way to the pier gate. There they both halted.

McCall jerked his head toward the far end of the long narrow pier where the cruise ship's pristine white launch bobbed on Tropical Storm Paulette's gentle swells, and said, again rather sarcastically, "There you go."

The pier was brightly lit. He could see the brief flash of a gold stud in her earlobe, then the sprinkle of freckles on her cheeks and across the bridge of her nose when she turned her face to him. From somewhere out in the harbor

came the sudden *thump-thump-thump* of a helicopter's rotors. He listened to it fade rapidly into the distance while he
watched the reflections of the pier lamps in her golden eyes.

They searched his for a long moment, those eyes, and
then he heard the soft intake of her breath, as if she was
on the brink of saying something.

Still she hesitated, and he wondered if, in different
light, he might have seen her blush. Then, as if she'd
come to some sort of decision, she held out her hand.
"I'm Ellie. Thank you." She said it on the breath's delayed exhalation, in that scratchy voice he was beginning
to get used to…even find sort of sexy. And impatiently,
as if she thought he might not believe her, "I mean that
sincerely, Mr.—"

"Just McCall. And you're welcome—sincerely." But
he made a lie of that as he sardonically tipped the brim
of an imaginary hat.

She gave him one long level look that made him feel
vaguely ashamed he'd mocked her before she nodded,
then turned and walked away down the long pier.

"And I sincerely hope I never set eyes on you again…
Mrs. Whatever," McCall muttered grumpily to himself as
he jammed his hands into the pockets of his paint-stained
dungarees and headed for the friendlier bustle of the plaza.
Damned shame the best-looking and most interesting
woman he'd run into in a long time turned out to be married, but…what the hell. Just as well. *Live and let live.*

He was wading into the swirl of tourists' laughter and
party music before it came to him—the reason for that
nagging little sense of disappointment: he'd been
waiting…hoping, one last time, to see her smile.

By the time the launch had delivered Ellie back to the
cruise ship, both the adrenaline rush that had sustained

her through the incident outside José's Cantina and its embarrassingly trembly aftermath had faded to a hazy memory. What was left was the Alice-in-Wonderland feeling, that sense of sheer disbelief that such events could be happening to *her*.

Had she, Rose Ellen Lanagan, really struck a man in the…um…in such an *effective* place? Had she really managed to disable two large—admittedly clumsy—male attackers? It didn't seem possible. She'd always been such a *nonviolent* person, gentle and sunny-natured to a fault. Even in her animal-rights activist days her protests had been limited to peaceful demonstrations, sit-ins, parades and picket lines. Even though, true to Ken Burnside's promise, the government had seen to it that she was well trained in the necessary law-enforcement skills, including the use of firearms and basic martial arts techniques, it had never really occurred to her that she might one day be called upon to *use* that training. At heart she was still a nice Iowa farm girl who happened to have a doctorate in biology—and a badge.

A badge! Lord above—as Great-aunt Gwen might have said—if anyone had even suggested, back in her teenaged years and college days, that she, Ellie Lanagan, would one day be a special agent working undercover for the United States government, she would have fallen down and rolled on the floor with laughter. How had such a thing happened?

The only answer Ellie could come up with was that it had seemed like a good idea at the time. She'd been so sickened by the carnage the traffickers in endangered species were inflicting on some of the earth's rarest and most beautiful creatures…so enraged by their callous disregard for living things…. Okay, Ken had gotten to her in a weak moment, maybe, but she'd certainly had plenty of opportunities to change her mind since. The fact was, she'd truly believed in what she was doing. She still did.

But what was all this *physical* stuff? She was supposed to be the brains of this operation—the technical advisor, the wildlife expert. Ken Burnside, former cop and FBI agent, was supposed to provide the muscle—not that they'd expected to need much. Their purpose, after all, was simply to make contact with the smugglers, a band so elusive and cunning they'd managed for years to elude every attempt on the parts of both American and Mexican authorities to put an end to their operation. One reason for that, it was believed, was that the smugglers seemed to have no permanent camp, and always managed, like guerilla fighters, to slip away into the jungle one step ahead of a raid. It was hoped that Ellie and Ken, posing as eager American buyers with more money than sense, might manage to gain the confidence of the smugglers enough to work their way into their camp. If they were successful, their job was to record evidence and plant a tracking device that would enable government forces to locate them and put them out of commission once and for all. Their mission was nonviolent; the weapon of choice would be American dollars, not bullets. And so far, things had been moving slowly, but according to plan.

How was it, then, that in her first day on Mexican soil she'd already been involved in not one, but *two* incidents involving physical violence? And both times, if it hadn't been for that American artist stepping in when he had....

Both times. She'd thought about that on the way back to the pier, thought about it as she walked beside the man—a stranger—through dark and empty streets, her adrenaline-charged brain worrying the notion like a starving wolf attacking a bone.

*What is he doing there? Coming to my rescue—again?
Can this be coincidence? Could he be one of them? Could
he be the contact? If so, why doesn't he say so? Why
hasn't he identified himself, or at least slipped me something with the meeting information on it?*

All the way back to the pier, on the alert and aware of
his body so close beside hers, remembering the wiry
strength in his hands when they'd gripped her arms, she'd
waited for him to make his move. He hadn't. In the end
she'd felt foolish, out of her depth, questioning her own
judgment. Of course he wasn't involved. He was exactly
what he appeared to be—an American artist and social
dropout trying to make a living hustling tourists. His being
there to rescue her twice in one day was just coincidence.
Those things happened.

Besides, according to all the information so far, the
smugglers were Mexican—back-country Mexican, as
Ken put it. Old-fashioned Macho Mexican Males who
wouldn't lower themselves to deal with a woman.

That was fine. But people in law enforcement are taught
to distrust coincidence as a matter of principle. *And there
were those paintings.* Parrots. Macaws. Tropical birds of
all kinds, many of them the very same ones that so often
turned up dead in customs inspections. Gaudy and God-
awful Mr. McCall's paintings might be, but there was no
denying he had the details right.

Still the question remained: If the American was a
member of the smuggling ring, why hadn't he established
contact with her?

She was still pondering those questions as she stood
before the door to her stateroom, key in hand, frowning
and gnawing on her lip as was her habit when deep in
thought. Consequently she didn't notice the white-
uniformed ship's steward hurrying toward her down the

long passageway, not until he spoke to her with alarming and breathless urgency.

"Mrs. Burnside—Mrs. Burnside, thank God you're back. We've been trying to reach you...."

A few tense and worried minutes later she was shown into a small cluttered office where two men were already engaged in grave consultation. They both straightened at Ellie's entrance to murmur, "Come in, Mrs. Burnside." One, a dark-skinned, salt-and-pepper-haired man with kind, liquid eyes, shook her hand and identified himself as the ship's physician, Dr. Singh; the other, judging by his frown and the resplendence of his uniform, she took to be the captain.

The fear that had clutched Ellie's stomach with the steward's first breathless words outside her stateroom squeezed even tighter. Even though Burnside wasn't really her husband, and there were times, in fact, when he annoyed her beyond bearing, he was still her partner, mentor and even, in an odd sort of way, a friend.

She gasped out, before anyone else could say a word, "Ken—my husband—is he all right? What's happened? Is he—he's not—"

The doctor's tone was stern, even though his voice was limpid with the accent of his native India. "It is very fortunate that he called us when he did, Mrs. Burnside. If he had waited even one more hour.... You should have come to us when his symptoms first occurred. As it is—"

"He had an upset stomach," Ellie cried, defensive in the face of the two men's unspoken disapproval, though she wasn't quite sure what she was supposed to be guilty of. "He said—he *insisted* it was just a twenty-four-hour bug!" She carefully made no mention of food poisoning; apparently her stock with ship's personnel was plummeting as it was. "I *asked* him—" She paused to draw a shaky breath, one hand pressed to her forehead. After a moment she said testily, fighting for calm, "So—what's wrong with him? Where is he? I want to see him."

"He has acute appendicitis," the doctor said gravely. After a polite pause for Ellie's horrified gasp, he continued, "At this moment he is on his way by helicoptor to the airport at Cozumel. From there he will be flown to Miami for immediate surgery."

Ellie was groping for a chair. The captain unfolded his arms from across his chest long enough to guide her to one. "We will, of course, make arrangements for you to join him as soon as possible," he said politely as she sank into the chair, limp with shock. Oh, what she would have given for a Hershey's Kiss just then.

The censure in the captain's voice and expression seemed to have softened somewhat at this evidence of appropriate wifely concern, but his opinion was no longer of any concern at all to Ellie. Having been reassured that her partner was alive and in good hands, what concerned her now was the fate of their undercover operation. This, after all, was the mission, the goal, the *crusade* she'd dedicated her life to for over a year—*dedicated* being the operative word and one people often used to describe Ellie Lanagan...although members of her immediate family would probably have been more inclined to say *pigheaded,* or *stubborn as a mule.* This also was no concern of Ellie's; it was just the way she was, the way she'd always been. When Ellie got involved in something she tended to develop tunnel vision, or what Ken referred to as a "pit-bull mentality."

Now, thinking hard and once again frowning and chewing on her lip, she muttered, "No...no...I can't. I can't leave now—"

Well, tough, was her annoyed thought when she saw

the captain's face freeze up again. Even the doctor looked slightly taken aback. But Ellie's mind was starting to function, although still in the crazily spinning, drunken wobble of an out-of-balance top.

"You don't understand," she went on. "We—my husband and I—had some business here. It was very important." The wobble had sneaked into her voice now, and for once to her advantage. She cast an appealing look from one disapproving face to the other and back again. "That's why he didn't want to believe there was anything seriously wrong. He was convinced it was just an upset stomach. He convinced me…." She gulped a breath and pushed resolutely to her feet. "I know he'd want me to stay and try to take care of…our business…for him. I don't know if I can, by myself, but…I have to try. And," she added with a touch of asperity, "there's not really anything I can do for him *there,* is there? In Miami I mean? Except wait?"

She looked at Dr. Singh, who was looking slightly dazed. He nodded and murmured, "Of course. I understand…."

The captain cleared his throat and finally growled an ambiguous, "Well." He coughed, then continued, "As you know, we'll be staying in port for several days to allow our passengers an opportunity to explore the Mayan ruins, visit the biosphere reserve, or dive the reefs, if that's their preference. You have until day after tomorrow, seventeen hundred hours, to let us know whether or not you'll be continuing on with us." He paused with one hand on the door. "Or, whether you wish us to make arrangements for you to join your husband." He opened the door and waited for Ellie to precede him. "It's up to you."

"Thank you." She was looking past the captain's out-

stretched arm at the doctor. "You'll let me know…
how—"

"Yes, of course, Mrs. Burnside," said Dr. Singh with
a slight bow. "As soon as I know anything I will contact
you immediately."

Ellie nodded and turned to go, then, spotting the steward hovering just outside the door, halted once more to
ask whether there had been any messages for her, or
rather, for her "husband."

While the captain took his leave with poorly concealed
impatience, the steward promised to check for messages
as soon as he'd seen her back to her stateroom.

That turned out not to be necessary. When Ellie unlocked her stateroom door she found an envelope lying
on the carpet, where it had apparently been slipped under
the door.

"Well, there you are," the steward said, showing
friendly white teeth. "Must have just come in." He hovered while Ellie tore open the envelope and read the brief
handwritten message inside. "Is that the message you
were expecting, Miss, uh…ma'am?"

"Mmm…" she murmured absently. "Yes…I think so.
Thank you…" For a moment longer the steward hovered,
then shrugged and went out, closing the door behind him.
Belatedly, the word *tip* flashed into Ellie's mind. But only
fleetingly; she had more important things on her mind.

*Mañana—twelve o'clock noon. Take a taxi from the
plaza. Give driver this following instruction….*

Noon. Tomorrow.

Ellie's knees suddenly went weak, and she sank onto
her smooth undisturbed bed, reaching automatically for
the bag of Kisses. A few feet away, tumbled sheets

dragged half onto the floor bore mute testimony to the disaster that had befallen her—or more accurately, her partner.

Her partner. Wait a minute. Ken was the one with appendicitis. There was nothing whatsoever wrong with *her*.

Heart thumping, even chocolate momentarily forgotten, she stared down at the piece of paper in her hands. *Tomorrow noon.* Okay. This was it. The meeting they'd been working toward, hoping for, for months. Okay, so Ken was out of the picture, but *she* was still here. There was nothing wrong with *her*. Why couldn't she still go through with it? Why *shouldn't* she?

Okay, Ellie, think about this logically.

On the downside, according to Ken these smugglers were a backward lot, with some annoyingly primitive ideas about women. He'd said they probably wouldn't even do business with a woman alone. Probably.

All right, so what? At the worst they wouldn't do business with her—a little humiliating, maybe, but she could handle that. And at least she would have a chance to explain what had happened, perhaps try to postpone the meeting until Ken was back in action.

But what if that *wasn't* the worst?

Memories of the evening's incident at José's Cantina crowded fresh and vivid into her mind, complete with the residuals of sour breath and hot, unwashed bodies. Reluctantly, she thought about the number one rule in law enforcement: never go into anything without backup.

Tonight she'd had backup—unplanned, but backup nonetheless. She forced herself to consider what would have happened if that artist hadn't arrived when he had. Probably nothing—she really did believe she could have handled those two drunks without any help. But that was just it—the men who'd accosted her had been a couple of relatively harmless neighborhood punks, and drunk to boot. The smugglers, she was certain, would be a different breed entirely.

But if she didn't keep the rendezvous, what then? How many months would it take to win back the smugglers' trust and set up another meeting? And in the meantime, how many hundreds, even thousands, of rare and beautiful animals would die in horrible, cruel ways? As always, that thought made Ellie's stomach clench and her skin go clammy.

She jumped up and began to pace—to the extent such an activity was possible in the cramped stateroom.

I should at least contact General Reyes, she thought, nibbling furiously at her lip. General Cristobal Reyes was the head of the Mexican government agency that had been working in close partnership with the USFWS and the man in charge of the Mexican phase of the operation. Though she'd never actually met him, he was, in effect, at this juncture, anyway, her boss. He would have to be told about this latest development. Of course he would.

And the general would call off the operation, or at least postpone it until Ken was back in action. He would tell her in no uncertain terms not to go to this meeting alone. Of course he would.

What shall I do? Think, Ellie, think! Use your wits....

It was the word *wits* that made her stop pacing and begin instead to smile. *Keep your wits about you.* It had always been one of her mother's favorite sayings, and Ellie could hear Lucy's stern and scratchy voice as clearly as if she'd been standing there beside her. *Keep your wits about you, Rose Ellen Lanagan.*

A sweet and childish longing swept over her as she sank onto the bed, popped a Kiss into her mouth and reached for the telephone.

* * *

Ordinarily Lucy found October's lull a welcome respite after the busy rush of September and its jam-packed schedule of back-to-school, 4-H meetings, fairs and live-stock sales. For a little while, between harvest and the hardships of winter, she could spend time with Mike, or simply relax and enjoy the cool, crisp mornings and bright, golden noontimes—as much as Lucy had it in her nature to relax.

Oh, but she did like the lovely sense of satisfaction that came with having once again, against all the odds man and nature could throw at her, successfully brought in a decent harvest. And though she always felt a small twinge of regret at the first soft furring of frost on the corn stub-ble, she never failed to feel her spirits lift when she heard the distant honking of migrating geese and paused, shad-ing her eyes against the glare, to watch the fluid arrows dipping and floating through a crystal-clear autumn sky.

Infused with restless energy, she spent those days clean-ing the house, raking leaves, or, something she'd always enjoyed much more, working in the barn, piling the stalls full of sweet-smelling straw and declaring all-out war on the summer's accumulation of spiders.

Her husband Mike, the journalist, attributed all this ac-tivity to a primitive, instinctive fear of winter, the same instinct, he said, that prompts squirrels to run about gath-ering nuts.

Well, of course, Mike was a writer, and Lucy was used to his tendency to over-verbalize—not to mention dram-atize. She certainly was *not* afraid of winter, or anything else, for that matter. Except maybe thunderstorms, which she considered only basic good sense; as far as Lucy was concerned, thunderstorms were violent, dangerous and de-structive, and anybody with half a brain *ought* to be afraid of them. And as far as instinct went, why, it seemed only natural that someone who'd spent her whole life on a farm would be more sensitive than some people to the rhythms of nature…the turn of the seasons…the cycles of life and death.

For everything there is a season, and a time to every purpose under Heaven…. That had been one of Aunt Gwen's favorite passages of scripture and she'd quoted it often and taken comfort from it. So had Lucy.

But this year, for some reason, she acknowledged a certain…*sadness* at the turning of the seasons. Perhaps it was partly because Gwen was no longer here to share them with her, but this year the autumn evenings seemed longer to her than usual, the big old farmhouse emptier, the silence…lonelier.

When the phone rang that particular evening, Lucy was curled up on the couch in what had once been, and what Lucy still considered to be, Aunt Gwen's parlor.

Earlier she and Mike had eaten supper together off trays while watching the *CBS Evening News* and *Jeopardy*. Then, while Lucy clicked irritably through the channels looking for her favorite shows, which seemed to be all out of place since the start of the new TV season, Mike had returned to work on his weekly column for *Newsweek* magazine.

He'd moved his computer into the parlor after Gwen's death the previous year, since it was cooler there than any of the spare bedrooms upstairs. In the summer it was a dim and peaceful working place, with dappled shade from the big old oaks that grew on that side of the house. In the fall, afternoon sunlight diffused through autumn's leaves filled the room with a lovely golden warmth, and in winter, the last of each day's meager ration of sunshine found its way between the filigree of bare branches. It had always been Lucy's favorite room, with the upright piano and its collection of family photographs on top, the white-painted mantelpiece covered with still more photos, the shelves full of books. And of course, Gwen's ancient recliner, empty now this past year, and yet…sometimes Lucy swore she could still feel Gwen in that room, and hear the musical grace note of her laughter.

The telephone's polite trill made Lucy jump; calls late in the evening weren't all that common in rural Iowa, and seldom meant good news. As she reached for the cordless that had replaced the old kitchen wall phone a few years back, Mike stopped typing and peered at her expectantly, blind as a mole in his special computer glasses, the dark-rimmed ones that give him a distinctly Harry Potter look.

"Mom?"

Lucy came bolt upright on the couch. "Ellie? Well, for goodness' sake!" Her mom-radar was lighting up like a Christmas tree. Across the room, Mike took off his Harry Potter glasses. "What's wrong?"

"Nothing's wrong, Mom, just called to say hi."

Lucy was unconvinced. "Your voice sounds funny."

"Probably because I'm eating chocolate. Plus, I'm on a cell phone. Mom, I'm fine, really."

"A cell phone!" Lucy was just getting used to cordless. "Well, you sound like you're a million miles away."

"Not quite—I'm in Mexico. On a ship. Listen, Mom—"

"Oh Lord. Not that Save the Whales stuff again? I thought you were through with—"

"It's not that kind of ship. Mom, listen—I need some advice."

"Advice!" Once again Lucy jerked as if she'd been poked. Across the room, Mike's eyebrows had shot up. As they both knew, Rose Ellen, being her mother's daughter, had never been one to take, much less seek, *anyone's* advice. "From me? Are you sure you wouldn't rather ask your dad? He's right here."

"Hey—give him a big hug and a kiss for me." Ellie's voice sounded odd again—slightly muffled, which Lucy knew meant she probably had her mouth full of chocolate. Which made her radar light up even more; Ellie always turned to chocolate in times of stress.

"Mom—I need to ask you something. I haven't got a lot of time…. There's something I need to do—at least, it's something *I* believe I should do—I think other people would probably tell me I *shouldn't* do it—they might even tell me absolutely *not* to do it, and then I'd have to do it anyway, and probably—"

"Ellie—slow down. You're not making sense. What is this thing you think you have to do?"

There was a pause, and then, "I can't really tell you that, Mom."

"I see. Is it dangerous?" Lucy's voice cracked on the last word. She cleared her throat while Mike pushed back his chair.

After an even longer pause, Ellie said, in the voice nearly everyone said was very like her mother's, "I think maybe…it could be, yes."

Lucy sat very still. Mike came to sit beside her, dipping the cushions so that she had to lean back against him. But she straightened herself and said very quietly, "Rose Ellen, you have a good level head on your shoulders. I know you wouldn't do anything foolhardy."

"No, Mama." Now she sounded like she had as a little girl, angelically, breathlessly protesting her innocence. Ellie never had been able to lie convincingly.

Lucy said, in what Mike always called her rusty-nail voice, "But, I know how you are when you really believe in something. If there's something you think you have to do...." She felt Mike's arms come around her and hurriedly cleared her throat as she gripped the phone hard. As if she could somehow force her strength of will and passion through those nonexistent wires. "Listen...honey—you just have to trust yourself. We've taught you to use your head and think for yourself, so you use your own judgment—your own *good* judgment, no one else's. You do what you have to do, honey. But you keep a level head, now, you hear me? You keep your wits about you."

"Yes, Mama. Thanks...I love you." Ellie was laughing...wasn't she? "Mom—tell Dad I love him, too, okay? Hey, listen, I'm sure it'll be okay. So don't worry about me, okay? I'll call you later and tell you all about it."

"Ellie, wait—"

"Bye Mom, bye, Dad. *Don't worry.*"

"Wait—" But the line had gone dead. Lucy punched the disconnect button and swiped angrily at her cheeks. "Damn," she rasped, "I didn't even get to tell her the news about Ethan getting married. You know he was always her favorite cousin."

Mike cleared his throat as he pulled her back against him. "Probably not a good idea, if she was on a wireless phone."

Lucy sniffed. "You think?"

"Not unless you want to read all about it in tomorrow's headlines: President's Son to Wed Notorious Rock Star!"

Lucy laughed...and sniffed again. Mike's arms tightened and he kissed the top of her head. "Hey, love, why're you crying? Ellie'll be fine—like you said, she's got a good head on her shoulders."

Lucy burrowed her face against the chest of the only

person in the world who was allowed to see her cry. "Our children are so far away, Mike. Rose Ellen off on some ship, and Lord only knows where Eric is—it's been months since he's called."

"A little delayed empty-nest syndrome, love?" Mike said softly, holding her close. "It's been quite a few years since our kids flew the coop."

"Yes," Lucy gulped, "but I think it just hit me that they're not coming back."

Chapter 3

McCall was packing it in early. Business had been slow all morning, which was more or less normal for the day after a cruise ship dropped anchor. Today was everybody's day to be off in the jungle swatting mosquitos and climbing pyramids or bird-watching in the biosphere reserves, or, for the younger and more athletically inclined, diving the wrecks and reefs offshore. Tomorrow there'd be another big flurry of shopping just before the ship set sail, everybody stocking up on trinkets and souvenirs to take home, put away in a drawer somewhere and eventually forget all about. But right now the heat and tropical-storm humidity were settling in and siesta time was coming on. He figured he'd just as well call it a day.

He was working up a sweat in the late October heat, trying to wedge the last of his canvasses into his ancient faded blue Volkswagen when he heard a sound that made his blood run cold.

"Taxi? Excuse me, *señor...por favor,* is this, uh... *¿este...esta un taxi?*"

There was no mistaking that raggedy voice.

Sure enough, across the street at the taxi stand near the entrance to the plaza, the cinnamon girl was attempting to rouse the driver of the lone cab parked there from his noonday siesta.

Oh Lord, McCall thought, what's she up to now?

But as much as he tried, he couldn't keep himself from stopping what he was doing to watch her. It didn't help that she was wearing a bright yellow tank top with one of those wraparound things that can't decide whether to be shorts or a skirt, this one in a loud Hawaiian print— hibiscus blossoms and palm fronds in clear shades of red, green and yellow—something like his own paintings, in fact, only a lot prettier. It would probably have hit her a couple inches above the knee if she'd been standing up straight, but since she was bending over to talk to the cab driver through his open window, McCall's view of her legs was extended considerably, and most pleasingly. All in all, she looked like a walking ad for some kind of tropical suntan lotion, and yummy enough to make a man's mouth water.

Except for the big clunky running shoes and the dorky-looking hot-pink sunshade on her head, anyway. McCall couldn't understand why so many tourists wore those sun visor things; he'd never seen a woman yet who looked good in one. Though Cinnamon Girl came close.

Those thoughts were distracting enough that it took him a moment to realize that she was having some trouble making the taxi driver understand where she wanted to go. It looked like she'd given him a piece of paper with the address written on it, but in spite of that the driver kept shaking his head and gesturing in a decidedly negative fashion. Even from where he stood McCall was getting *his* message loud and clear: *Lady, you are loco!*

In her exasperation, Cinnamon Girl snatched back the paper and read what was on it in a loud voice, the way people do, for some reason, when they try to communicate in a foreign language—as if they think deafness is the root of the problem. When she did that, her words carried clearly to McCall's ears, and what he heard made him swear out loud.

What *was* the woman trying to do, get herself killed?

There had to be some mistake. Either that or she was crazy. That was obviously the taxi driver's opinion, and McCall was beginning to think he might have the right idea. No one of sound mind, certainly not a foreigner—*definitely* not a woman—would be caught dead in the area she was asking to be taken to. Well, maybe *dead* was the operative word, all right. What it was, was probably the meanest slum in the whole Yucatan, brush and tin shacks on baked-dirt streets, the principal inhabitants of which seemed to be drug dealers and their customers, and roving bands of mean, scrawny dogs and even meaner and scrawnier children. The few "legitimate" places of business made José's Cantina look like the Ritz; next to their clientele, the two rowdies who'd accosted Cinnamon last night were the Hardy Boys.

The taxi driver was dead on. Clearly this woman was loco.

None of my business. Live and let live.

McCall told himself that, standing there in the street beside his jam-packed VW Bug and shaking his head, for about as long as it took the cab driver to give a classic Latino shrug of surrender as he accepted a handful of dollar bills; for Cinnamon to climb into the taxi's back seat and for it to pull away from the stand with a clashing of gears that clearly expressed its driver's opinion of the whole enterprise.

Well, hell. The only thing McCall could think of that would be worse than wading into this lady's business once again was the way he was going to feel when her cute, tidy little body washed up on the *playa*. Not to mention how bad a murdered *turista* would be for business.

He fought the impulse for a moment or two longer, grinding his teeth on the butt of his cigarette and muttering a few extra choice swearwords. Then he spat what was left of the cigarette into the sandy gutter, shoe-horned himself into the VW and slammed the door. As usual, it took several tries and more swearing before the engine fired, by which time the taxi was long gone. Not that it mattered. With some expressive gear-grinding of his own—and a few silent prayers to the gods who protect fools and children—McCall headed for the wrong side of town.

"Are you sure this is the right place?" Ellie asked, peering through the film of dust on the taxi's window.

The driver pointed toward a jumble of scrap lumber and tin on the opposite side of the rutted dirt road and muttered something Ellie couldn't understand.

With a sigh—really, the crash course in Spanish she'd been given in preparation for this assignment was proving worse than useless—she opened the door and stuck one foot out. Then for a moment she hesitated. She could still call this off. Go back to the ship, notify General Reyes and let him take it from there.

But…*no*. A sense of failure washed over her and when it receded she felt more determined than ever. Her parents hadn't raised her to be either a coward or a quitter. She'd worked too long and hard on this mission—cared about it too much—to let everything fall apart now. Resolute once more, she got out of the taxi.

She'd barely slammed the door behind her when she heard a terrible sound: the roar of an engine and the gnashing of gears.

"Oh—wait! Please—I wanted you to wait for me!" She grabbed for the door handle, but it was too late; the taxi jounced off, leaving her sputtering in its dust cloud.

For a few moments, then, she just stood there, too stunned to think. Fear came slowly, creeping insidiously into her consciousness disguised first as anger, then as a cold little sense of shame. *How could I have done something so stupid? And after what Mama said about me having such a good head on my shoulders. She and Dad will be so disappointed in me.*

Keep your wits about you, Rose Ellen Lanagan.

Take a deep breath. Think, Ellie. Think.

First things first. She'd come here to do a job. She'd come here to make contact with some people. And that was what she was bound and determined to do. She'd worry about how she was going to get back to the plaza later.

Maybe I *should* have left a trail of bread crumbs, she thought.

And for some reason, remembering that, remembering last night and the artist named McCall, made her smile. She even caught herself looking around, squinting in the noonday glare, with the thought in the back of her mind that he might magically turn up again, just in the nick of time. And then she laughed at herself for the twinge of disappointment she felt when she didn't see a slightly disreputable and untidy form shuffling toward her, wearing a loud shirt and a Panama hat, sandals slapping dust and teeth clamped on the butt of an ever-present cigarette.

But…it was siesta time; except for a skinny brown dog that growled at her from between the slats of a fence that looked far too fragile to contain it, the street—using that term loosely—was deserted. There'd be no miraculous rescue today.

Well. So be it. Resolutely, she straightened her sun visor, took a good wrap-grip on the strap of her shoulder bag and started toward the ramshackle building indicated by the taxi driver.

She could see now that it was actually a cantina, of sorts—at least that was the indication of the cardboard signs advertising beer tacked to the walls on either side of a door opening, some so sun-faded they were all but unreadable. That made her feel a little better, actually. At least it appeared to be a legitimate place of business. They'll have a phone, Ellie told herself, ever the optimist. Yes, surely they would. She could call for a cab after her business was concluded.

If… If they show up at all. *If* they'll even talk to me, a woman….

Roused by that thought, she snorted defiantly and stepped through the doorway.

The dimness and the smell inside the cantina hit her like a physical blow. It smelled like old outhouses. New vomit. And a sweet smokiness she remembered from her college days that was either incense or hashish—she never had been certain which. Fortunately, Ellie wasn't squeamish; between her farm upbringing, her crusades on behalf of endangered wildlife and a chosen profession that involved animals at all stages of life and death, she was accustomed to sights and smells some would probably consider revolting.

After that reflexive pause and another moment to let her senses adjust, she crossed the room to a wooden bar that was leaning drunkenly against the back wall. A man sat there on a high, three-legged stool, elbows propped on the bar, drinking a milky liquid from a bottle and lazily smoking a brownish, handrolled cigarette. Perhaps the source of that cloyingly sweet smell? Ellie decided she'd rather not know.

"Señor Avila?" she asked, placing the note with her handwritten instructions on the bar.

The man regarded it with silent disdain, one eye closed against curling smoke.

Ellie was about to resort to her extremely limited knowledge of Spanish when inspiration struck. Feeling quite astute, she reached into her handbag and found the crumpled bills she'd thrust there after paying the taxi driver. She pulled one out and laid it on top of the note-paper. A ten, she noticed with some chagrin; probably a five would have been more than enough. Oh well.

The man slowly picked it up and stuffed it into the pocket of his sweat-stained blue shirt, then jerked his head toward the front of the cantina.

Turning, Ellie saw for the first time that there were three men sitting silently at the table in the corner, half hidden in the shadows behind the shaft of sunlight slanting in through the open doorway. A little chill shivered down her back as two of the men rose and moved unhurriedly to form a silhouetted phalanx across the entrance, blocking her only escape.

McCall drove slowly down the deserted road, squinting into the midday glare and mentally gnashing his teeth. Not a creature was stirring, save for one evil-looking dog shambling idly from one disgusting discovery to another, pausing to sniff them all and occasionally eating one. On the one hand, McCall figured that was a good sign; at least, all things being equal, he thought he could probably handle the dog. On the other, it was obvious the taxi had departed for safer pastures, with or without its passenger, it was impossible to know for certain.

Or rather, there was only one way to know for certain.

Resigned to the inevitable, he parked the Beetle next to a more-or-less vacant lot, arousing the immediate interest of the dog, who shuffled over to investigate and wasted no time in marking this new addition to his territory. With a sigh that was more like a growl, McCall locked up the VW—aware that it was probably going to be futile—and crossed the road to the cantina.

When he stepped through the doorway, he really believed he was ready for anything. A nice little tickle of adrenaline was making his skin tingle in a way that wasn't entirely unpleasant; probably if he'd been of a species possessed of hackles, they'd have been rising. He felt like Clint Eastwood walking into one of those dusty desert bars looking for bad guys to shoot—except that the way he remembered it, Clint never had to contend with the effects of that glare, which made the inside of the cantina black as a cave and McCall consequently blind as a bat for as long as it took his eyes to adjust.

But as it turned out, there was probably nothing that could have prepared him for what did happen.

His first warning was a little rush of air, a whiff of a sweet flowery scent that jolted him with a memory he couldn't place. He threw up his arms reflexively, but instead of a fist or a knife, they met with soft, yielding flesh.

There was a gasp, then a cry, breathless with joy and relief. "Darling—thank God you're here!"

A pair of arms, small but strong, hooked around his neck. A pair of lips, soft but firm, pressed against his. Pressed, not brushed. And for a heady, heart-stopping moment, clung. He tasted moisture and warmth, and sweet, clean woman.

Adrenaline hit him, big-time. Response was automatic; his mind had become incapable of thought. Clutching reflexively, his hands found and closed around a small, firm waist covered in something soft and clingy, but that was as far as he got before the lips peeled themselves from his and he felt instead the skin-shivering brush of breath on his cheek. And then a whisper in his ear, along with enough of that breath to blast the shivers clear through his body.

"You're my husband. You've been sick. *Please* play along...."

Play along? Hell, he didn't even know what the game was!

Now that his eyes had adjusted to the gloom, McCall could see that he and Cinnamon—the owner of the lips and source of that delicious scent—were not alone in that corner of the cantina. Two men wearing jungle camouflage khakis and a faintly military air stood flanking the woman and a little behind, arms folded across outthrust chests, legs planted firmly and apart. Behind them a third man, obviously the one in charge, half sat, half leaned against a rickety wooden table, smoking a cigar. The aura of menace in the room was as unmistakable as the cloud of sweetish smoke that hung in the air like ground fog.

"*¿Quien este?*" The smoker spat the words into a tense and ringing silence.

The woman's golden eyes, bright with fear and pleading, were fastened on McCall's face. What could he do?

So—though with a mental shrug and a familiar sense of foreboding—he hooked his arm around the woman's waist and pulled her against his side.

"I am her husband," he said in Spanish, and added in

silent afterthought, *Just, please God, don't let him ask me what our last name is.*

The cigar smoker watched him with narrowed eyes through the swirling golden fog. "She told us you were sick. You look very healthy to me."

McCall glanced down at Cinnamon—okay, she'd told him her name but he'd forgotten it, dammit—who was either frozen with fear or not very fluent in Spanish. In either case oblivious, and no help to him at all. "I'm feeling much better now," he ventured, and taking a chance that the malady afflicting the absent husband was the one most common to tourists in that region, added with a wan smile, "Something I ate."

The smoker's narrow-eyed stare didn't alter, but around the cigar his lips lifted in a sneer. "So…a little *turista* and you send your woman to do your business for you?"

"I did not send her. She came without my knowledge or permission." McCall added a snort that gave the words a definite ring of sincerity.

"You do not seem to have much control over your woman, señor."

"She has a mind of her own." McCall shrugged. "What is a man to do?"

"I would know what to do with her if she were my woman." The smoker made a gesture, one even Cinnamon had no trouble understanding. She sucked in air in an incensed gasp. The two men flanking them laughed, and McCall, recognizing a male-bonding moment when he saw it, joined in.

"Unfortunately, such things are illegal in my country," he said dryly, as Cinnamon squirmed in his arm to give him a dirty look. Under his breath he snarled at her in English, "Not a word. You're my wife. *Play along.*"

The smoker placed his cigar on the tabletop with an air

of getting down to business. "Enough. We have important matters to discuss. You have brought the money?"

Money? This just keeps getting better and better, thought McCall. But while his hackles were perking up, preparing for the worst, the woman was already pulling a fat envelope out of her handbag.

She held it out to the smoker. "It's all there."

The smoker regarded the envelope with hooded eyes. Recovering his senses, McCall snatched it out of his "wife's" hand and took a quick peek inside. *Yikes.* American bills—hundreds, it looked like—lots of them. Now his hackles not only perked, they positively crawled. What was this he'd gotten himself mixed up in? A drug deal of some kind? Surely not—Lord, the girl might be a little bit loco, but she looked wholesome as cornflakes.

"Your woman handles your financial affairs, too, señor?" The smoker's voice, like his eyes, oozed contempt.

"Like I told you—not with my permission," McCall said with what he hoped was unconcern, lifting a shoulder as he handed over the envelope. The smoker took it and like McCall before him, glanced inside.

"You—" That was as far as Cinnamon got before McCall got his hand clamped across her mouth.

"Shut up," he growled, "for the love of God." He was watching Smoker's face, which had darkened ominously.

"Why are you trying my patience, señor?" McCall stared at him blankly. The smoker smacked the envelope down hard on the tabletop, making the cigar jump. "Where is the rest?"

The woman was squirming frantically against McCall's side, causing his hand to shift just enough. He sucked in air as he felt the sharp sting of her teeth in the fleshy base of his thumb. Stifling shameful urges, he eased the pressure of his hand enough to allow her furious whisper, "Tell him he'll get the rest when we meet his boss."

McCall delivered that message in a carefully neutral voice. Mentally he was grinding his teeth and vowing that if he got out of this mess in one piece and without committing manslaughter, he was going to be faithful and true to his live and let live creed for the rest of his days.

The smoker picked up his cigar and mouthed it while he thought things over—while tension sang like locusts in McCall's ears, and Cinnamon's heart thumped against his side. For some reason that made McCall feel a little less ticked off at her. Maybe even a little bit soft-hearted. Damn his Sir Galahad tendencies all to hell.

Apparently satisfied, for the moment, at least, the smoker gave a little shrug and tucked the envelope full of cash inside his shirt. At the same time he pulled out another, smaller envelope, which he passed to McCall. It felt unpleasantly damp, and McCall had to stifle a fastidious urge to handle it with a thumb and forefinger.

"My boss will speak with you," Smoker said in staccato Spanish, "but not here. Those are your instructions. Be at the designated location tomorrow evening. Come alone, just you two. If you do not..." He narrowed his eyes thoughtfully at the woman huddled against McCall's side. "Perhaps...I should take your wife with me, eh? To insure that you follow these instructions."

The thug closest to Cinnamon grinned in anticipation, showing missing teeth. She didn't make a sound, but McCall felt her shrinking. He jerked her around and thrust her behind him, beyond the reach of either thug. Without going through McCall first, anyway.

"That won't be necessary," he said easily, though his heart was pounding so hard he could hear it himself. "I will follow your instructions—I am not stupid."

There was another tense pause, and then unexpectedly the smoker laughed. "Keep your wife, señor. I do not envy you. But take my advice, eh? A woman needs a firm hand."

"Yeah," said McCall, "I'll consider it." With a firm hand on his "wife's" upper arm, he was already steering her toward the door of the cantina. After a nod from their boss, the two soldier bees stepped reluctantly aside to let them pass.

Outside the door he paused, cringing in the light, once again momentarily blinded, lungs in a state of shock from their first contact in a while with nontoxic air. The arm he still held had gone slack and quiescent—for the moment.

And then... "Thank you," Cinnamon said, in a voice so clipped and prim he'd have found it comical, maybe, if he hadn't been so damned angry.

"Thank you?" he muttered under his breath as he towed her across the sunbaked street. "She says, 'Thank you'?" McCall couldn't remember the last time he'd been this angry.

"You can let go of my arm now," she breathed. She sounded winded, but he ignored that as well as the suggestion.

No longer the least bit quiescent, she struggled and tugged against his grip. "I said, let *go* of me."

"I will let go of you when I'm damn good and ready. Which is when and *if* we get out of this hellhole with our hides intact, *and* you've told me exactly what in the hell you've got me mixed up in."

She hissed at him like an angry cat. "What if they're watching? They'll think we're quarreling."

"Quarreling?" He didn't know whether to laugh at her or yell. "We're *married*, remember? I'm your *husband*.

That's what married people do, isn't it? They *fight*."
They'd reached the car, so he figured it was safe to let go
of her arm.

She eyed him sideways while he pulled his crumpled
pack of cigarettes out of his shirt pocket. She kept rubbing
sullenly at the marks his fingers had left on her upper arm,
and since he didn't much like looking at those marks,
himself, McCall shifted his gaze away from her and fixed
a narrow-eyed stare on the door of the cantina instead.

"Don't you think we should be leaving?" she asked
after a moment, sounding nervous as her gaze followed
his.

He deliberately waited until he'd finished lighting up,
taking his time about it, then glanced at her, eyebrows
raised. "We?"

Behind the cinnamon sprinkle of freckles her skin
looked flushed, though he conceded that might have been
from the sun. "You wouldn't just…leave me here." Her
voice was flat, certain.

Which naturally made him contrary. He inhaled and
held it, counting pulsebeats, then blew smoke. "Don't
tempt me."

"But…they could come out of there any minute. If they
see this car—"

He pretended to be affronted. "What's wrong with my
car?"

"Well, it's not a tourist's car, that's for sure," she
snapped in that crusty voice of hers. "My God, how old
is this thing?"

"Ancient—probably about as old as I am," McCall
muttered, and then, bristling, "Hey—it got me here,
didn't it? Good thing for you. And it'll get us both out of
here. That's what counts." He planted the cigarette between his teeth and hauled out his keys.

But she was staring at the Beetle as if seeing it for the first time. "How, exactly?" she asked in a fascinated tone.

McCall didn't think that required a reply. He threw her a withering look as he opened the door. Then for a while he stood in silence, considering the piles of paintings wedged into the VW's every nook and cranny, including the front passenger seat.

Ah, hell. What was he going to do? Much as he'd like to have done so, he really couldn't go off and leave the woman there. Not after what he'd just gone through to rescue her. Growling to himself, he manhandled the stack of canvasses out of the front seat and leaned them lovingly, one by one, against the weathered fence nearby. I'll come back for you, he promised, giving the outermost one a pat.

Just then the dog, who'd been watching all this activity from the middle of the street while lethargically scratching himself, trotted over to the paintings and lifted his leg.

"Everybody's an art critic," McCall muttered, as Cinnamon clapped a hand over her mouth to stifle either laughter or dismay. Since he couldn't be certain which, he just jerked his head toward the open door and snarled, "Get in." Then he went around to the driver's side without waiting for her.

She gave him a sideways look as she settled into the seat, which he ignored while he sent up a prayer and set about the complicated process of getting the VW's engine fired up and running. When he had it settled down to a more or less reliable rattle, she cleared her throat and said in her Miss Prissy voice, "I really wish you wouldn't smoke in here."

McCall couldn't believe it. Here, he'd just hauled the woman's cute little behind out of the fire for the third time in two days, and she was telling him where he could smoke? He was beginning less and less to think about how cute those cinnamon freckles were.

He took the cigarette from his mouth and pointed past her toward the window with it clamped between his first two fingers. "Listen, sister, it's my car. If you don't like it, you can always call a cab." Okay, he was being boorish—he did know how to be a courteous, unobtrusive smoker. But at the moment he was feeling a mite used and abused, and not in much of a mood to be accommodating.

Still, he felt a *little* bit ashamed of himself as he clamped the cigarette back between his teeth and yanked the VW into gear. So, when they were underway, he glanced over at the woman now sitting silent and pensive beside him and said calmly enough, "You know, you've got a lot of gall, sister. Pulling that Goody Two-Shoes routine after you've just been doing business with three of the meanest-looking characters I've ever seen, in one of the worst dives in this or any other town."

He waited for an explanation, but instead of giving him one she scrunched her face into a look of irritation and snapped, "I really wish you'd stop calling me sister. Sounds like a bad Humphrey Bogart impression."

That surprised him. He gave a snort of laughter, then threw her a measuring look. "What do you know? You're way too young to remember Bogie."

She met his eyes for one fleeting moment. "And you're not?" She shrugged and faced forward again. "I used to watch old movies on satellite TV with my Aunt Gwen when I was a kid."

He wanted to leave it there, he really did. There wasn't anything he wanted to know about this lady except what it was she'd gotten him mixed up in that was likely to land him in a Mexican jail. Still, he heard himself say, "Yeah? Where was it you grew up that you needed a satellite dish to watch old movies on TV?"

"Iowa." Her exhalation had almost a wistful sound. "On a farm."

A farm… "Figures," he muttered sourly. But he kept hearing that sigh.

It was a few minutes later when she said softly, just as if she'd read his mind, "It's not drugs or anything like that. If that's what you're worried about."

He could only hope she was telling him the truth. He glanced at her but didn't say anything more as he guided the Beetle, jerking and wheezing, through streets slowly returning to life after the midday siesta. She didn't say anything either, though she seemed restless and edgy, as if she sure did want to.

Impulsively, he pulled into a sandy parking area overlooking the *playa* and shut off the motor. When he did that she straightened up in a hurry, peering through the windshield.

"Why are we stopping here?"

McCall was busy cranking down his window and lighting up a new cigarette, making himself comfortable. Leaning back, he gestured toward the vista spread out before them—aquamarine water, blue sky brushed with the first of Tropical Storm Paulette's cloudy fingers…white sandy beach sheltered on the right by brown cliffs topped with Mayan ruins, where tourists without sense enough to get out of the midday sun could be seen scurrying about in it like ants, and on the left, by a point furry with the palm trees that marked the beginnings of the tourist hotels.

"What," he said with exaggerated innocence, "you don't like the view?"

She just looked at him, studiously ignoring it.

And he looked back at her, this time holding those hot golden eyes of hers for a lot longer than a moment. Until he felt himself running short of breath. Then he shrugged and nodded toward the beach, the other cars parked nearby. "This is a safe enough part of town—probably farther from that cruise ship pier of yours than you'd care to walk in this heat—" he glanced at her running shoes "—even in those." He took a drag from his cigarette while she waited silently. "This is as far as you go, sister. Unless you care to tell me exactly what it is you've got me mixed up in. And why."

Chapter 4

Ellie was caught, as her mom might have said, between a rock and a hard place. The man deserved an explanation, he really did. But how *much* could she tell him?

What did she really know about him, after all?

As far as she could tell he was just some kind of expatriate American beach bum who scratched out a living selling dreadful paintings to gullible tourists. A beach bum who, for some reason, kept showing up just in time to bail her out of trouble. Three times, now. *Three.*

That made her think of something she'd read once, she couldn't recall where. Something like...once is happenstance, twice is coincidence and the third time is enemy action.

Though, unpleasant as he tried to be, he seemed like anything but an enemy. Could he possibly be another undercover agent? One of General Reyes's men, perhaps? He was certainly fluent enough in Spanish.

She blurted out before she could stop herself. "Who *are* you?"

Her rescuer seemed startled by the question at first, then more like...uncomfortable with it. "Just a guy," he growled, shifting his shoulders against the back of the seat as if they itched. "A guy trying to mind his own business. *And* make a living—" he jabbed a finger angrily in her direction "—which you aren't making easy to do, sister."

Ellie sat back with an exhalation, suddenly feeling deflated, flattened by the weight of guilt. "I'm sorry about the paintings," she said, her eyes on the beach, crowded at this hour with sunbathers. "I really am. I—I'll pay you for them." Well, the government would, probably. But she would feel better knowing they had. "It's the least—"

"No. That's not the least, sister, not by a long shot. The *least* you can do is tell me what the hell's—"

But at that point Ellie jerked straight up in her seat, her brain belatedly registering what she'd been staring at. "Is this—" she croaked, "—is this beach *topless?*"

The man beside her turned his head to glare wickedly at her, lips stretched in a mirthless grin around the cigarette clamped between his teeth. "Yeah, it is—why?" Before she could answer he gave a bark of laughter and tossed the cigarette out the window in a gesture of pure frustration. "Lady, I can't figure you out, I really can't. One minute there you are, involved in business transactions with thugs in a slum dive I wouldn't take my worst enemy—or my ex-wife—to, and the next you're doing this little Miss-Goody-Two-Shoes-from-Iowa number and expecting me to buy it."

"I'm not expecting you to buy anything," she shot back, both stung and embarrassed. It had been a long time since she'd felt like such a little hick. "It's just that—I thought—well, isn't it illegal here?"

Staring straight ahead, he lifted an indifferent shoulder. "Technically, I suppose. This is a pretty laid-back town. Who's going to file a complaint?" He shot her a glance that was half challenge, half contempt. *"You?"*

"Of course not." Ooh, she was really starting to dislike this guy—rescuer or not. Temper simmered, then exploded. "Oh wait—I get it. You brought me here on purpose, didn't you? Just to make me uncomfortable. To get me to talk, I suppose. What—I'm supposed to get so flustered I'll spill all my dirty little secrets?"

He let his gaze drop slowly, appraisingly to her chest. Inexplicably and in spite of her anger, she felt her nipples contract. Then he looked away again, with that shrug of indifference that to Ellie was more incendiary than a slap. "Never occurred to me. Frankly, my dear, I didn't even think about it. It was just a good place to park."

"Well, it's not going to work," Ellie snapped, ignoring that. "I grew up on a farm. I've lived on fishing boats and in tents. You think I'm going to go all wimpy at the sight of a few bare boobs? Listen, I've probably seen more stuff than you have, *buster.*"

He was looking at her again, this time with eyebrows raised and blue eyes glinting in what appeared, unbelievably, to be amusement. A fan of laugh lines had deepened at their corners. Something about those eyes made Ellie's anger evaporate as quickly as it had come, like the rain puddles back home on a hot summer's day.

"Besides," she said on a grudging exhalation, settling back in her seat, "it wouldn't have been necessary. I was going to explain."

"So...explain," he said softly.

So...explain. But it came back to the same question: How much could she say? How far could she trust him?

She couldn't possibly tell him everything. Where should she begin?

It was getting warm in the car. She pulled off her sun visor and laid it carefully in her lap, lifted her arms and raked her fingers through her hair, then rolled down her window and closed her eyes as a damp ocean breeze stirred the hair on her temples. She could feel it tightening into corkscrew curls. When she opened her eyes again, she saw that the man—beach bum, artist, rescuer, whoever he was—was gazing in fascination at her hair, at those very same curls.

What was the matter with the man, she wondered? With all those naked bodies out there, right in front of him, he was looking at *her*…at her *hair,* yet? A moment ago he'd been gazing at her breasts, erect nipples and all, with complete boredom. Just now, the look in his eyes had been that of a starving man at a banquet-hall window.

It suddenly struck her how small the car was…how close to him she was sitting. She felt much too warm. Claustrophobic. Her heart was beating much too fast—faster even than in the cantina, facing those three smugglers.

She half turned in her seat and pulled up a knee, making a little more space between them. "First," she said, clearing her throat, "I just want to remind you that I did not ask you to show up in that cantina today." She narrowed her eyes and fired the question, much like a cat pouncing. "Why did you, by the way?" He didn't answer immediately, just shifted his gaze slightly to meet hers. Uncomfortable again, she mumbled, "Not that I'm sorry you did, you understand. I'd just like to know what you were doing there. It *is* kind of odd…."

He waved that off with a grimace. "Coincidence.

Heard you talking to the taxi driver.'' And now it was he who seemed uncomfortable.

''And you just…decided to follow me?''

He muttered defensively under his breath, shifting in that irritable way he had. ''Well, hell, I thought I'd better. You were heading for a dangerous part of town.'' He halted to stare fixedly through the windshield, eyes narrowed in an angry squint.

But for some reason Ellie found herself remembering how blue those eyes were…how clear and clean. Remembering a look she'd caught in them once or twice. Now she wondered if the look could possibly have been… compassion.

What a strange man he is, she thought. So rude and cranky, determined to seem crude and cynical, and yet…

''Do you really have a husband?'' he asked suddenly, turning his head to look at her.

It seemed two could play the cat-and-mouse game. Caught by surprise, she answered quickly, ''Yes, of course.'' Too quickly. Too breathlessly. She could feel the heat of the lie in her cheeks, and looked away, fighting for composure. ''He…he was supposed to go with me, you see—yesterday evening, too. We both thought it was just a stomach upset—you know, the *turista* thing? But then last night they had to fly him to Florida for emergency surgery. Appendicitis.''

''So, you decided you'd go it alone.'' He spoke very quietly, staring straight ahead again, only his staccato fingers on the steering wheel betraying inner turmoil. ''Jeez. Must have been some important business.''

Ellie nodded eagerly. ''Oh, it was. We'd been working for months to set up a meeting. That's why I couldn't just let it all be for nothing.''

''Uh-huh.'' He reached into his shirt pocket and took

out a battered pack of cigarettes, tapped one out, put it in his mouth and lit it. When he had everything stored away in his pocket again, he settled back, blew smoke carefully out the window and said in a gravelly voice, "So tell me—what *was* it you were buying with that wad of cash?"

"I told you—it's not drugs," Ellie said stiffly.

"Not drugs?"

"That I promise you." But he held her eyes, refusing to let it go at that, and after a tense few moments more she folded. "Animals," she said on a gust of released breath.

"Animals?" He repeated the word as if he'd never heard it before.

She nodded. "Birds...reptiles...you know. Some of them are very rare, and worth a lot of money. A *lot*." She paused, and when he continued to stare at her in frowning incomprehension, added lamely, "I told you last night, remember? We own a pet shop. In Portland, Oregon."

"Rare..." he said slowly, as if he hadn't heard that. "As in...endangered?"

"Well, *some* maybe, but—"

"As in...*illegal?*"

She could feel the warmth in her cheeks again. "Oh, I wouldn't know about *that*," she hurriedly said. "The important thing is that these animals are being shipped regardless—"

"Smuggled, you mean."

"—and most of them die en route. Because the people who do the...shipping...don't know anything about animals, you see? My husband and I do know about animals. So, we thought, if we could go directly to the source—"

"The source."

She really wished he'd stop repeating everything she said. "That's right—the man in charge of shipping—"

"The head smuggler, you mean."

Ellie just looked at him, fighting hard to hold on to her temper. "That envelope he gave you back there in the cantina," she said, speaking slowly and carefully. "It should have the instructions—directions, I mean—for the meeting. Maybe a map. If we're supposed to be at the meeting place by day after tomorrow.... By the way, can I see it, please?"

Her rescuer parked his cigarette between his teeth and pulled the envelope from his shirt pocket. "You mean this one?" But instead of handing it over he just went on holding the envelope and looking at her, an odd, wary look in his eyes.

Almost as if he was waiting for something.

She held out her hand. "Yes—can I see it? We have to—" And that was when it hit her.

"Oh...no..." she whispered. She felt herself go cold.

Her companion took a long drag from his cigarette and said mildly, "Just who in the hell is this *we,* Kemo Sabe? You and your *husband?*" His lips had a sardonic tilt, but the glint in his eyes was anything but amused. "Ah—that's right." He snapped his fingers. "According to you, he's in a hospital somewhere in Florida. Man, I hope he heals fast. But then..."

He'd been wondering when it was going to occur to her.

She'd clamped a hand over her mouth. Now she peeled it away, leaving a white, pinched look around her lips and the imprint of fingers on her flaming cheeks. Her voice was uneven, hushed with dismay. "As far as those guys are concerned, *you're* my husband."

"Uh-uh," said McCall flatly, shaking his head. "Don't even think about it, sister."

She opened her mouth, then closed it again without saying anything. Just went on looking at him. Looked at him for so long those golden eyes of hers seemed to shimmer. It struck him suddenly that begging and pleading weren't in this woman's repertoire. That asking for—even *needing*—help would never be easy for her.

It also struck him that the fact she'd had to accept *his* help, not once but *three* times, meant that he was probably never going to make it on to her top ten list of favorite people. He didn't know why he minded that, but he did.

"What are you looking for?"

She'd dragged her handbag onto her lap and was rummaging around in it like a hungry dog digging for a bone.

"Chocolate," she said shortly, without looking up. "I don't suppose…ah!" She fished a small plastic bag with several foil-wrapped lumps in it out of the depths of the purse and held it up with an air of triumph that reminded him of himself, out of smokes and discovering a lost pack with a couple of bent and crumpled cigarettes still left in it.

He watched with a kind of revolted fascination as she unwrapped one of the lumps.

"Damn—melted…" She made a face at the brown goo that had oozed out of the foil, but managed to suck the mess into her mouth—most of it, anyway. She carefully licked her fingers, then her lips, and crumpled the foil into a tiny ball before diving back into the bag for another lump. She repeated the whole process for the second chocolate, then a third, each time returning the foil wrapper to the plastic bag after it had been licked clean of chocolate. Then she briefly closed her eyes, took a deep breath and paused, before finally dropping the plastic bag back into her purse.

"So? Some people smoke," she said pointedly when she looked over and saw him staring at her. "I eat chocolate—so what?"

"Hey," he said with a shrug, "whatever works." But he hoped she hadn't noticed the way *he* kept swallowing. He for *sure* hoped she never guessed how the sight of those ripe-cherry lips of hers drenched in melted chocolate was making his mouth water.

He had his hand on the ignition key when she said quietly, "I'd pay you. *Very* well. There's a lot at stake...."

"A lot of money, you mean."

She jerked her head to give him a sharp, almost guilty look. "Of course, what did you think I meant? Yes, there's a *lot* of money involved. I—my husband and I— would be willing to split it with you—" she paused, and he could see her thinking it over "—three ways."

McCall shook his head, but he couldn't keep from smiling as he turned the key. "Sorry," he said, as the Beetle's ignition, for the first time in memory, fired on the first try.

"Fifty-fifty," she said breathlessly. He put his hand on the gearshift. She reached over and placed her hand on his. "Please—think about it. That's a lot of money. I don't think you realize—"

"I have all the money I need," he growled, shaking his head. Not looking at her. Wishing she'd take her hand off his. Hoping she'd leave it there.

She made a little sound of frustration as she took her hand from his, finally, and gestured with it toward the jumble of canvasses in the back seat. "Business must be *very* good." Hard to miss the sarcasm.

In spite of it, he kept his face and tone serene. "My

needs are simple.'' He tossed away his cigarette and waited for a bus full of tourists returning from a visit to the ruins to go by, then pulled out into its exhaust wake.

He thought about lighting up another cigarette, but for some reason didn't. Beside him, Cinnamon sat in silence, staring as intently as he at the road ahead. After a while she said in a voice that was even scratchier than usual: ''What if I said to name your price?''

He didn't know why that got to him, but it did. He smacked the steering wheel hard with his open palm. ''*Damn* it, woman, it's not about money.''

Again that breathlessness. ''I said *price*. It doesn't have to be money.''

He shot her a look. Surely she hadn't meant that the way she *could* have meant it. Not this woman—Miss Goody Two-Shoes from Iowa with her cinnamon freckles and Nikes, smuggler of illegal animals, wholesome as molasses cookies…. *Ah, hell.*

''I *meant*,'' he said between clenched teeth, ''that money isn't everything. Maybe you're not old enough to have found that out yet, but it's true. Some things are more important than money—like my life, for instance. I mean, my life*style*. I like my life. I live simply, quietly, no hassles. Live and let live. I don't bother anybody and nobody bothers me. Zero stress—you get it? That's the way I want it. And one thing I've found out, sister, is that the more money you have, the more stress. Let me tell you, I've had it and I don't want it anymore. You can keep your money.''

''You could give it away. There must be something you care about.'' Her voice sounded shaken; he could feel her eyes on him, so intense he felt their heat. Like sitting in the sun.

He stuck his lip out, pretending to think about it, then

shook his head. "Nope," he said, "can't think of a thing. Just numero uno..."

"So," she said tightly, suddenly angry, "you've dropped out of the world, is that it? Now you just...*sit* here with your head in the sand and let somebody else take responsibility for what happens to this planet and the creatures that live on it."

He gave a hoot of astounded laughter. "Listen to you, Miss Goody Two-Shoes! Don't tell me *you* care about this earth's poor creatures."

"Of course I care," she shouted, and to his astonishment her voice cracked, as if she were only a good breath away from crying. "I own a pet shop, remember? Do you know what it's like to see those animals, the way they ship them? Those parrots you paint—can you imagine one of those beautiful creatures crammed into a cardboard tube designed to hold tennis balls? They even stuff them into the wheelwells of cars. To cross deserts! They arrived *cooked*." She paused, breathing hard. "I'm just trying to put a stop to it," she said, and after a moment finished in a whisper, "That's all."

Well, *damn*. She sure *sounded* as if she meant that. Damned if he didn't almost believe her. Which was more than he could say for some of the things she'd told him. That way she had of blushing, sometimes, while she was telling him something ordinary. He had to wonder about that blush.

He drove in silence, thinking about it as he threaded his way along the main tourist street, pastel tourist hotels on one side, palm trees and beach and aquamarine water on the other, para-sailers gliding through the afternoon sky like butterflies darting and dipping above the lazy surf. Familiar sights to him, after so many years.

I like my life...it's the way I want it. No hassles...

He pulled into the taxi zone closest to the pier and parked, putting the VW in neutral but keeping the motor putt-putting away.

His passenger had her door open almost before he'd stopped, but then, instead of getting out, she turned to him and in that oddly prim little way she had, all stiffened up with pride, said once again, "Thank you." Then she let out a breath and smiled—wryly, but a smile nonetheless. He realized it had been a long time since he'd seen it. "For saving me—again. I'm not sure what you saved me from, but I'm sure it wouldn't have been pleasant. So…thank you. I mean it. Mister—it's McCall, right?"

"No mister. Just McCall." He took the hand she offered. It was unbelievably small, almost childlike. He found himself suddenly remembering her kiss, and the feel of her body tucked up against him. Nothing childlike about that. No sir.

"And you're…Ellie." Yeah, he remembered it now. Such a gentle name for a cinnamon girl. "Ellie…what?" He asked her that belatedly, remembering that she had a husband. Asking himself what did it matter what her name was, in that case. He was many things, but a seducer of other men's wives wasn't one of them.

"Ellie's enough." But she gave him her smile—the real one, briefly—before she got out of the car. Then she leaned down and said through the open window, "It's short for Rose Ellen Lanagan. My dad's Mike Lanagan." She straightened and walked away quickly, toward the pier.

McCall stared after her. *Mike Lanagan.* Was that supposed to mean something? Why did that sound so familiar to him? Something from his former life…. He shook his head once, hard, forcing the memory back into the dusty attic of his past.

More germane to the present, if that was her dad's name—Lanagan—why had she given him her maiden instead of her married name?

And something else. Why didn't she seem worried about having told him all this? Hadn't it even occurred to her that he might go straight to the police?

And what about that, McCall? What *are* you going to do? Live and let live?

He was chewing on that when he noticed something that turned him cold all over. The envelope, the one the cigar-smoking boss-thug had given him. The one containing directions to a meeting with smugglers of illegal animals. Smugglers who, according to Miss Ellie, didn't seem to care how many of their cargo lived or died. People, therefore, with little or no regard for life, animal or human.

She had that envelope in her hand.

He shut off the motor and got out of the VW and called to her over the roof. She paused and turned to look back at him. "What are you going to do?" he asked her, nodding toward the envelope.

She glanced down as if surprised to see it there, then lifted it, gazed at it, turned it over once. Shrugged. "I don't know," she said, and started walking again.

Live and let live. It seemed a fading memory to him now.

He jammed his keys into his pocket and set out after her at a jog trot. Which was more exercise than he was used to on a hot muggy afternoon, which, he told himself, was why he was out of breath and his heart beating hard when he caught up with her.

"Come on, Ellie," he panted, shortening his customary lazy stride to match her short quick one. "Can't you just let it go? For now, at least? Hey, at least until your husband's back on his feet?''

She stopped walking and looked up at him, rosy from the sun and the heat and the exertion. He had a sudden and thoroughly shameful urge to take her in his arms and kiss her, husband or no.

''First of all,'' she said in a matter-of-fact tone, ''these people are incredibly paranoid. Do you know how hard it's been to win their trust, even *this* much? Any kind of delay, any glitches, and I'm afraid they'll call the whole thing off. But besides that…aren't you forgetting something?'' She looked at him for a long time, but he waited for her to say it. She did at last, in a voice soft and scratchy as wool. ''What happens if we happen to run into those three who were there today? As we surely would. As far as they're concerned, *you* are my husband.'' Her lips tilted wryly. ''And let me tell you, McCall, you look nothing at all like my p—like Ken. How do I account for the fact that I'm now married to somebody completely different?''

McCall didn't have much of an answer for that, so after a while he said, through a grimace of helplessness and a tightness in his belly, ''You're going to go through with this, aren't you? On your own?''

She shrugged and turned to walk on. ''I don't know. Maybe. If I have to.''

He caught her arm and held on to it when she would have jerked away. ''I can't let you do that.''

She gave a small, incensed gasp. ''You mean you think you can stop me?''

''No,'' McCall said with a weary sigh, ''I mean I'm going with you.''

He didn't know what he'd expected her response to

be—a little Snoopy-dance, maybe; a small "Yippee," or at the very least a restrained, "Okay, cool."

What she did was look at him for a long time without saying a word, a long enough time for him to begin to get good and uncomfortable with what he'd done. *Way* long enough for him to start to have second—and third— thoughts.

Then she put her palms flat against his chest, stood up on her tippy toes, and kissed him.

On the cheek. Nothing at all like last time—the Hello-Hubby kiss. And the effect it had on him was a whole lot different, too, though both had left him dazed and con-fused, and aching in places he hadn't felt much of any-thing in for a long, long time.

For one thing, he suddenly remembered what that scent of hers was and where he knew it from. Orange blossoms, that's what it was. It made him think of when he was a kid, and the road between his dad's garage on the outskirts of Bakersfield, California, and his school in town was still lined with groves instead of subdivisions, and sometimes when the trees were in bloom the air would smell so sweet he'd roll down his window and suck it in with all his might, just trying to drink that air....

That and the kiss—sweet, impulsive, genuine—left him with an ache in his throat and a rough, cranky feeling that was like hearing certain old songs on top of too much tequila.

"Thank you," she said. Nothing prissy about it this time, just soft and real, and sweet, like the kiss.

"I'll need to see that envelope," he said gruffly. "See where it is they want us to go. See if there's a map, at least." He held out his hand.

She held on to the envelope, enfolding it in both hands against her chest, eyes going wary again. "You really do mean it? You'll come with me to the meeting? Pretend to be my husband?''

"I said I would." McCall waggled his fingers impatiently. "Come on, hand it over—before I change my mind."

"How do I know you aren't just trying to get the directions away from me?" she demanded, flushed and breathless again. "To keep me from going?"

He gave an exasperated snort—though in his heart he rather admired her for thinking of that. And wished he'd thought of it first. "Come on," he growled, "if I'm going to be your husband, don't you think you should start trusting me?"

Trust you? A beach-bum-slash-artist I don't know from Adam? Ellie wanted to say it, but didn't. "We'll both look at it—together," she said firmly, then paused, chewing on her lip. "Is there someplace we can go? Not the ship," she hurriedly added, before he could suggest it. "They know my husband there. They already think I'm a terrible wife for not going to the hospital with him—God knows what they'd think if I showed up with you. No—what about a restaurant? We can have lunch while we're at it." She was starving, actually; she'd been too nervous to eat before the meeting. Except for the Hershey's Kisses, she'd had nothing to eat since breakfast.

McCall glanced at his watch. "Best thing would probably be if we just go to my place."

"Your place?" *Mamas warn their little girls about guys like this.* And yet, try as she would, Ellie couldn't find anything sinister or even suggestive in the invitation. Not the way he'd said it. Just business. She wondered if the funny little twinge she felt could possibly be disappointment.

"What, you still don't trust me?" He was scowling at

her, an impatient, sideways look. "No worries, sister. You're probably young enough to be my daughter." She made a small sound of insulted surprise, which he ignored. "Look, I'm going to have to unload the Beetle anyway, if we're going to be heading south first thing in the morning. Not to mention one or two things *I* need to take care of. Believe it or not, I do have a life. Hey, look—suit yourself. Stay here, if you want to. I'll pick you up tomorrow morning." And he was heading back up the pier, sandals slapping and shirttail fluttering, muttering grumpily to himself.

"Wait!" Ellie yelled. Her mind was awhirl. Trust him? In spite of his overwhelmingly generous offer, about as far as she could throw him—which was why she was no way in hell about to let him out of her sight. What if he didn't come back? She'd have no idea how to find him again. *Young enough to be your daughter? What is that?*

He paused and looked back at her long enough to bark, "What? Are you coming or not?"

"Coming!" she snapped back. Dammit, there was no way she was young enough to be this man's daughter— and she was furious with him for making her feel as if she was. With that in mind she took a deep breath and fought down her temper. "Excuse me," she said with what sounded to her like simpering politeness, "but I have to tell the captain I'm leaving the ship. And I'll need to get my stuff."

He took a few steps back toward her, warily, as if approaching a possibly dangerous animal. "Why? I told you—we don't have to leave until tomorrow." She didn't say anything, just looked at him. Realization came to him a moment later, and he halted, teeth bared in a sardonic smile. "Ah. I see. You really *don't* trust me, do you?" He ambled toward her, still smiling, arms folded across his chest. "Kind of got you on the horns of a dilemma, hasn't it, sister? Don't trust me enough to come home with me, but don't trust me enough to let me out of your sight, either." He made a brief, tsking sound. "Must be tough, being so suspicious all the time."

She held her ground as he came closer, though her heartbeat seemed to accelerate with every step he took. When he came to a stop in front of her, folded arms almost brushing her chest, she felt as if she were standing on a moving boat, as if the pier under her feet were rocking with the force of her own pulse. Her eyes were on a level with his beard-stubbled chin. Gray stubble mixed with reddish brown. Hurriedly, she dropped her gaze—and saw dense, sun-bronzed skin, sun-bleached hair nestled in the deep V of a tropical-print shirt. Were there a few gray hairs mixed in? She caught a quick breath. *Oh, good grief...*

"I'm going to tell you something," he said in a soft-rough growl that seemed to resonate in her very bones. "And listen carefully, because I'm only gonna say it once. I don't like to let it get around too much. I do have a reputation to think about. However. In my own way, I am a man of honor. There are certain rules for living that, for completely selfish reasons, I try never to break. You, sister, are a married woman. I make it a point never to mess around with other men's wives, for the same reason I make it a point never to cheat at cards. Saves me having to watch my back all the time. See, I'm a live-and-let-live kind of guy. No hassles—that's my motto.

"Oh—and one other thing. I am also a man of my word. I told you I'd go with you to meet these...guys. We shook hands on it. I don't go back on my handshake."

Incomprehensibly rattled, Ellie sucked in a breath and

retorted, "Yes, well, unfortunately, I have only your word for that."

She was even more unnerved when he threw back his head and laughed. So unnerved that her gaze jerked upward and collided with his. And—oh, Lord, why did she keep forgetting how blue his eyes were? How clear and clean and...*honest?* And right now, bright with amusement.

"I guess you're right about that," he said, still softly chuckling.

And Ellie, still in thrall of those eyes, heard herself murmur, "I'm sorry."

"Hey—if you *were* my daughter, I'd probably be the first one to tell you not to trust me. I think." He seemed to think about that, then shrugged it off. "So, what's it gonna be? Coming or staying?"

"Both," Ellie said firmly, having just at that very moment made up her mind. "Coming with you and staying with you. But I still have to get my stuff."

"Where you gonna put it? On the roof? My car's full up, if you remember. And," he added darkly, "I'm not sacrificing any more paintings for you, lady. At the rate my stock is being depleted, if I hang around with you much longer I'm going to be out of business. We'll go and unload first, have some lunch and take a look at those directions. Check out a map. Then I'll bring you back here so you can check out of your floating hotel. How's that?"

"Fine," said Ellie meekly. She was wondering what her parents would think of their nice level-headed daughter if they knew she was about to go home with a beach bum she'd only just met.

Chapter 5

MᴄCall's house was a surprise to Ellie. She'd imagined him living in a rickety beach shack with palm thatch on the roof and no glass in the windows. Instead, his house sat on a small cliff just outside of town, reached by wooden stairs that scaled the cliff in a series of short zig-zags, and while it *was* slightly rickety and did have a thatched roof, it was much too substantial ever to be called a shack. Made of stone covered with dingy white plaster, it rather reminded Ellie of a sulky seagull squatting on a pile of rocks.

On the other hand, she thought, in a way it was just like him—scruffy and eccentric, but with a certain rakish charm.

Rakish charm? She sucked in a breath as somewhere in the back of her mind alarms began beeping a steady warning, like the monitors in an ICU. Not the ones that bring the crash cart at a dead run, more like the ones that cause the nurses on duty to glance up, maybe come over and make a few minor adjustments, then go on about their business. Nothing to worry about, not yet, the alarms said. Just be on the alert.

McCall parked the VW on a widened-out spot on the dirt road, close to the side of the cliff near the base of the steps.

"Do you mind taking a load up now?" he asked as he got out of the car, pocketing his keys, and began pulling canvasses out of the back seat. "Saves a trip."

"Sure." Already out of the car herself, Ellie folded her seat forward and began tugging on canvasses.

"Here, take these." He dumped his own load into her outstretched arms. "I've got a system. Go on up—it's unlocked. I'll catch up with you."

"Right," said Ellie as she cast a dubious look upward.

But the steps were neither as steep nor as rickety as they looked, and she arrived at the top safely and only slightly winded. The steps ended at a flagstone pathway, flanked by bird-of-paradise and lily-of-the-Nile and some drought-resistant succulents, which led to a wide three-arched veranda. The veranda was the same stone and plaster as the house itself, with the same type of thatched roof, and a floor made of flagstone, like the path. Unexpectedly enchanted, Ellie paused in its deep shade to look out on the view of thatched roofs, palm trees, and pale aqua-blue water. Clouds were building along the horizon, where a line of ultramarine marked the beginning of deep water, like a line drawn with a dark blue Magic Marker.

"Nice view," she said to McCall, who was just then stepping onto the flagstone pathway, canvasses tucked under both arms.

It occurred to her that in spite of being a fairly heavy smoker, he seemed to be in good physical condition. Certainly no more out of breath after that climb than she was.

She told herself that was a good thing to know, given the fact that he was going to be her temporary partner in what could very well be a dangerous assignment. She told herself that was the only reason she'd noticed.

"Hadn't noticed," McCall grunted, in response to her comment. But he gave her a look as he passed her, and even in the veranda's deep shadows she could see the bright blue gleam of irony in his eyes.

McCall held his body rigid and hoped she wouldn't hear his heart beating as he reached past her to open the heavy wooden door, then waited for her to enter his house ahead of him. He held his breath, too, but it didn't help much; it seemed her orange-blossom scent was already in his senses to stay. He wondered if he'd absorbed it through his pores.

She gave him back the look as she stepped carefully around him, the same amused, sardonic one he'd given her. "You don't lock your door?"

He followed her into his house and kicked the door shut behind him. "Everybody around here knows I don't have anything worth stealing. Like I said—my needs are simple. I live a hassle-free life. At least, I used to," he added darkly, looking around for a place to stash the canvasses. Normally they'd go on the couch, but since it looked as if he was going to be needing that later on, it didn't seem like a good choice. Finally he just lowered the whole stack to the floor near the front door and leaned them against the wall. Good enough—they'd be going back out soon enough.

He devoutly hoped. *If* this whole smuggling mess didn't wind up getting him killed, which, given what he'd seen of these people so far, seemed a distinct possibility.

And this his first Good Samaritan act since he'd

adopted this new care-and-hassle-free life. The irony in that made him laugh, a brief and mirthless snort.

"Here—let me have those." He relieved Cinnamon of her burden—he supposed he was going to have to call her Ellie now that he knew her name, but in his mind she was always going to be Cinnamon—and added those canvasses to the stack on the floor.

Then he straightened, and was suddenly aware of the fact that for the first time in a long time there was a strange woman occupying his house. A woman he was intensely attracted to. And had no business being attracted to. Dammit. He had to resist the impulse to fidget, couldn't find any worthwhile use for his hands.

"Ah...okay. That'll do for now. We can get the rest later. You, uh...want to go look at that envelope now, or you want something to eat first?"

"I'm kind of hungry, actually." She said that absently, with her back to him as she was strolling toward the French doors that opened out onto his garden. Enclosed on two sides by stone and plaster walls and on the back by the same rock that formed the foundation of his house, it was pretty much the way he'd found it—an untamed riot of bougainvillea and hibiscus and lots of other stuff he'd never bothered to learn the names of.

"I believe in the 'live-and-let-live' method of gardening," he explained as he hurried to beat her there, nervous as a new mama dog with one pup, wondering what she'd be thinking about it—about the garden, his house...him. Wondering why in hell it mattered.

She was looking at him, smiling, eyes glowing with it. Then she sort of started and gasped, "Oh—my God!" when he opened the doors. But it was in pleasure, not dismay.

"Meet Carmen," he said gruffly, as a raccoon trotted

huffily past his feet and, pausing only to give him a scolding growl, trundled off toward the kitchen. "She's not really tame," he went on to explain, as Ellie turned her fascinated gaze on him. He felt obscurely pleased with her reaction, and awkward and self-conscious because of it. "Just thinks my kitchen is part of her scavenging territory, and gets testy when I shut the door on her and she can't get to it. Actually, I'm not even sure she isn't a he—" he batted at a monarch butterfly that was bobbing drunkenly through the doorway just then, managed to shoo it back outside then quickly shut the doors "—but it didn't seem polite to ask."

"Live and let live," Ellie said, in a voice thick with suppressed laughter.

"Right…"

"Won't he—or she—need to, uh…" she gestured toward the closed doors.

"Oh, Carmen lets me know when she wants to go—" He broke off, swearing, interrupted by a racket of furious squeals and screeches. Ellie was right behind him as he dodged into the kitchen. He wasn't surprised to find the raccoon on the countertop with her paws up on the side of the refrigerator. From the top of the fridge a pair of round, wide eyes stared down at him in sleepy outrage.

McCall clapped his hands—a futile exercise, he knew, but it allowed him to maintain the illusion that he was still boss of his domain. "Okay, get down from there. That's not part of the deal. Come on—*get.*"

From behind him came a whispered, "That's a *potos flavus.*"

He waited while the raccoon—taking her sweet time about it—selected a plum from the bowl of fruit on the counter and made her way down the row of partly open drawers to the floor. Then he reached up to retrieve the smaller of the two combatants from the top of the fridge. "It's a kinkajou, actually," he said, keeping his tone bland. "She doesn't much like having her nap interrupted." But his self-consciousness was gone, and he wondered how it was that a run-of-the-mill pet-shop owner happened to know the scientific name of such an obscure little animal.

"I've never seen one." Ellie was extending a cautious hand toward the kinkajou, who was now occupying her favorite perch on McCall's left shoulder with her long tail wrapped around his neck.

"She doesn't take much to strangers," he said, just as the kinkajou was perking up and leaning toward Ellie, nose quivering to beat the band.

"What's her name?" Her voice had gone soft and sing-songy, with almost none of that rough little edge he was getting used to and, in fact, beginning to like. And he saw now that the fingers she was extending toward his passenger were holding a grape.

"Inky," he answered, holding his breath. He wasn't surprised about the grape, not really. After all, he'd learned from personal experience that this woman's arsenal of weapons included bribery. He just wondered how she could have known that grapes were Ink's all-time favorite treat.

Her eyes flicked to his face. They had that glow again, that warm golden shimmer that made him feel a tickle of laughter under his own breastbone, and farther down, a nice little nugget of a different kind of pleasure altogether. "Not Kinky?"

He grimaced. "Cute—but obvious, don't you think? No—I started calling her Inky because she likes to annoy me while I'm painting. I paint in the evenings, mostly, which is her active time. She gets into the paint...you know, makes a mess of things.''

Ellie gave a delighted laugh as the kinkajou flicked out a hand and snatched the grape from her fingers, then retreated with it in triumph to her nest on top of the refrigerator. She turned back to her host, shivering and giddy with the particular thrill she always got from a close encounter with a wild creature. She was breathless, dusting her hands, ready to say something...she didn't know what, maybe something about her pleasure and excitement at actually meeting a kinkajou. Then her eyes met McCall's, and her hands went still and her breathing stopped, and every thought of kinkajous and conversation went right out of her head.

Those alarms were going off for real now—the crash cart was undoubtedly on its way.

''What?'' she asked. McCall had said something, and she was utterly at a loss.

''Would you like to wash up?'' A polite host's question, but his voice sounded sharp, edgy.

''Oh—yes, thanks.'' She was almost to the kitchen door in what felt like full and ignominious retreat before it occurred to her to ask, ''Where is it? You do have a bathroom...inside?''

His skewed smile flashed briefly. ''To me, hassle-free includes indoor plumbing. Go through the big room— there's a door opposite this one, that's my bedroom. Bathroom's on your right.''

''Right,'' said Ellie, breathing again. Breathing as if she'd just come up those stairs of his at a dead run. What *was* the matter with her?

She finally left the kitchen on wobbly legs, and with a stomach full of butterflies such as she'd not felt in years— probably not since eighth grade, standing on the steps of the school gym waiting for Jimmy Rockingham to screw up enough courage to ask her to the Halloween dance.

She was halfway across the living room when she heard her host say—apparently to the kinkajou, "What're *you* looking at? Thirty seconds, and she's got *you* eating out of her hand."

Laughter bubbled up inside her and she clamped a hand over her mouth to stifle it. The laughter felt good, but it didn't do a thing to banish the butterflies.

She made her way across the big central living room— and *living* did describe it, for it seemed to serve many purposes—walking carefully, mindful of her still-wobbly knees and the hand-woven Mexican rugs scattered here and there on the uneven quarry-tile floor. She paused to smile at the raccoon, who was crouched on the rug closest to the French doors fastidiously washing her face and hands, having apparently already polished off the plum. When she saw Ellie she waddled over to the doors and paused there to throw an imperious look over one shoulder.

"Yes, Your Majesty, *of course,* Your Majesty," Ellie murmured as she went to open the door for her. Or him. Given the raccoon's size, she suspected it really was the latter.

Her butterflies and spaghetti legs were gradually fading, to be replaced once more by that Alice-in-Wonderland sense of bemusement. Since she'd arrived in this town, nothing seemed to be turning out the way she'd expected. She, who had always been so sensible and careful, had had her purse stolen, then recovered by a man who'd have made her hold on to her purse a little tighter if she'd seen him coming toward her down the street. She'd been accosted by thugs in a bar, then "rescued" by that same man, who incidentally was the very image of the kind of man women were warned to stay away from in bars.

Finally, and most incomprehensibly, she'd lost her partner, and acquired a new one—yes, that very same unsavory-seeming beach bum, in spite of the fact that he claimed to have no interest in helping anybody. Live and let live, wasn't that his motto? He seemed a confirmed and unrepentant social dropout, with no concern for anyone or anything but numero uno—but he'd refused the money she'd offered him. He barely knew her, seemed not even to like her very much, but he'd agreed to help her out of an impossible dilemma. He behaved the way she'd imagined an antisocial dropout would behave—cranky and sarcastic and downright rude—but today in the cantina he'd put his body between her and an armed thug. He looked like a beach bum—sunburned, scruffy and unshaven, perpetually scowling—but seemed clean and smelled like nothing more unpleasant than paint and turpentine. And his mouth, when she'd kissed him, had felt warm and firm and had tasted, not at all unpleasantly, of tobacco.

Her stomach fluttered alarmingly, and she drew a quick hard breath as she pulled the French doors shut and latched them. Another surprise, she thought as she watched the raccoon disappear into the garden's riotous foliage. In her experience it took a man with a gentle and generous soul to respect and appreciate wild creatures, much less form bonds of mutual trust with one.

Gentle? Generous? Cranky, crotchety McCall? It seemed unlikely, and yet…who would have guessed he'd have a house like this? So simple, only three rooms, not counting the bathroom—this one in the middle, with kitchen on one side, sleeping quarters on the other—but in a modest way, gracious, with sturdy rattan furniture, couch and chairs with cushions big enough for relaxing in, tables laden with reading material and artists' supplies, an artist's easel, and ceiling fans lazily swishing. Small, but with a feeling of light and space. Cool, even on a hot afternoon like this one. The word *comfortable* came to mind.

And yet, this McCall didn't seem at all a comfortable sort of man.

Who was he, really? Or rather, who had he been? Where had he come from, and what had brought him to this place, and this life?

Did he have a first name?

Curiouser and curiouser...

Noises were coming from the kitchen—cupboard doors banging, dishes clinking, water running, and a tuneless whistle that might have been annoying if it hadn't reminded her so much of her brother, Eric. Eric, whom she seldom saw these days, and missed so much....

Like an unexpected rain shower, the sadness of that thought dampened her curiosity and scattered the last of the butterflies. Quickly, now, she found her way to the bathroom, trying hard not to notice the bedroom as she swept through—which was, of course, impossible. She'd been prepared for the dimness of drawn shades, the clutter of clothing and unmade bed, and so wasn't really surprised, since everything else about McCall had been so unexpected, to find light and space instead, and the bed neatly made beneath its veil of mosquito netting.

The bathroom was spartan but clean. She made use of its facilities as quickly as possible, then paused on the way back through the bedroom to study a framed photo that was standing on top of a high dresser near the door. She'd noticed it on her first pass through the room, probably because it was the only photo of any kind she'd seen in the house—in contrast to her own apartment in Portland and her parents' house near Sioux City, Iowa, where every available space was always crowded with photographs and family mementos.

This one was most likely a blowup of an old snapshot, black and white and slightly blurry, of a man and a woman—or boy and girl, actually; they looked very young, probably still in their teens. The couple were dressed in the style of the late 1950s. The girl wore a Lucille Ball hairdo, a white blouse with the collar turned up in back and a scarf tied around her neck, pedal pushers and flat-heeled shoes. The boy wore his dark hair in a James Dean ducktail and was dressed in skin-tight jeans and a Marlon Brando-style white T-shirt. Ellie could see a pack of cigarettes tucked into one rolled-up sleeve. The boy was slouching against the front fender of a late-fifties model car, the kind that was all chrome and fins, while the girl stood by smiling at him adoringly—if perhaps a little too indulgently.

Ellie pulled the photo closer and peered at it, searching for a resemblence between this young man and the artist she knew only as McCall. Impossible to tell, really; the styles were too different, the details blurred...

"Yeah, that's my parents," McCall said, startling her so much she gasped and knocked over the picture with a clatter. He reached calmly past her to set it to rights. "That was taken when they were in high school. About a year before my mother got pregnant with me."

"I wasn't trying to be nosy," Ellie said, her voice gone raspy with embarrassment, heart beating like a jack-hammer. "It was right there, I couldn't help but notice—"

"It's all right," he drawled. But his eyes, for once, seemed shielded. "I just came to tell you lunch is ready—if you're interested."

"Oh, yes—thank you. I'm starving..."

What the heck, she thought. In for a penny... "So, is that the only picture you have?" she brazenly asked as she followed her host into the living room. "Of your family, I mean. Brothers and sisters?" *A wife?* He'd mentioned an ex... "Do you have any children?"

"Nope." He waved her past him toward the round rattan table, cleared now of painting supplies and set with woven place mats, heavy glazed crockery plates with a bright Mexican design, and the kind of inexpensive flatware that sometimes comes in picnic baskets—flimsy metal with bright red plastic handles. And as a centerpiece, the fruit bowl from the kitchen—blue and white ceramic, piled high with tropical fruits. It reminded Ellie of a still-life painting by...she couldn't think of his name, the French impressionist who'd fallen in love with the South Seas.

"No napkins," McCall said gruffly, handing her a folded dish towel. "I don't have company very often."

The Alice-in-Wonderland feeling was back again; she wondered when she was going to stop being surprised by this man. She felt like the kinkajou, nose a-tremble, all but beside herself with curiosity, but all she said as she took the chair indicated—in an abrupt, almost afterthought way—by her host, was, "Thanks. Looks good."

"Don't sound so surprised," he said dryly, shifting a dish-towel-covered plate closer to her before sitting down himself. "I do eat." The corners of his mouth twitched—as if he'd heard her thoughts. "Occasionally even sitting down."

Ellie lifted a corner of the dish towel. Tortillas—of course. She took one and put it on her plate, then passed the plate to McCall, who did the same. He picked up a shallow white bowl and ladeled a spoonful of its contents onto his tortilla, then passed the bowl to Ellie. Ignoring good manners, she held the bowl to her nose and took a good sniff. Rather like oranges, she thought. Spicy... Her stomach rumbled.

"Smells good," she said. "What is it?"

"Chicken," muttered McCall. "Mostly."

Chicken...loops of onion, chunks of red, yellow and green— peppers, perhaps. And something orange.... Mango? With McCall, even the food came in bright, simple colors, she thought, like a child's first box of crayons.

My needs are simple....

She spooned some of the mixture onto her tortilla and rolled it up, following McCall's example, into a taco—the Mexican version of a sandwich. She picked it up and bit into it, closing her eyes. Sweet-sour... hot...spicy...exotic. Heavenly. "Good," she said, nodding.

"Glad you approve." Again his tone was dry, ironic.

"No, I mean it. Different, though. What's it called? Where'd you learn to make it?"

He shrugged, busy building himself another taco. "Hell, I don't know. It's pretty much local, I guess. No particular way to make it—everybody does it their own way." He gave her a look and a half smile. "Kind of like meat loaf in New Jersey."

But he hadn't answered her questions, Ellie noticed. She thought about that as she polished off her taco, then reached for another. "How long have you lived here—in Mexico, I mean?"

"All my life," said McCall.

Her eyes snapped to his face. He returned her look with a long, direct stare, and she felt her cheeks grow warm and the food she'd just eaten form a lump in her chest. It had seemed to her an innocent enough question. Hey—

just making normal conversation, right? But such a blatant and obvious lie in reply carried its own equally obvious message: *Back off...don't ask questions.* Far from being intimidated by the warning, Ellie took it as a personal challenge.

She cleared her throat. "You mentioned an ex-wife," she said evenly, returning the stare.

His eyes shifted away from her as he nodded in time with his chewing. "I have one."

"Then I assume she must be Mexican?"

Again their gazes locked—hers wide-eyed innocence, his veiled...secretive. Again he was first to break the contact. "Your mother ever tell you it's rude to ask so many questions?" *he* asked rudely as he reached for a long-necked bottle beside his plate.

Her eyes followed the bottle as he lifted it to his lips. Her own throat, tight with shame and anger, convulsed when he swallowed. "We're going to be working together," she said in a low voice. "You're supposed to be my husband. It would be nice to know something about you besides your last name."

The corners of his mouth lifted. "What you see is what you get." But it was almost insultingly glib. After a moment he tipped the mouth of the bottle toward her and said very softly, "*Pretending* to be your husband. Pretending. Big difference. Or have you forgotten you have the real thing stashed away somewhere? In a hospital, wasn't it? In Miami?"

This time it was Ellie who jerked her eyes away from a touch that had become too intense. Her cheeks felt so hot she thought they must be glowing. "As if I would forget that," she said in a choked voice. But she had. *She had.*

This undercover stuff was turning out to be a lot harder

than she'd expected. Or, maybe, she thought dismally, she was just too fundamentally honest for this kind of work. Too open. She'd always found it hard to lie. Even harder to hide her feelings. She didn't know how to think like a married woman, much less act like one. She hadn't had any practice. And this man, this McCall, it seemed, missed nothing. She was going to have to be very, very careful.

"What's that you're drinking?" She changed the subject almost violently, hurling the inquiry at him in a voice that was too loud and raspy with self-consciousness.

He glanced at the bottle in his hand, as if surprised to see it there. Or surprised by the question. "This? *Pulque*. The local beer, I guess you'd call it. Want one? Gotta warn you, it's an acquired taste."

"Sure—" she gave a savage little shrug "—why not? When in Rome…"

McCall pushed back his chair and went off to the kitchen. He came back a moment later with a second bottle, which he placed in front of Ellie. She lifted it to her lips, sipped and gamely suppressed a shudder.

"You want anything more to eat?"

"No, thank you," Ellie said, determinedly taking another, longer swig of the beer and repressing an urge to gag. She watched resentfully from the corner of her eye as her host gathered the dishes, stacking everything except the fruit bowl into a haphazard tower, then shifted to more blatant, almost defiant observation when he started off with them to the kitchen.

Oddly, watching him walk away from her, dish towel flung casually over one shoulder, shirttail flapping, sandals slapping on the Mexican tiles, she felt her resentment and frustration melt into something else…something she couldn't recall ever having felt before, at least about a man. A warm and achy little pool of disappointment…of wistfulness...of regret. She wanted to *know* this man. She didn't know why, but she did. Not just out of curiosity, or because he represented a challenge to her—so determined to be a man of mystery!—but something deeper. A sense of connection, perhaps. A feeling that, given half a chance, she could really *like* him.

And it sure didn't look as though she was ever going to get that chance.

She took another swig—a big one—of pulque. It didn't seem so bad this time; perhaps she was acquiring the taste for it after all.

When McCall returned, the kinkajou was riding on his shoulder, once again with her tail curled around McCall's neck. Ellie's heart did a peculiar little stutter-step which she blamed, wishfully, on the *pulque*.

"She was hunting for the fruit bowl," McCall explained when he saw Ellie's eyes on him. "There you go, Ink—" He held out his arm, offering the kinkajou a bridge from his shoulder to the table. Instead of using it, she took a flying leap onto Ellie's shoulder. Ellie gave a gasp of surprised laughter. "Hey—sorry 'bout that," McCall muttered. "Here—let me get her—"

"No, no—that's okay—" Ellie turned, shifting her passenger away from the hands that had reached to take her, and one closed instead on her bare shoulder. Just for a moment she felt the warmth and weight of it—altogether different from that of the kinkajou. But she blamed the shiver that rippled down her back on the animal, anyway—just the thrill, she told herself, of having such an elusive little wild creature snuggled next to her ear.

"There," she said shakily, as she plucked a grape from the bowl and offered it to the kinkajou, "is that what you're looking for?"

And suddenly, because she couldn't bring herself to

look at the man, feeding the little animal became intensely important, the focus of her total concentration. But she felt the man there beside her…close enough to touch, but not. She could feel him watching her and wondered, if she were to look at him, what she'd see in those eyes of his, whether they'd be that clean, clear blue she remembered, or clouded over with secrets.

That intense awareness and the strange unease that went along with it, were beginning to nibble away at Ellie's natural good nature. Dammit, she wasn't accustomed to feeling shaky and self-conscious with people—especially men. She'd always *liked* men, as friends. She'd never been in love and was sensible enough to realize it, refusing to mistake the giddy crushes of adolescence or the mildly exciting attractions she'd experienced since for anything other than what they were. Maybe she could be so sure of herself because she knew what the real thing— real love—looked like. She'd grown up with it, witnessed it every day in her own parents. She was sure she'd recognize it when and if it ever came her way, and she wasn't about to settle for anything less. Meanwhile, the way she saw it, men either liked her or they didn't; it was out of her hands and therefore—possibly because most people did like her—she never concerned herself about it.

She didn't think she'd ever been in the position before of *wanting* someone to like her, and being completely clueless as to whether or not they did.

"Excuse me," she said, covering testiness with exaggerated courtesy, "I don't mean to pry…but is it all right if I ask you a question? About Inky, I mean?"

McCall's lips curved wryly in acknowledgment of the sarcasm, but he nodded solemnly and said, "Sure—go ahead."

"Where—and how—on earth did you get her? She didn't just wander in out of the garden, like the raccoon?"

"Nope—I bought her."

Surprise—or the fact that he'd finally moved away from her—gave Ellie the courage to risk a glance at him. Again, he'd managed to catch her completely off guard. Surely, he had to be the last man she'd have thought would buy an exotic pet. But damned if she'd ask. Not if it killed her.

So, while Inky smacked and munched her way through a third grape, she silently watched him rummage through the drawers of a small rattan desk until, with a little grunt of triumph, he came up with a rumpled and badly folded road map. She pretended to give her full attention to the kinkajou when he brought the map back to the table and slapped it down in front of her.

"Some street kids had her," he said as he took his own chair. He pulled a pack of cigarettes from his shirt pocket, but instead of lighting one, glanced at Ellie, then laid them on the table. Tapped the pack once, gave it a little push, then spoke to it, frowning. "She was just a baby. I figured she wasn't going to have much of a chance where she was, so I…bought her. I was going to, you know…wait until she got bigger, then turn her loose." He paused to clear his throat, squirming in his chair. "But then…well, hell, it didn't seem like she'd have much chance in the wild, either, since she was so young when I got her. So," he said gloomily, "it looks like I'm stuck with her."

"What happened to 'live and let live'?" Ellie asked softly, addressing the kinkajou. The shakiness was back—though that may have been due to the fact that Inky, having finally had her fill of grapes, was currently exploring the nape of Ellie's neck.

McCall gave a little snort. "I occasionally have lapses," he said darkly. "Fits of temporary insanity."

"Is that what it was?" Ellie's voice was hushed with suppressed shivers; the kinkajou was snuffling along the topmost bumps of her spine. Oh, and she hoped McCall wasn't noticing the way her nipples were sticking out, hard as buttons under the soft knit of her shirt. She didn't dare look at him to see. "Stopping that boy from stealing my purse. Temporary insanity?"

"Hell, I don't know." And his voice was like someone shoveling gravel. "What was I supposed to do—let him get away with it? I was there. It just *happened*."

Happenstance. "And last night…José's Cantina?"

"Coincidence," growled McCall. "All I wanted was my usual shot of tequila. Walked into the bar and there you were. Wearing this big sign: Stupid Tourist—Please Mug Me."

Ellie felt the heat throbbing in her cheeks—odd, because the shivers were still cascading down her back, and her nipples were beaded so hard and tight they hurt. In a voice rigidly controlled and barely audible, she said, "And today? You said you followed me. Couldn't have been coincidence. Must have been—"

"Insanity—definitely."

"You didn't have to help me." Bracing herself, she shot him a look. "You could have walked away, there on the pier. Why didn't you?"

In the waiting, ringing silence, Inky crept in under Ellie's ear and paused there, staring at McCall with eyes wide, nose quivering, for all the world, Ellie, thought, as if she, too, was waiting for his answer. McCall's eyes dropped to the kinkajou, then lifted slowly back to Ellie's, and the corners of his mouth curved in a sardonic little smile. He didn't answer, but he didn't have to. His eyes and the smile said it plainly enough.

Just like the kinkajou, Ellie thought. He doesn't think I'd have much of a chance out there in the wild…on my own.

"Let's have a look at that envelope," McCall said abruptly, reaching again for his cigarettes. "See if we can figure out where it is we're supposed to be going. Then I'll take you back to the ship so you can get your things."

Chapter 6

"Hi, Mom, it's me."

"Ellie!" Lucy sat bolt upright under her afghan, gesturing frantically at Mike, who had already hit Save on his computer and was making his way over to join her on the couch. She shifted her feet around to make room for him beside her. "Honey, I'm so glad you called." *Your dad and I have been worried about you.* But of course she didn't say that; she knew Ellie didn't like to be fussed over. Consequently Lucy made sure her tone was casual when she added, "We've been wondering about that…thing you mentioned you had to do. How'd that come out?"

"Well, that's mostly why I'm calling. I think it's going to work out fine, Mom, so you and Dad don't have to worry, okay?" There was a pause, which Lucy wisely didn't interrupt. Then a small, decisive breath. "The problem was, my partner on this…project I'm working on, he'd gotten sick, and it looked like I was going to have to finish it up by myself. But as it turns out, I've found somebody to help me out. So I won't be going it alone after all.''

''Well,'' said Lucy, ''that's nice.'' She waited, watching her husband's eyes, then cautiously ventured, ''This new partner—is it someone you know?'' Darn, but it was hard, being the mother of independent grown-up children. Hard to know which questions she was allowed to ask and which ones would be considered prying. Hard to know how much concern she was allowed to show without being a buttinsky. She looked at Mike for support once more before adding bravely, ''Someone you can trust?''

There was another pause, and then an oddly thoughtful, ''Yes, Mom, I believe I can.''

But, thought Lucy, she didn't answer the first question.

''Anyway, Mom, Dad, I just wanted to let you know I'm going to be leaving the ship, so I probably won't be able to check in with you for a few days. Okay? Everything's fine, so don't worry about me. I'm going to be staying with…my partner, and he doesn't have a phone—''

He, thought Lucy. She said, *He.* At least that was something.

''This partner,'' Mike said loudly, leaning closer to Lucy and the receiver, ''does he have a name?'' He gave his wife a smug look, well aware that fathers were allowed more slack in the prying department than mothers.

Even so, this time the pause was so long that Lucy finally said, ''Honey, did you—''

''Yeah, Mom, I heard. It's…McCall.''

''McCall,'' said Lucy. ''Is that—''

''Listen, Mom, I have to go now, okay? Tell Dad I love

him—love you both. And *don't worry.* I promise I'll keep my wits about me.''

Lucy could hear a smile in her daughter's voice when she said that. She wished she felt like smiling herself, but she had an edgy, uncertain feeling as she pushed the cordless phone's disconnect button...kind of a tingle between her shoulder blades. Still holding the phone in her lap, she said to her husband, ''She said his name's—''

''McCall,'' said Mike. ''I heard.'' He tapped a fingertip against his lips. ''I knew a McCall once.''

''Oh, surely not the same one,'' said Lucy, in an ''Oh, pshaw'' sort of tone. ''McCall's not that uncommon a name.''

''She didn't mention a first name, did she? Unless McCall—''

''I'm sure that would be the last name—can you imagine anybody naming a little baby *McCall?*''

''McCall...'' Mike Lanagan said under his breath. ''I wonder...'' He was frowning thoughtfully as he went back to his computer.

McCall lay awake listening to the small sounds that marked Ink's progress on her usual nightly rounds, thinking about the woman currently occupying his not-very-comfortable couch.

He'd offered her his bed, of course; he wasn't a complete jerk. He'd apologized for not having a hammock—one Yucatan custom he'd never quite taken to—and told her how lumpy the couch's cushions were, how they had a tendency to separate, allowing various body parts to fall through onto the rattan underpinnings.

She'd told him again about how she'd slept on the decks of ships, on bare ground and open beaches, on sidewalks and the steps of government buildings. A couch with actual cushions, she'd assured him, would be a luxury.

He'd have to leave his bedroom door open a few inches to allow Ink hunting access, he'd told her, adding a sly remark about how it might be a bit of an inconvenience, but it kept the lizard and scorpion population down. But instead of a horrified "Eeuw!" or a shudder or a change of heart about sleeping on the couch, all she'd done was smile and tell him she'd slept through worse.

So it wasn't as though he hadn't tried. And it wasn't guilt that kept him wide awake and tense long past the time when he'd normally be deep in untroubled, unhassled, live-and-let-live sleep. Awake, and all his senses keyed to the slightest sound or movement from beyond his half-open bedroom door.

Dammit, the woman just didn't add up. She didn't *fit*. Miss Goody Two-Shoes from Iowa, raised on a farm, now grown up and married and owner of a pet shop in Portland, Oregon. Disapproves of smoking, scarfs chocolate when upset; discomfitted by a topless beach but doesn't hesitate to dispatch a mugger with a swift kick to the *cojones*. Says she's slept on boats, beaches and sidewalks, isn't put off by lizards and scorpions, and knows the scientific name for a kinkajou.

None of which seemed to McCall to fit with the kind of woman who'd do business with thugs and smugglers in dangerous backstreet bars. At least not for the sake of the money involved.

Unless her husband had gotten her into this. He supposed that might make sense; he'd heard there were women out there who'd do anything for the men they loved. Never met one in his lifetime, but...hey, who knew?

But—that was another thing—what about that blush?

The one that showed up every time she mentioned that absent husband of hers. What the hell was *that* all about?

He stirred angrily—then froze as he heard rustlings from the other room. The creak of rattan. His houseguest was restless, too, it seemed. He wondered if she could be lying awake as he was, staring wide-eyed into the shadows and wondering about *him.*

Just for a moment—though it might have been his imagination—he caught a whiff of her orange-blossom scent, carrying him back once again to a distant past, and the sweet, sad ache that always came over him when he thought about his beginnings...his boyhood...his parents. From across the room the photograph on the dresser was only a faint rectangular edge in the darkness, but he could see his mom's and dad's faces in his mind, looking, as always, not out at him but toward each other. It was the way he remembered them—high-school sweethearts, lovers first, parents only a distant second to that.

McCall knew he'd come a long way from Bakersfield, California, in more ways than one. Why was it, looking back at times like this, he always got the feeling he'd missed a turn somewhere along the way?

Damnation, he needed to sleep; he had what looked to be a long and uncertain day ahead of him. What he needed was a cigarette—that would help. Yeah...and a shot or two of tequila. But...since he had a guest in his living room and a hard and fast rule against smoking in bed, he got up as quietly as he knew how, pushed the window open and, cigarettes and lighter in hand, stepped onto the veranda.

Far down at the other end of the veranda, Ellie heard the window creak open on its hinges. When she saw the shadowy form emerge she tensed instinctively and flattened herself against the wall. A dumb thing to do, she immediately realized. Even without a moon she'd be plainly visible against the white wall, if he chose to look this way.

If he didn't hear her first. Counting her thudding heart-beats and trying not to breathe, she watched a lighter flare...a tiny bud, blossoming into a wider glow that included cupped hands...a face...deeply hooded eyes. There was a click, and the face slipped once more into shadow. She heard an exhalation...a soft, grateful sigh.

I have to let him know I'm here, Ellie thought. *Oh lord... But better now than later.*

Summoning her courage, she pushed herself away from the wall. "Don't freak out. Just wanted to let you know you weren't alone."

Other than a little grunt of surprise, he said nothing. She watched the glowing end of his cigarette arc upward, flare briefly, then wink out. Cupped in his hand, perhaps, or obscured by his body.

"Couldn't sleep," she explained, her voice gruff with nervousness. "Thought maybe some fresh air would help."

He cleared his throat, but when he spoke his voice was as gravelly as hers. "Told you that couch wasn't comfortable."

"No, no—it wasn't that." She smiled, even though he wouldn't see it. "Or Inky, either. I think maybe I'm just a little nervous—about tomorrow." That was true enough, but only partly. The other reasons for her sleeplessness she didn't want to think about or examine too closely.

She moved away from the wall, inhaling deeply as she looked out over dark rooftops and darker water toward a horizon that was fading to milky gray. "It's nice out here, though. I think there's going to be a moon. Not full though—not for a few more days."

Again the cigarette's tiny yellow eye winked at her, and again he said nothing. Finally, she let the breath out in a rush and leaned against the base of an arch, her back to the view. "This is awkward for you, isn't it? Having me here." She waited, and when he still didn't respond, added dryly, "I take it you don't have too many visitors." At least, not like me...not the kind of visitor that sleeps on the couch.

There was the faint hiss of an exhalation, and then a grudging, "Not many."

Okay, Ellie thought, he just stepped out for a smoke and doesn't feel like talking. I can handle that. Don't take it personally. It isn't like the man's a scintillating conversationalist at the best of times.

But the silence was like a tender tooth she couldn't stop herself from probing.

"Seems funny," she remarked after a moment. "It's your house, and you have to come outside for a cigarette?"

This time the winking yellow eye was accompanied by a grunt that *may* have been amusement. "Not generally." His voice was raspy in the darkness. "Just don't smoke in bed, is all. Habit I picked up a long time ago, when I was..."

"Married?" Ellie ventured when he left it unfinished. Then, momentarily emboldened by his soft affirming chuckle, she got as far as, "How did—" before stopping herself with a hand clapped across her mouth. "Sorry," she mumbled, more resentful than contrite. "Forgot myself there for a minute."

She listened to the night's sounds...the rustle of breezes in tropical foliage, the far-off barking of a dog. The faint sound of a throat being cleared. She pushed abruptly away from the arch and let out her breath in an exasperated rush. "Dammit, McCall. I don't think I'm a nosy person. Really. I mean, it's *normal* for strangers forced together by circumstances to ask each other questions. It's not prying, it's…it's just trying to find a common ground. Like, 'What do you do for a living? Where are you from? Are you married? Have any kids? Read any good books lately?' Then you go from there. Maybe you find out you don't have anything in common with this person and you never want to see them again as long as you live. Or, maybe you hit it off and you've made a new friend. How are you ever going to know if you don't *talk?*"

There was a long pause. Then, just as Ellie was uttering a whimper of pure frustration, the raspy voice came again. "Maybe I just like to maintain an air of mystery." Definitely amused.

Ellie's frustration morphed into a kind of cautious joy. A little frisson of excitement shivered through her, finding its way into her voice. "You mean, like Batman?"

The cigarette's ember arced away into the night, exploding in a tiny shower of sparks as it made contact with the ground. *"Batman?"* The chuckle seemed easier this time, though loaded with irony. "A superhero? Not hardly."

"Hey, if you don't want me to know the real story, you could always make something up," Ellie suggested. "Then, I'll tell you something back—"

"Make up something, you mean?"

"Maybe. Who knows?"

"So we stand here and tell each other lies."

"At least we'd be speaking." But she felt breathless, suddenly, and not from laughter. And a peculiar shaking deep inside. Did he know? Could he read her so easily? *Liar liar, pants on fire….*

For a moment there while they'd been talking she'd

begun to move closer to him, as if words were an invisible line pulling them together in the alienating darkness. Now she saw the space between them as a zone of safety and shrank back into it, the darkness an ally, protection for her own lies. Necessary lies, she told herself. It wasn't as if *she* had any choice.

"For instance," she went on, but too quickly, her voice too light and too glib, "you could tell me how you and your wife were childhood sweethearts, and she died tragically when she fell overboard on your honeymoon cruise, and that's why you don't have any children, and ever since—"

"Nothing so romantic, I'm afraid," he interrupted dryly. "My wife and I met in college. We're divorced. Not having kids was a mutual decision—a wise one, as it turned out."

"Ah," said Ellie. A dozen new questions were buzzing around in her brain. *College? You went to college? Where? How long were you married? Why didn't you want kids? Was it the divorce that brought you here?* Then she remembered. "Is that the true story?" she asked suspiciously. "Or did you make it up?"

"Ah, but that's the question, isn't it?" His chuckle was soft and dry as the wind in the bird-of-paradise. "That's the trouble with lies—after the first one, you can't ever know what to believe."

Now it was Ellie who had nothing to say. And suddenly, inexplicably, there were tears welling up in her eyes—where had *they* come from? Rose Ellen Lanagan was not and never had been a crybaby! But she'd never felt this overwhelming sense of loss and loneliness, either—an intense longing for something she couldn't even put a name to, but which she knew for certain did *not* involve lies.

"Your turn," McCall said softly.

"I beg your pardon?" Ellie mumbled. Had he asked her a question? She'd no idea what.

"Your husband. You told me his name—my name now, I suppose—is Ken."

"Right," said Ellie, trying surreptitiously to stop her nose from running without resorting to a telltale sniff. "Ken Burnside."

"And that the two of you own a pet shop in Portland, Oregon." There was a pause. "So...if you grew up on a farm in Iowa, how did you two meet?"

"At a 'Save the Whales' rally," Ellie returned instantly—defiantly. Well, it *could* have been true, dammit!

She heard him mutter, laughing, under his breath. Something that sounded like "Goody Two-Shoes," and then, "Figures..."

Goody Two-Shoes? Why did he always say that? She sucked in a breath, feeling vaguely insulted and gravely misunderstood. But after holding the breath for a half-dozen or so pulse-pounding beats, she let it out without a sound. What did it matter what he thought of her? The man obviously had no interest in knowing who she really was—even if she'd been free to tell him. She'd bent over backward to be friendly, and he didn't seem to want to meet her even halfway—which was particularly hard for her to swallow, since she'd always been the kind of person who made friends easily wherever she went. People just naturally *liked* Ellie Lanagan. Most people. Apparently not *this* person. Was *that* why it bothered her so much? Some perversity in her nature, some contrary streak that caused her to be attracted to the one person seemingly immune to her charms?

There. I said it: I am attracted to him. I'm fiercely at-

tracted to a scruffy and somewhat mysterious beach-bum-slash-artist-slash-social-dropout I know only as McCall.

It was almost a relief to admit it. She felt better immediately, though perhaps a little shaky—rather as if she'd finally pulled out a painfully inflamed splinter.

That's all it is, she thought. Just an attraction. I've had them before, though probably never one as dumb as this. Now I can laugh at myself and put it aside. Concentrate on the job ahead of me. Keep my wits about me. Now I can sleep.

"Well," she said abruptly, "I believe I'll give that couch another try. Good night, McCall."

She heard a click, a faint hiss and crackle, and then a soft and ironic, "Good night...Mrs. Burnside."

After she'd gone back inside, McCall sat for a long time on his bedroom windowsill, smoking and watching the moon rise out of Tropical Storm Paulette's cloudy veil, contemplating the nature of lust and sin. And, like most people confronted with their own guilt, trying as hard as he could to rationalize it.

Well, hell, he told himself, how was he supposed to remember she was a married woman when she kept forgetting to act like one? Not that she'd openly flirted with him, or done anything overtly improper—besides kissing him, of course, and there'd been extenuating circumstances for that. No, it wasn't so much what she'd done, as what she *didn't* do. She didn't *talk* about her husband, for one thing. Every married woman he'd ever met, happy or unhappy, it seemed like they couldn't seem to get a complete sentence out without mentioning hubby one way or another. It was, "my husband says this," or "my husband does that." This woman almost never brought up her husband's name, unless McCall did so first, and when he did, she'd blush. And that was another thing. It was true that, in McCall's experience at least, women in love generally tended to light up when speaking of their beloved. But with sort of a happy *glow,* not going all flustered like this woman did, as if she were embarrassed by even the suggestion of such intimacy.

No, he thought, there was definitely something not quite right with the Burnsides.

Not that it was any of McCall's business. Happy or unhappy, right or not right, he didn't get involved with married women. End of story.

Which brought him back to his internal debate on the nature of lust and of sin. For various reasons, McCall wasn't big on religion, but he did believe wholeheartedly in the concept of sin. Hey, there was right, and there was wrong, no getting around that. And no matter how hard a man might try to get around it, in his heart he mostly always knew the difference. Which was why, at the moment, he was having a little argument with himself over whether lusting after a married woman in his heart was actually a sin. Oh, sure, according to the gospel and Jimmy Carter, thinking was supposed to be the same as doing, but given the nature of human beings, McCall was pretty sure there'd be quite a bit of slack involved there. He figured a man was in the clear as long as he didn't *do* anything about his thoughts. Okay, there was that commandment—he couldn't remember which number—the one about not coveting thy neighbor's wife. But he felt certain he was okay on that score, too, because the way he understood it, *covet* meant wanting to have for himself, and the last thing McCall wanted was to have *any* woman for himself—married or otherwise.

For the past seven years he'd been careful to keep his liaisons with women uncomplicated and hassle-free— "safe sex" being a concept he took very seriously, in more ways than one. And if there was anything he was certain of right now it was that *this* woman—whether she went by Ellie Lanagan, Mrs. Ken Burnside or Cinnamon, as she would always be to McCall—could complicate his life in ways he hadn't even thought of yet.

He tossed away his cigarette, but instead of reaching immediately for another, sat very still for a while, listening to the sounds of the night: the singing of insects and of frogs, wind rustling through palm trees, the disconcerting crunching noises Inky was making somewhere in the dark bedroom behind him. The small voice inside him that kept saying, *Fool, she's already complicated your life, don't you know that?*

Oh, yeah. Forget about the perky little breasts, smooth, tan legs, cinnamon freckles, ratchety voice and killer smile. There was still the small fact that, as of this moment, he was guilty of aiding and abetting her in the commission of a felony. What was he going to do about *that?*

He had until tomorrow to think of something.

From the crossroads town of Tulum, the highway left the coast and angled abruptly inland. Ellie, who'd been dividing her attention between the view from the VW's windows and the map spread across her lap, rubbernecked so avidly when they passed the marked turnoffs to the Mayan ruins at Coba on the right, and the Punta Allen peninsula on the left, that McCall asked her about it.

"Oh, nothing," she said, but with a wistful sigh. "I was just wishing—"

"Say the word," he said roughly. "If you want to change your mind about going through with this—"

"No, no—I'd just like to see the Sian Ka'an Biosphere Reserve someday, that's all."

McCall gave her a quick, hard look. "Not the ruins?

That's where most tourists wind up—unless you're into reef diving.''

Ellie shrugged. ''I'm not much into ruins. It's the wild-life that interests me—you know, the birds, the animals.''

''Ah,'' said McCall. ''Of course.'' From Ellie's angle his smile looked wry, and without much humor.

''Well, have *you* ever been there?''

He threw her a glance. ''To the Reserve? Nah—been down the peninsula, though, many times. Diving.''

''What's it like?''

He gave her the same crooked smile, but it seemed easier, now. She could see the creases at the corner of his eye. ''It's a great place to go if you want to get away from the world. And don't mind a few inconveniences.''

''Well,'' said Ellie dryly, ''I can see why *you'd* love it.'' And she was pleased beyond proportion when he laughed.

It didn't take much encouragement, then, for him to tell her about his travels on the peninsula, and his adventures diving the reefs along the coast there. She listened to him talk, shivering with a strange happiness, marveling at how articulate he was, how comfortable with himself and with words when the subject wasn't his personal or past life. Questions rushed into her mind like an unexpected gust of wind, leaving her breathless, unsettled, off-balance.

What must he have been in his former life—a lawyer? Teacher? Used-car salesman? CEO? He was good with people, once. He had a wife. Money, too—he said so. What could have happened, to make him give it all up? What was it that brought him here?

For once, wisely, she kept her curiosity to herself, and instead opened her mind and allowed it to wander through the worries and uncertainty she'd been ruthlessly trying—without much luck—to squelch.

Who is this man? Can I really trust him? Just because he has kind eyes, and a kinkajou.... Am I out of my mind to be doing this?

At the time, of course, back there in that cantina, she'd felt as though she'd had no choice. She'd been scared, at a loss, and he'd walked in. And later, it had seemed unthinkable to let it all fall through, with the money paid, the arrangements in place...all the months of preparation...to let it all be for nothing. Now...oh, it seemed so clear to her now...she knew that what she should have done was inform General Reyes and let him break the news to the USFWS and let *them* figure out what to do about it.

She could still do that. It wasn't too late. *I can call the whole thing off.*

"You want to call it off?" McCall's voice rasped across her raw nerves.

She jumped and answered reflexively, "No! I don't want to call it off." She saw now that the VW had slowed almost to a crawl, and that he was staring at her, eyes the sharp, cold blue of the October skies back home in Iowa. She felt her stomach fill up with queasiness and butterflies.

"You still can, you know." And he was himself again, at least the McCall she knew—crusty, crude and cantankerous. "Give up this crazy idea. Go on back home—to Portland or Iowa, what-the-hell-ever. Forget about the damn money—it's only *money,* for God's sake!"

"I can't call it off. I told you—my husband—"

His fingers flexed on the steering wheel, as if what he really wanted to do was break it in half. "You sure your husband would want you doing this? Going into a Mexican jungle to meet up with armed criminals? They *are* armed, you know—I hope you noticed that. Does he even know—do *you* know—how dangerous this is? Jeez, what kind of man lets his wife—''

''He trusts me,'' Ellie said tightly. ''He knows I can handle it.''

''But you can't handle it, can you?'' His voice was suddenly very soft…gentle, almost. ''Not alone. Not without me.''

She went utterly still, staring at him. His face looked set, hard as stone. ''You promised—'' Her lips felt stiff; she licked them and finished hoarsely, ''You gave me your word.''

''Yeah…I know.'' He said that on an exhalation as he shifted gears. The VW's engine sputtered and slowly picked up speed.

She waited, nerves strung tight as wire, with a high-tension pulsing inside her head: *You promised. You gave me your word. You promised…*

It seemed a long time before he spoke again. ''We should be coming close to Felipe Carillo. We'll stop there—fill up the tanks. It's the last chance for gas, unless we want to detour to Chetumal.'' He said that in a disconcertingly normal voice, as if the tense little exchange had never happened. But Ellie had a sense of a crossroads passed…a moment of truth come and gone. Decisions made. Things settled.

It's going to be all right, she told herself, relaxing a little. Maybe he really is a man of honor.

In any case, for better or worse, she felt certain he wouldn't try again to talk her out of doing what she had to do.

McCall considered himself a man of his word. He'd promised a crazy woman he'd accompany her into a Yucatan jungle and pose as her husband in a meeting with armed smugglers, and if she insisted on going through with it, by God, he'd be right there with her, keeping his word. That didn't mean he couldn't try every way he knew of to keep her from going through with it. Backed up against a wall, all reasonable appeals having failed, he'd come up with a plan. A brilliant plan it was, too, in his opinion; devious but simple. Practically foolproof.

It was late morning when they reached the bustling jungle crossroads town of Felipe Carillo Puerto. It was too early for a full midday meal, but since McCall knew it was going to be a good long way to the next decent restaurant, he suggested they stop for a *botana*—Mexican for a light snack—of *garnachas,* which was basically fried masa patties topped with pork and chicken, onions, tomatoes and avocados. After that, on the way out of town they stopped at a gas station where a big hand-lettered sign reminded travelers: *Ultimo Gas.* While Ellie bought bottled water from a vending machine, McCall topped off the VW's tanks and to make it look good, checked the oil, hoses and tire pressure.

He was hunkered down and peering into the engine in a businesslike way when Ellie came up to him, holding out a bottle of cold water. He saw her, of course; felt her in his bones, muscles, nerves...in the very pit of his stomach. But he didn't acknowledge her presence until she said, "Are you sure this car can make it all the way to Chetumal?"

He gave an exaggerated wince. "Ssh—she'll hear you." He slammed the engine cover and straightened up, smiling at her as he tipped back the brim of his hat and took the bottle she offered. He was feeling amazingly good-humored.

Which seemed to befuddle her, for some reason. She gave her head a quick little shake, and in that abrupt, scratchy way of hers said, "No, no—I was just thinking—no gas also means no garages. This car's probably about a hundred and ten in human years. What happens if we break down?"

McCall cracked the cap, twisted it open and took a long drink. "No problemo," he said with an airy wave toward the Beetle's front end. "That's why I carry my tools with me wherever I go."

"Tools!" She gave him a sharp, startled look across the car's rounded roof. "Don't tell me you're a mechanic." Her gaze lingered…puzzled…quizzical, and he suddenly wished he could have read her mind just then. But the only thing he saw in those golden eyes of hers that he could be certain of was surprise.

"Not me," he said as he opened his door and got in. She did the same, and he handed her his water bottle to hold while he fired up the VW's engine and shifted gears. "My dad was, though. I worked for him weekends and summers all through high school, so anything around the mid 1970s or earlier I'm pretty comfortable with. These modern cars, though—all the electronics, computer-controlled everything—forget it. That's one reason I drive the Beetle. At least I know if anything goes wrong I can probably fix it."

He heard a faint sound, quickly stifled. He glanced at Ellie and found her gazing at him, lips parted, eyes glowing with frustrated curiosity. Smiling to himself—hell, he was in a mood to be generous—he waited until he'd got them back on the highway and headed south once again before he went on in a conversational tone, "I'd have probably been a mechanic, too—I liked it well enough—but my parents had their hearts set on sending me off to college. I was their only child, you see, and they had big plans for me." He didn't tell her what he'd always suspected, which was that his parents' real reason for wanting him gone had been because they'd wanted their own lives and privacy back. Or how hard it had been, sometimes, feeling like the fifth wheel, the unwanted third party tagging along on someone else's date.

"Where did you go?" Her voice was breathless and brave. "To college, I mean."

"Harvard." He punched it at her and waited for her reaction.

"Harvard!"

And he laughed, because, as he'd known it would be, it was so clearly the last thing she'd expected. "Not bad, on a mechanic's income, huh?" But when he glanced at her, the look on her face seemed more gratified than surprised.

"You're not—you weren't—a lawyer, were you?"

He smiled, but irony and memory were crowding in on him again, constricting his heart and making the smile feel strained and wry. "Nope," he said, still trying to keep it light and low-key. "Business. MBA."

"Your parents...your dad—they must have been very proud." Her tone was pensive, only slightly ironic, and her face was turned away, toward the window. But McCall could hear the thought as clearly as if she'd spoken it. *What must they think of you now?*

"I imagine they would have been," he said with gentle defiance. "Unfortunately they died in a car accident my junior year—" he continued relentlessly over her gasp of dismay and whispered "I'm sorry..." "—coming home from the beach on a Sunday evening. Somebody in a hurry tried to pass on a two-lane stretch of highway and hit them head-on. Matter of fact, it happened not far from the spot where James Dean died...."

Chapter 7

About thirty miles south of Felipe Carillo Puerto, Ellie's broken night's sleep began to take its toll. She was dozing off intermittently, shaking her head and fighting it as hard as she could, when McCall suddenly yelled, "Wild turkeys—look out!"

Adrenaline slammed into her like a truck. Her head jerked up and her eyes snapped open, and she managed to utter one gasped word: *"Where?"* as the Volkswagen braked hard, then swerved sharply to the right. For several very busy moments the VW bumped and jounced along the narrow shoulder, managing to avoid rocks, shrubs, small trees and major potholes before coming to a bone-jarring halt, safely back on the paved road.

"Are you okay?" McCall asked. His tone was solicitous, but with a suspicious little croak of excitement.

Ellie felt a sudden urge to hit him. "I didn't see them," she wailed. "The turkeys! I didn't even see them."

McCall looked shocked. "How could you miss 'em? They were all over the road. What were you, asleep?"

"Yes! Maybe...I don't know, I must have been. Why didn't you wake me?"

"I thought I did."

"No, I mean *before* you plowed into the middle of them."

"How was I supposed to know you'd dozed off?" And he was laughing as he shifted gears and the VW sputtered to life once more. Ellie subsided in a disappointed if now wide-awake sulk.

A few hundred feet farther down the highway, the VW slowed...sputtered...gasped one last time...and died.

"What?" Ellie demanded, looking at McCall.

"I don't know." Frowning, he tried turning the ignition key. The starter coughed and growled like a bad-tempered tiger. "Feels like we just ran out of gas, but that's..."

"We can't be out of gas. We just filled up," Ellie said, flatly stating the obvious. And after a moment, "Maybe something happened when we were bouncing around back there."

"Maybe," McCall grunted as he opened his door and stepped out of the car. "Come on, help me get it out of the road."

With both of them pushing on the doorjambs and McCall steering one-handed, they managed to maneuver the VW more or less onto the shoulder. McCall opened the hood and took out a serious-looking metal toolbox which he carried around to the back of the Bug.

"I thought you said you could fix it," Ellie said when she saw him standing there, scowling at the open engine compartment and absently swatting at mosquitos.

"Gotta find the problem first. Might be a ruptured fuel line...maybe the pump. If it's the pump...only thing I can think of is to flag somebody down and hitch a ride to Los Limones, see if we can order a part. Car this old...I don't know. Probably have to come from Merida...someplace with some good-sized salvage yards. Maybe take two...three days—''

He broke off, primarily because his audience had deserted him. And secondly because he suddenly had a sinking feeling in his stomach. Because Ellie was just then crawling into the Beetle's front seat, where she had no business being. That was not good. Not good at all.

His worst fears were confirmed when she sang out happily, "Hey, I think I've found the problem."

"What the hell do you mean, you found the problem?" McCall stalked around to the open passenger-side door just as she was squirming out from under the dash, looking flushed and radiant—and so damned delicious she'd have made his mouth water if he hadn't been frustrated enough to spit nails.

"This is what—a '58, '59? Must be, because only the really old VWs had it. It was because they didn't have fuel gauges then. There's this little switch down here, see? So you can manually switch over to the reserve tank. Or, you can also shut it all the way off. That's what happened—you must've hit it with your knee when we were bouncing all over the place back there. Try it now."

Damn. He didn't know whether to admire her or shoot her.

Mentally gnashing his teeth and silently using up every swearword he knew, McCall stomped around to the driver's side and got in. He turned the key, and, of course, after only the usual amount of pumping, begging and growling, the engine fired.

"Don't forget your toolbox," Ellie said in a tone that tried too hard not to be smug.

"How come you know so much about a car that's probably twenty years older than you are?" he grudgingly asked when he had his tools stowed and they were on their way again. "I never even thought of that fuel switch." Well, okay, he was a liar. May that be the least of the sins I commit this week, he thought.

"I'm not that young," Ellie cried, which in McCall's opinion only proved she was. It had been his experience that only very young women objected to having their ages *under*estimated. "For heaven's sake, I have a doctor's—" She clamped it off there as a look of dismay flashed across her face, then looked away out the window and finished with a testy, "Just because I'm short, don't underestimate me."

"I'd never make that mistake," McCall said fervently, meaning it—and also mightily intrigued by what she'd been about to say. A doctor's...*what?* Permission slip? "But seriously—how come you knew about that switch?"

She flashed him a uniquely feminine look, lashes lowered, pleased with herself again. "Old VWs are very popular with us Save-the-Whales types, you know." Practically purring with satisfaction, she gave her head a toss, and he was so distracted by the way the wind played with her cinnamon curls he allowed the VW to wander briefly onto the shoulder again. "I once rode all the way from Portland to the tip of Baja in one that was probably older than this. It was a convertible. Hardly anything was left of the top and you could see the road going by through the floorboards. There aren't too many service stations in some parts of Baja, either, so you'd *better* know some basic auto mechanics."

"And you do?" Just my luck, he thought sourly. Of all the women in this world, he had to hook up with Tillie Tune-up. "They teach you that back on the farm?"

"Well, it's something you just sort of learn, actually, when you grow up on a farm. At least we—my brother and I—did. My mom made sure of that. At least the basics—things like how to change your own oil and tires and stuff."

"Your mom?" He snapped her a look, thinking about his own fifties-style mother with her bright red nail polish and soft hands, leaning in admiring feminine helplessness over her mechanic husband's shoulder while he checked the oil in her car. Ellie, he suddenly noticed, had almost boyish hands, freckled as her face, with short, unpolished nails. "Not your dad?"

She gave a light, gurgling laugh, full of amused affection. "My dad's a newspaper columnist—Mike Lanagan, maybe you've heard of him? I don't know, maybe he knew something about fixing cars once, but these days the most complicated piece of equipment he deals with is his new all-in-one-printer-scanner-fax machine."

"Mike Lanagan." McCall never knew how he kept his face blank, his voice neutral, utterly without inflection. Because it had suddenly dawned on him. *Jeez. Mike Lanagan. Newspaper columnist. No wonder that name sounded so familiar.* He took his time lighting a cigarette, and by the time he'd finished that task he was able to say in a normal, no more than mildly interested tone, "Newsweek, right?"

"Right!" She turned her head to beam at him, like a little girl delighted that he'd correctly answered her riddle.

McCall stared resolutely at the road ahead, not trusting himself to look at her. He cleared his throat and said carefully, "I thought he was based in Chicago. Doesn't he also write for one of their big dailies?"

"Yeah, he does. When my brother and I were growing up he used to spend a lot of time in Chicago, but nowa-

days, with modems and stuff, he mostly works at home.
Which is nice for my mom. Dad, too, I guess. He's writing
a book—nobody's allowed to know what's in it except
Mom, but supposedly it's about his early days as a journalist in Chicago, and how he and Mom met..."

"Yeah? How *did* they meet? A Chicago journalist and
an Iowa farmer..."

"Are you sure you're interested? It's kind of a long
story."

McCall waved a hand at the ribbon of road walled in
by jungle ahead of them and said dryly, "We've got a
long way to go." That's the ticket, he thought. Keep her
talking. Then maybe she won't notice how rattled you are.

"It's a pretty exciting story, actually," said Ellie, shifting around in her seat in an eager, preparatory way.
"First, Dad almost got killed by some hit men, because
of this story he was working on. So he thought he'd better
get out of Chicago for a while, but then he got lost in a
thunderstorm and drove his car into a ditch, and that's
how he wound up in my mom's barn...."

It probably was an exciting story, but McCall barely
heard it. He just kept hearing the name *Mike Lanagan*,
over and over again in his mind. Jeez, he thought, of all
the women in the world I pick to get mixed up with...first
Goody Two-Shoes, then Tillie Tune-up, and now...Mike
Lanagan's daughter.

Lucy came in for lunch red-cheeked and blowing on
her hands. "Whoo—that storm's coming in fast," she
said to her husband, who was sitting at the kitchen table
waiting for her. "You know, I think it might even snow.
I sure hope it doesn't. Hope it holds off until after tomorrow, at least. Makes it so tough for the trick-'r-

treaters." She paused, noticing the manila file folder. "What's that you've got?"

Mike shoved it forward a few inches with a forefinger, then brought it back. "It's that file I was looking for— the one on Quinn McCall."

"Quinn McCall? Who's—"

"I told you I remembered a McCall. Did a whole series of columns on him a few years back. Seven, to be exact." He tilted his head and made a small, appreciative sound. "He's not a man you forget."

Lucy had picked up the file and was flipping through it. She looked up, frowning and skeptical. "Oh, Mike, you can't think *Ellie's* McCall is this same person. Out of all the McCalls there must be in this world? That would be just too...I mean, coincidences like that don't happen, except in books."

Mike's smile was wry. "No, actually, they *don't* happen in books, at least not fiction, because people wouldn't believe it. The fact is, they happen in real life all the time. The difference is, if it's true, people *have* to believe it. Then they say, in awe, 'My goodness, isn't it a small world!'"

"Gwen always believed in Providence," Lucy mused. Her smile, as she gazed at the man she'd been happily married to for...oh, so many years, was perhaps a tad misty. "You know she always said it was Providence made you take refuge in my barn—"

"—the very day your hired man quit," Mike chimed in with her, laughing. "I know, I know."

The laughter died, and his eyes grew thoughtful again. "I just keep remembering the last thing Quinn McCall ever said to me. It was after the last interview, the tape recorders were turned off, and we were packing up, saying goodbye. I asked him what he was going to do with himself, now that it was all over.''

"And?" Lucy prompted. "What did he say?"

"He said, 'I'm gonna find me a beach. A long, long way from here.'"

They came to the hotel on the shores of Lago Bacalar late in the afternoon. They'd missed the turnoff specified in their instructions on the first pass and were halfway to Chetumal before they realized they'd gone too far. Then they'd had to ask directions twice before they found it, to McCall's obvious irritation.

It had amused Ellie, actually, to discover that her new partner had such a tender ego—and oh, how that incident with the car had ticked him off, her knowing about that switch and being the one to find and fix the VW's problem. Somehow, though, that common male malady only made him seem more human. Less...mysterious. In an odd way, more likeable. Maybe.

"Yes, Señor and Señora Burnside, your room has been reserved for you," the desk clerk assured them, in the cordial but haughty manner of hotel desk clerks the world over. "And will you be staying more than one night?"

Ellie shot a quick glance at McCall, who was gazing around the lobby as if he hadn't heard a word. She felt her cheeks grow warm. Dammit, why hadn't she thought of this? Why hadn't he? Clearing her throat, she stepped closer to the counter and inquired in a low voice, "Excuse me, but do you have any vacant rooms? My husband—"

The desk clerk looked alarmed. "Yes, *señora,* we do have rooms, but surely—"

"We have friends who may possibly be joining us later," McCall interrupted in a voice as smooth as silk.

"They weren't certain what day they'd be arriving. Just checking…"

Ellie turned her head to stare at him. He was smiling at the desk clerk, showing more teeth than she'd have guessed he possessed, and carefully *not* looking at Ellie.

The desk clerk returned the smile—fleetingly. "Ah yes—I see. This time of year there should be no problem. Later, after the Day of the Dead…that is our busy time. Right now…plenty of rooms. Will you be paying with your credit card, Señor Burnside?"

McCall turned his smile on Ellie with a breezy, "Pay the man, dear."

As she handed over the credit card that had been issued to her and her partner by the United States Government, her mind was racing jerkily to and fro—like a rabbit in a cage, she thought. Trapped. Nowhere to go.

Why didn't I think of this? Spend the night in the same room with him? Impossible. No way. But he's right, we can't ask for two rooms. How would it look? We're supposed to be married.

Funny thing was, it had never bothered her to share a room with Ken. Anyway, not like this. Of course, she and Ken had always had separate beds….

"Excuse me," she said as she calmly and without a visible tremor signed *Rose Ellen Burnside* on the registration slip, "is that one bed or two?"

"One bed," said the desk clerk with obvious satisfaction. "Queen size."

Ellie nodded and became very involved, suddenly, with the task of putting the credit card back in her wallet, and the wallet back in her purse.

"Will that be all right, *señora?*"

"Yes, that's fine." But her mind was doing the frightened rabbit thing again. *Impossible. A king…maybe. But a queen? No way.* She could feel McCall close beside her, casually turned a little toward her so that his Panama hat, squashed under one arm, brushed against her shoulder. She could feel the heat from his body. Smell his scent— like hers, mostly insect repellent. She could feel her own pulse thumping in the hollow at the base of her throat. *One of us will just have to sleep on the floor. I will....*

The desk clerk had turned away to look for their room key. In desperation, Ellie gazed upward, as if somehow the answer to her dilemma might be found written on the wall above the registration desk.

And—lo and behold, there it was. A sign, neatly hand-lettered in both Spanish and English. The English part read: Hammocks Available on Request.

"Oh, look, dear," she said in a sweet girlish voice that was nothing like her own, and with a breathlessness that was more relief than excitement, "they have hammocks! I used to love hammocks when I was a little girl." Turning toward McCall, she twined herself around his arm and purred, "Let's get one, shall we, darling? Just for fun?"

Was it her imagination, or did his breathing catch—just a little? At any rate, his voice, when he spoke, was thick with gravel—though admittedly, that wasn't unusual for McCall.

"Sure, why not? Anything you want, *dear.*" His teeth were showing again. She couldn't see his eyes.

The clerk disappeared through a door behind the desk and came back with a tightly rolled webby bundle, which he placed on the counter. "There you are, *señor...señora.* You will find hooks on your veranda. And there is a message for you, Señor Burnside." He handed McCall a sealed white envelope. Ellie could hardly keep herself from snatching it out of his hands. "Perhaps it is from your friends...."

"Perhaps," said McCall as he tucked the envelope in his shirt pocket.

The desk clerk gave them the key and directions to their room, which turned out to be not in the main hotel but one of a string of tiny cottages arranged along a path overlooking the lakeshore. McCall passed the key to Ellie and tucked the bundled hammock under one arm. They thanked the hovering desk clerk, who beamed at them as they turned to go and said something in Spanish that Ellie didn't quite understand.

"What did he say?" she muttered as soon as they were out of earshot, glancing up at McCall. His face was curiously deadpan. "It definitely wasn't 'Enjoy your stay.' I understood *feliz* and *luna,* but what's *miel?*"

His lips twitched slightly, and it was a moment before he answered, in a voice as determinedly devoid of expression as his face. "It means honey. He was wishing us happiness on our honeymoon."

"Oh," said Ellie, and her heart did an odd little stumble-step. She gnawed her lip and frowned at the ground, trying hard to think of something to say. She couldn't remember the last time she'd felt this self-conscious...walking close beside McCall, not touching him but aware of every breath and muscle twitch, his heat and scent melting into her very pores. Both of them carefully not looking at each other and her feeling as though the eyes of the entire world were watching *them,* even though not a soul was in sight. "I'm sorry," she finally said on a shaken exhalation. "I should have thought of this."

You should have thought of a lot of things, McCall thought grimly but didn't say. *Before you elected a complete stranger to stand in for your absent husband. Before you dragged me into your life...your mess. Before you kissed me....*

He cleared his throat and said aloud, "Couldn't be helped. Look—this is a remote part of the world. Everybody around here's probably related—hell, for all you know, that desk clerk could be the head smuggler's brother-in-law. We're supposed to be husband and wife—how's it gonna look if we'd asked for separate rooms?"

"Well," said Ellie, getting a staunch, determined look he was beginning to recognize, "I'll sleep in the hammock. It's the least I can do."

She wouldn't get any argument from him there. So why *was* he arguing? He wondered about that as he heard himself say, "Come on, you'll get eaten alive by mosquitos."

"Maybe we can rig up some netting. Besides, I'll douse myself with plenty of repellent. Don't worry about me." And she gave her head an intrepid little toss as she jerked open the door to the VW and plunked herself inside.

"Sister, you're the last person I'm worried about," he muttered, going around to the driver's side and easing in under the wheel.

But why did that always get to him—that arrogant, overconfident little way she had that made him want to either kick her in the butt or gather her into his arms and shield and protect her? Maybe because he knew it for what it was? Because he'd worn it often enough himself in a past life...the mask of bravado people wear to hide the fact that they're really scared to death...and bound and determined to go ahead anyway.

Some people might have said that was the definition of courage. As far as McCall was concerned, it was just plain stupidity.

Neither of them said anything more as he drove the VW to a parking space as close as he could get to their cottage. The silence held while he was hauling their over-nighters out of the back seat, along with Ellie's purse and a big cloth beach bag that held her sun visor, flashlights, insect repellent, bottles of water, and of course, a dozen or so bars of chocolate. It persisted while Ellie stood in the VW's open doorway with her elbows resting on the roof, one hand holding down her wind-ruffled hair as she gazed out across the lake…and while McCall tried every way he knew how not to look at her, or notice how rich and warm the colors of her skin and hair were against the cool greens of the jungle, the vivid blues of water and sky.

Then he heard a soft sound, a deeply inhaled breath. "Mmm…you can smell the sea," she murmured.

"Huh," he said, scowling at the overnighter he'd just wrestled out of the car. "Wind must be just right. Probably that tropical storm moving in."

She turned her back on the car and the lake and lifted her face to the sun, which retaliated by making a coppery halo of her hair. Wind stirred through orange and mango, oak and banana leaves, and a flock of small green birds—parrots of some kind—flitted, chattering, from tree to tree. McCall caught the scent of orange blossoms.

"It's so beautiful here," she said softly, as if to herself. "It *would* be a lovely place for a honeymoon."

It wasn't so much the words, as the way she looked when she said them. A kind of wistful innocence, McCall thought, like a young girl gazing at bridal gowns. He didn't know what it was about it that made his throat tighten up, what made anger flare hot behind his eyes…or what made him pounce almost without thought, like a cat smacking a paw down on a hapless mouse.

"One to a customer," he said in a rough, rude tone,

and then, firing her a challenging stare, "Where'd you go for yours, Mrs. Burnside?"

He didn't know what he'd expected to accomplish by asking that, except perhaps to punish himself by stirring up the little worm of jealousy that kept popping up so unexpectedly from dark cupboards in his subconscious mind. What he did *not* expect was the look that flitted across her face. Blank, pale panic, as if she had no idea whatsoever how to answer him.

And then... "Lake Tahoe!" she blurted it out angrily, almost defiantly. And he absolutely *knew* it was a lie.

"Really? Lake Tahoe..." he said in a calm, musing tone, aware suddenly that his pulse had quickened and that it was taking all his concentration to keep his breathing from doing the same. "I know it very well. Where, exactly?"

"None of your business," she snapped, then shot it right back at him. "Where'd you go on yours?"

She was standing very close to him, drawn up to her full height, such as it was, head thrown back so she could look him straight in the eyes. He gazed down at her, refusing to let himself dwell on how lush and lovely her mouth was. Suddenly feeling old and indefinably sad.

"What business is it of yours?" he said with sneering cruelty. "By my calculations you were probably in kindergarten at the time."

She inhaled sharply through her nose. "You know, McCall, I'm getting really tired of these little digs about my age. I'm twenty-eight years old. And you're what...thirty-five?"

"Forty," he admitted gloomily.

She let a couple of long, slow beats go by while her eyes shimmered into his and a sweet flush ripened under her freckles. He felt his own eyes burn and heat crawl beneath his skin, as if he'd been out in the sun too long.

"I don't know very many twelve-year-old fathers," she said in a soft-rough voice like a kitten's purr. Then she turned a shoulder toward him and walked away up the graveled path.

As he seemed to find himself doing so often, he stood there and just watched her, watched her going away from him, looking, in her shorts, T-shirt and Nikes, every inch the teenager he knew she wasn't. She was a full-grown woman with a strong will and a mind of her own—bull-headed and lion-hearted, a terrifying combination—a fact he'd known all along, he now realized. He knew, too, with a frightening little sense of loneliness and loss, that he'd tried so hard to convince himself otherwise in order to make it easier to accept that he couldn't have her. Now here he was, thrown into forced intimacy with her, and only his conscience and a moral code she didn't seem to share to keep him from doing something shameful.

To keep him from doing...what? *Seducing her?*

The fear inside him grew as he acknowledged the thought, and realized it had been there in his mind for a while now. Disgraceful, but...what if he could? Married or not—and how could he know or judge what kind of marriage hers was?—she was susceptible to him in that particular way. He knew it. He could *feel* it.

The fact was, for reasons he couldn't begin to understand she seemed hell-bent on committing God knew how many felonies and dragging him right along with her. And for the life of him he couldn't figure out a way to stop her. He knew for darn sure he wasn't going to be able to talk her out of it, and if he pulled out she was just going to go ahead on her own, and how was he going to live with himself if something happened to her? Physical force might work—hog-tying her, maybe, or locking her in a closet—but then what? What proof did he have that he was doing it for her own good? He could very well wind up in jail himself, on kidnapping charges, no less.

Seduce her? It seemed a long shot, at best, but maybe…just maybe, if he could get her all soft and vulnerable and acquiescent in his bed, he might be able to talk some sense into her…get her to listen to reason. Get her to listen to *him,* and forget that absent husband of hers and this crazy suicidal plan he'd gotten her mixed up in. It *could* work…couldn't it?

Forget it, McCall. All you're trying to do is justify doing what you want to do anyhow. But it's still not right. And it's not who you are. Forget about it.

But as he hitched his load and set off after her, all his senses were still on red alert and tuned to her wavelength, and his body was humming in ways it hadn't in…so many years, aching and tingling like long-frozen tissues coming back to life.

Chapter 8

"Are you sure you want to do this?" McCall asked. They were standing together on the veranda. Twilight was coming down and he'd just finished putting up the hammock and was testing the tension in the anchor rope, plucking it like a guitar string. "Look," he heard himself gruffly say, "why don't you take the bed? I'll sleep on the floor."

"What about those lizards and scorpions?" Ellie gave him a solemn look that had laughter lurking in it.

He rejected the laughter with an angry gesture. "The chair, then."

"No—really, I'm looking forward to this. Unless *you*—" she hurriedly and politely added, lifting her eyebrows and making an offering gesture with her spread hands.

He shook his head and shuddered. "Damn things remind me of giant spiderwebs."

"I used to love playing in one of these when I was a

kid,'' she said musingly, setting the hammock to swaying, gazing at it but obviously seeing something else. Something long ago and far away. ''In the summertime we had one strung between these two big trees in our yard. The one we had was different, though, not woven like this. It was canvas—green and white stripes—and really tippy. You had to be careful getting in and out, and you had to get balanced just so or it would dump you. My brother Eric and I used to play this game, sort of King of the Mountain only it was King of the Hammock. We'd play Rock-Paper-Scissors to see who'd get to be in the hammock first, and then the other person would try to dump him out and claim it for himself. It could get pretty rough—about the only thing that wasn't allowed was the garden hose—squirting with water, I mean. Or mud-throwing—that was a *big* no-no.'' She gave McCall a sideways look and a wicked little smile that let him know how well she'd stuck to those rules.

He smiled back, trying, as he had all through dinner, as she'd talked about her family and her childhood on the farm, to see her the way she must have been back then. Trying now to see her as a laughing, squealing little girl roughhousing on a farmhouse lawn on a hot Iowa summer day, with bits of grass and mud in her hair. But the image wouldn't come. The top half of her was covered by a tank-type bathing suit in an unbecoming dark shade of blue, some silky fabric that molded itself to her body like paint, and from waist to six inches above the knees by that wrap-around shorts or skirt thing she'd worn before, with no regard whatsoever for color compatibility. A soft breeze was blowing and the humid air smelled sweet, a heady mix of flowers and foliage and the distant sea. The last of the sunset colors were fading from a sky full of billowing thunderheads, darkness was folding itself like a warm embrace around one of the most beautiful places on the planet, and all he could think about was how the woman beside him smelled like the night, and how warm her body would be, and how much he wanted to put his arms around her and breathe in the sweet scent of her hair.

"You know what I really loved most, though?" Her voice was soft as the air, and almost lost in the awakening chorus of frog song and insect hum. "The times when I was all by myself, with my book, maybe an apple. And I'd lie there and be really, really quiet...and after a while the birds and animals would forget I was there. Birds would be sitting and singing right above my head, sometimes even on the hammock's strings, close enough to touch. Squirrels would be digging in the grass for acorns right underneath me. One time this rabbit came hopping onto the grass with three of her babies, and they just sat there, munching away, not even seeing me...."

Right then McCall thought he knew how she must have felt. *She's so close to me,* he thought. *If I move just slightly, if I even draw a deep breath, I'd be touching her....*

And so, carefully *not* breathing, he said in a tight, airless voice, "So, you've always had a thing for animals, then."

"Oh yes...for as long as I can remember."

"Did you always think you'd have a pet shop someday?"

She threw him one of those quick, mysteriously guilty looks, then laughed—a low, husky chuckle that stirred like a stroking hand across his already sensitized nerves. "Oh no—I always thought I'd be a vet. Farm animals, you know? I never imagined I'd ever leave Iowa."

Sister, you're a long way from Iowa now, he thought, helpless frustration a pressure inside him, squeezing his heart. Aloud he said softly, "What happened to change your mind?"

He felt her shrug, then turn to face him. "College happened, I guess. I found out there was a big world out there, and a lot of things in it—a lot of causes—that needed me more than my mom's cattle and hogs did."

Causes? My God, thought McCall, what happened to you? How could you go from "causes" to wildlife smuggling for profit and not even bat an eye? He wanted to grab her by the arms and shake some sense into her....

He wanted to take her by the arms and *kiss* some sense into her.

To keep himself from it, he folded his arms across his chest and tucked his hands against his sides and held himself so tightly in his own embrace that his body quivered with the strain.

He didn't have anything to say to her. He stood there looking down at her and she looked back at him, and messages flew back and forth between them as night swallowed up their features, leaving faces like pale blank places in the darkness. Anonymous, covering darkness. It would be so easy to forget who she was...who *he* was.

Don't do it, McCall. It's not who you are. Don't do it.

"I'm going for a swim in the lake," she announced, hurling herself away from him in a jerky pirouette. "There are lights on the hotel's dock. Coming?"

She fled from him without waiting for his answer, on legs that had suddenly become unreliable—like so many other parts of her. Her mind and body seemed bent on betraying her lately, and she couldn't find a way to stop it. *Coming?* Why had she asked him that? It was the last thing she wanted. The last thing she needed. What she desperately needed was to get away from him, to clear her mind and cool her overheated body in the fresh cold waters of a tropical lake fed, according to the guidebooks, by underground streams.

Oh, but, be honest—there was a part of her that just as desperately wanted him to come after her. And try as she would to block them, the images came to her of two bodies coming together in the soft purple night, meeting and touching with the water like cool silk between them…then slowly warming, melting together, heat soaking through skin and muscle and deep into their very core…. She ran faster, fleeing in vain from the images, and felt frightened and frustrated and filled again with that unfamiliar urge to cry.

Why are you doing this to me? Ellie asked of God-knows-who, breathing hard in silent fury as she dropped shorts and sandals on the end of the dock and knifed into the air in a clean, sure arc.

The water's embrace was a sweet, exhilarating shock, like stepping from a hot sultry day into a cool shower. She swam hard for a few minutes with her mind a blessed blank, concentrating on things that usually took no thought at all—like the rhythm of muscles, and breathing and heartbeat. When she paused at last, winded, and turned to float languidly on the gentle wake of her own making and gaze up at the vastness of sky and stars, her mind felt calmer, if no less concerned.

This isn't the real thing, she told herself. It can't be. But, she told herself, it's probably normal—certainly understandable. A combination of circumstances. A tropical setting as romantic and beautiful as anything she could possibly have dreamed…a man who kept showing up on her radar screen as her white, if somewhat tarnished, knight. Who knows, maybe some sort of biological clock kicking in, though well ahead of schedule, as far as she was concerned. *Normal. Understandable.*

Oh, but why *now?* Why did such a thing have to happen to her now, distracting her mind when she so needed all her wits about her, undermining her self-confidence just when she needed it most?

She swam back to the dock with slow, measured strokes, concentrating once again on breathing and rhythm, on relaxing her body and clearing her mind. All for nothing, as it turned out. A familiar form was standing on the end of the dock, haloed by the strings of lights overhead, looking somehow incongruous in cutoffs, tropical-print shirt and the Panama hat she was beginning to think of as his trademark—rather like Indiana Jones's stained fedora. Just short of the ladder she pulled up, treading water, and heat rose to her head like magma, and her heart was pounding beyond all reason.

"What are you doing here?" she asked as she glided over to the ladder through water that had become as viscous as honey. She kept her voice light, breathless, but no more so than normal for someone who'd just completed a vigorous swim; he would never know how her heart was banging against her ribs.

"Brought you a towel," he said, strolling unhurriedly toward her. "I noticed you forgot to take one with you."

"Didn't think I needed one." She pulled herself up the ladder, ignoring the hand he offered, and straightened bravely and defiantly before him, smoothing her wet hair back with both hands. "It's a warm night."

"Then why are you shivering?"

She said nothing for a moment, but aimed a hard, meaningful look straight into his eyes. Then... "It'll pass," she snapped. "It's no big deal. Nothing I can't handle."

His chuckle stirred like a breeze over her already shivered skin. "Yeah, I know. There's not much you can't handle."

She turned her back to him in rejection, then closed her eyes as she felt the towel embrace her anyway. Her throat ached and tears burned behind her eyelids. Through the thick and slightly scratchy toweling she felt the warmth and weight of his hands on her shoulders.

"Besides..." he growled the words close to her ear "...what if someone's watching? We're supposed to be honeymooners. How's it gonna look, you out here swimming all alone?" He gave her shoulders a little shake and a squeeze, and she thought if her heart beat any louder he would surely have to hear it.

Oh, she thought, *if I were to lean only a little...hardly at all...that would be it. That's all it would take.*

Yes, and then what?

What was she thinking? She barely knew this man. She was in the middle of a mission. Who knew what tomorrow would bring?

She stood utterly still, frozen inside, holding the towel together with a fist so tightly clenched it hurt. "The water's nice," she said with barely a hint of a tremor in her voice. "You should try it."

He gave his patented snort, soft and wry. "Maybe after all this is over. *If* I'm still alive..."

They had started walking together, McCall with his arm still draped across her shoulders in what must appear to be a casual, comfortable intimacy. To Ellie it seemed an impossible weight. "Don't do that," she said in a choked voice.

"Do what?" He sounded truly puzzled.

"Put your arm around me."

The weight of his arm slipped away, but the warmth, the *feel* of it remained, a tingling awareness in her muscles, a cringing in her spine. "Solely for appearances' sake, I assure you," he said dryly, taking cigarettes and lighter from his shirt pocket.

"Do you really think it's necessary? Just because we're supposed to be married?" She gave her shoulders an impatient little wiggle, trying to shake off the residual effects of his touch as she bent over to scoop up her shorts. She shot him a look as she struggled to force her still-damp feet into her sandals. "I mean, all married people don't grope each other in public, do they?"

"I don't know," he said in a mild tone, blowing away smoke. "Do they?"

They began walking, close together and in silence, McCall methodically smoking, Ellie carrying her shorts clutched against her chest underneath the towel because putting them on in front of him seemed too great an intimacy. When they came to their cottage, she stopped abruptly and for a moment simply stood gazing at the cloud of mosquito netting cascading down over the hammock from a coat hanger hooked in the veranda's thatched roof. She looked up at McCall. He gazed back at her, but the light over the door cast his face in unfamiliar shadows, making it unreadable.

"Thank you," she said, once again dangerously and inexplicably close to tears. She remembered how she'd thanked him once before, standing on tiptoes to kiss him on the cheek. She thought how strange it was that what had seemed so natural to her then now seemed utterly impossible.

He shrugged and unlocked the door. "No problemo." He pushed open the door and flipped the light switch, then gave the inside of the cottage a quick once-over before turning back to her. "Well," he said. And there was an awkward pause.

Ellie finally muttered, "We should probably—" just as

he was starting to say something. So she stopped and said, "Go ahead."

He cleared his throat and made a careless, throwaway gesture. "No, I was just going to say that according to our new instructions we're going to need to get an early start tomorrow morning."

She nodded, her head bobbing foolishly. "Right. So we should probably call it a night...."

"Turn in early, try to get a good night's sleep..."

"Plus," said Ellie, her voice rusty and blunt as an old trowel, "I don't know about you, but I didn't get much sleep last night. I'm beat."

He glanced at the hammock and his lips curved in a rueful smile. "Don't know that you'll fare much better on that thing."

"I'll be fine. Don't worry about me."

He hesitated, while her heart hammered out-of-sync rhythms. Then he jerked his head toward the open door. "Okay, then. Why don't you go in and do whatever it is you need to do? I'll wait out here."

"Right...okay." Still clutching her towel across her chest, she stepped past him into the cottage and shut the door behind her. Then, instead of crossing immediately to her overnight bag or the bathroom, for a few minutes she just stayed there, leaning against the door and drawing long, deep breaths, and waiting for her legs to stop trembling.

She'd been in there a long time.

Sure taking her time about it, McCall thought, grumpy with the awareness that he—and she—were fast becoming a genuine honeymoon cliché. Woman taking forever in the bathroom...man pacing impatiently while his pulses pounded and his blood backed up in predictable places. It might have struck him as funny if he hadn't been so damned uncomfortable, what with needing the bathroom himself, and way too much nicotine in his system and not nearly enough tequila. Not to mention the fact that his mosquito repellent was wearing off.

Five more minutes, he promised himself. Then he was going in.

He noted the time on his watch, then ambled the length of the veranda and back. Glanced in the window, not expecting to see much of anything with the curtains drawn…then did a double take and looked again.

The curtains were open only a crack, but the angle was just right, and Ellie was in just the right place. He could see her clearly. She was kneeling on the quarry-tile floor in front of her open overnight bag. She had her back to him and was dressed in an oversized T-shirt and baggy shorts, and the turned-up bottoms of her feet looked pink and wrinkled and childlike.

And there was nothing childlike at all about the gun she was holding in her hands.

He hadn't meant to spy on her; for God's sake, he wasn't a Peeping Tom. But when he saw that gun, what the hell was he supposed to do? Shock had already exploded through him in gusty, whispered swearing he'd had enough presence of mind—after the first word, at least—to stifle. After that he just held his breath and shrank back as far as he could and still see through that crack in the curtains and prayed to God she didn't turn around and see him there.

What's this? What the hell is this?

For a few more minutes that was all he could think of, the only thing in his mind. And then he thought, Goody Two-Shoes, Tillie Tune-up, Mike Lanagan's daughter and now...what? Mata Hari? Annie Oaklie? Who *was* this woman?

One thing for sure, she didn't have that gun in her bag by accident. He watched her run through preparations for firing the thing—slap in the clip, check the chamber—*click-click*—set the safety—with professional efficiency. She knew what she was doing, all right. He didn't know a whole lot about handguns, but this one looked efficient—slim, dark and deadly. He felt a cold and alarming clamminess creep over him as he saw her fasten it into an ankle holster, strap it in place, then pull on a pair of boots to cover both of those and check them for fit and comfort, and the gun for accessibility.

How much longer could he stand here and watch this? He could remember only one other time in his life when he'd made so shocking a discovery. He remembered how he'd felt then, too...cold like this, and a little sick. He remembered how disappointed he'd been, and angry and—hell, he wasn't ashamed to admit it—scared. And just like then, wondering what in the world he was going to do about it.

Then, just when he thought he was either going to have to sit down and put his head between his knees or barge in and confront her, she did something that sent his thoughts careening wildly off in another direction entirely.

She'd taken off the boots, holster and gun and laid them carefully aside. Now she took something else from her bag, something he couldn't immediately see. Then he heard the unmistakable *r-r-rip* of a Velcro fastening and a moment later her hot pink sun visor with the rainbow-colored Acapulco embroidered across the headband was placed to one side as well. Only...it looked different, somehow. It took him a moment to make sense of what he was seeing—to realize that the headband part of the sun visor had been opened along its top seam like a pea pod to reveal a hidden compartment lined with some sort of light-absorbing material.

And that was all the time he had to wonder about it before she picked up the sun visor and inserted something into the compartment, then held the visor up to the light while she painstakingly fitted it, whatever *it* was—camera? Recorder? Some kind of secret weapon?—into position, directly under the embroidered Acapulco. Then the newly "armed" visor went into the neat pile beside her along with the boots, holster and gun.

Next to come out of the bag was her watch, which she put on her wrist and then proceeded to fiddle with, but not in any way he'd ever seen, turning the watch this way and that while she stared at it—more like a compass than a timepiece. Apparently satisfied that it was working the way it should, she then, of all things, took off her earrings—the tiny gold studs he'd seen her wearing—and replaced them with a different, much larger pair.

Did that make sense? One minute the woman was calmly prepping lethal weapons and James Bond spy toys, and the next she was primping like a teenager going to a party. *Who the hell is she? What the devil's going on?*

By this time, McCall was just about beside himself with impotent fury and unsatisfied curiosity. It was taking long-forgotten reserves of self-discipline—the kind he hadn't thought he'd ever be called upon to use again—in order to maintain his silence, his distance and his calm. While his mind was busy jumping to impossible conclusions and shrieking questions at him for which he had no answers, he had to force himself to stand utterly still and watch with narrowed and burning eyes as she took a fat manila envelope from her bag and dumped its contents onto the tile. He wasn't all that surprised to see money—lots of it,

American bills, thick stacks of them, bundled with paper strips, the kind banks use. What did seem odd to him—though by this time he didn't think anything could *really* shock him—was when Ellie carefully removed all the paper strips, then divided the pile of money into two roughly equal parts, one half of which she returned to the manila envelope. The other half she wrapped up tightly in a plastic bag and placed in the overnight bag, then covered it with the casual jumble of her clothes.

That done, she sat motionless for a moment with her hands in her lap, the rigidity of her spine and the slump of her shoulders betraying both tension and exhaustion. Her head was turned to one side as if she were deep in thought, going over a mental checklist one more time, perhaps. Though her profile was set in lines of grim resolve, she looked pale…vulnerable but determined. Watching her, McCall felt a sudden twisting sensation in his chest, a manifestation of emotions he'd hoped never to feel again and angrily squelched.

Since it was obvious she'd just about reached the end of her preparations, he moved quickly and silently away from the window. When she came onto the veranda a few minutes later he was standing on the pathway at the bottom of the steps, smoking a cigarette, depending on the nicotine to quiet his vibrating nerves and provide an excuse for the harshness he couldn't keep from his voice when he spoke to her.

"So soon? I was beginning to think you'd changed your mind about taking the bed."

"Sorry it took so long." Her voice sounded breathless—with nerves, he wondered? Or guilt? "I was getting things ready for tomorrow—my clothes and things." It was too dark to see if she'd blushed.

But then, he told himself, she wouldn't, would she? Not

if, as he suspected, she only blushed when she lied. After all, "clothes and *things*" covered a lot of territory.

Resentment simmered inside him, a slow burn underneath his breastbone. He thought of a dozen things he could have said to her, hinting of his knowledge, offering her openings to tell all. He couldn't utter a one; all the words in his mind seemed to be stuck there, dammed up behind a bitter disappointment and sense of betrayal he didn't understand at all.

Instead he took a final drag from his cigarette, threw it down onto the pea-gravel path and ground it viciously under his shoe, then started up the steps to where Ellie stood waiting for him, looking wholesome and innocent and lovely…and about as dangerous and deceitful as a handful of sunflowers.

And as he passed her, his heartbeat provided a timpani accompaniment to his soft, "Well, I'll say good night, then…sleep well."

As he knew he would not.

First light and the birds' raucous wake-up calls came as a welcome relief to Ellie. For all its exotic and nostalgic allure and her eagerness to give it a try, the hammock had not served her well—through no fault of its own, she was sure. It had turned out to be every bit as comfortable as she'd thought it might be. The problem wasn't her body; it was her thoughts that gave her no peace. And since in a hammock she couldn't very well toss and turn, the only option she had was to stare wide-eyed into moonlit palm thatch and think about tomorrow.

No matter how hard she tried she didn't seem to be able to talk herself out of self-doubts and forebodings— especially in the wee hours…the worrying hours, as Mom would have called them. She'd gone back over the sequence of events leading up to this moment a hundred times in her mind, giving herself every chance to second-guess her decisions. And it still came up the same: she was doing what she had to do in order to complete her mission. Any other alternative was failure, pure and simple. So what was the problem? She was ready; she'd been trained for this. All possible preparations had been made. Why was she lying here wide awake with the cold and clammy feeling that things were just...*not right?*

You're scared, Ellie. Admit it—you've got cold feet and a jillion butterflies.

Well, okay. Maybe she was a little scared. Okay, a lot. And why shouldn't she be, on the eve of the resolution of her first field assignment? It was only natural, surely.

Face it, Ellie. You wouldn't be this nervous if it was your partner, Ken Burnside, asleep in that bed in there, instead of some stranger named McCall....

And just like that, like the records Gwen used to play on her old phonograph, when there was a flaw in one and the needle would catch in it and repeat the same word or part of a word over and over until somebody came along and bumped it off...just like that her mind caught on that word and replayed it endlessly, *McCall...McCall...McCall...*

McCall was the unknown. She didn't know what to expect from him. How could she, when *he* didn't know the truth about what was going on? She and Burnside had trained together, gone over every possible scenario, prepared for just about any eventuality. She knew that Ken, a former FBI agent, was capable of handling himself in dangerous situations, and that she could trust him to back her up—and vice versa. But McCall? He was a civilian, for God's sake! If things got ugly tomorrow he'd be more of a liability than a help to her.

Wouldn't he? Except…the other day in that cantina, hadn't he faced down those smugglers without batting an eye? Picked up the ball she'd pitched him out of the blue and run with it, even though he'd had no idea what was going on? And oh, how she remembered the sure, solid feel of his body, the strength in his hands and iron in his voice when he'd put himself without hesitation between her and those thugs. That was when it had really come to her that there might be more to this man named McCall than met the eye.

It would have helped if she could at least be certain he was one hundred percent on her side. But…as far as he was concerned, she was one of the bad guys. He'd tried so hard to talk her out of going through with the meeting, and she was *almost* certain he'd attempted to derail the whole mission with that little fuel-switch stunt of his— attempting to sabotage the VW. She'd offered him the face-saving way out—for reasons she still didn't entirely understand—but the truth was, it just wasn't that easy to turn that fuel switch off by bumping it with a knee. Not impossible…just highly improbable.

Okay, the man had his principles, she could say that for him. Under different circumstances she might even have to admire him. She *did* admire him, dammit. And more than anything she wished she could tell him the truth. Oh, how she wished…

Admit it, Rose Ellen. It hurts when he looks at you with contempt in his eyes. When he speaks to you so coldly, the way he did this evening. You care what he thinks of you.

Dammit, she did care. More than she'd have imagined possible. More than made any kind of sense, considering how short a time she'd known him. How little she knew about him. She cared a *lot*.

So, why can't I tell him who I really am and what I'm really doing? Why not?

Because, the voice of common sense and all her training calmly replied, if he doesn't know who you are he can't betray you. Even unwittingly. You can't tell him until after it's all over. Don't even think about it.

Oh, but...

End of story.

It was then that the hammock totally let her down. In a hammock she couldn't flop onto her stomach and pull a pillow over her head in a futile effort to shut out the din of her own thoughts.

"Where in the world are we, do you know?" Ellie's voice sounded more than a little uneasy. "I swear, I think we have to be in Belize by now. One thing's for sure—" and she gave the map spread across her knees a frustrated thump "—this road we're on isn't on any map."

"Road?" McCall said with heavy sarcasm as he tossed his half-smoked cigarette out the window onto the narrow mud-and-gravel track. His stomach was already on fire from the effects of too many cigarettes and not enough food...too little sleep and way too much tension. He was in a sour mood in more ways than one, and thinking that if this kept up he was going to have an ulcer for sure. Live and let live seemed very long ago and far away....

Except for short exchanges like that one, and Ellie calling out directions to him from the written instructions that had been left for them at the hotel, they'd said almost nothing to each other since leaving the resort at Laguna Bacalar. He hadn't been able to resist, though, when she was coming down the steps from the veranda wearing jeans and those boots and new earrings, and that pink sun visor with Acapulco emblazoned across the headband in rainbow letters.

"Boots?" he'd said in mock surprise. "What happened to your Nikes?"

"Snakes," she'd returned without batting an eye, giving the boot's leather upper a thump with her hand.

Good answer, he'd thought, and didn't know whether to be even angrier with her or just impressed. No doubt about it, the woman was really something. Aloud he'd shot back a gruff, "Got the directions? The money? Chocolate?"

"All here," she'd serenely replied, holding up the canvas beach bag.

He'd had to bite down hard on the urge to ask her if "all" the money meant *both* halves or not. Literally. He'd clamped his teeth down on his tongue until tears came to his eyes.

And it had taken just about all his willpower to maintain the lovey-dovey newlyweds charade when they stopped by the hotel lobby to ask the desk clerk to hold their room for them at least one more night—and no, they hadn't heard a word yet from their "friends."

In the restaurant they'd ordered a *botana* of foil-wrapped tacos and *garnachas*, fresh fruit and bottled water to take with them. Both of them had only nibbled warm tortillas while forcing down sweet black Mexican coffee; neither, apparently, were up to the *huevos Montulenos* offered as the breakfast special that morning.

The silence and tension seemed to grow thicker, louder, angrier with every second, until it seemed like a living thing...a third person sitting there between them, visible for all to see. And McCall, for one, didn't care. His head, his chest, his belly were filled with it, leaving no room for anything else—not food, not cigarette smoke, not even thought.

Dammit, McCall did *not* like being lied to. Never had. Never would.

This would have to stop. Now. He had to ask her. He had to know the truth. *Now.*

He'd lost count of how many times he'd said that to himself, gripping the gearshift lever until his knuckles went white, thigh muscles clenching, ready to stomp on the brakes...the clutch. And how many times he clenched his teeth together and just kept going....

And then all at once he *did* stomp the clutch and hit the brakes—*hard.*

The VW jolted to a halt. Not because of anything he might have wanted to say to her, but because the track ahead had suddenly filled with men wearing jungle-green camouflage and carrying guns.

Chapter 9

"What now?" McCall muttered, and it felt as if he were grinding each word between his teeth.

Ellie's hand was resting on his forearm, though he'd no memory of her putting it there. "It's okay...don't move." Amazingly, there was only the slightest hint of a tremor in her voice. Then she just kept muttering as if to herself, "I think it's okay...I think it's okay..."

He had to hand it to her, he really did. *He* was so jangled with adrenaline he didn't think he could have lit his own cigarette, while she just sat there looking...not frightened, so much as just...wary. As if she'd been half expecting something of this sort to happen. As she obviously had.

But all McCall could think about was what in the hell she'd thought she was going to do with that little bitty pistol of hers up against all those great big automatic rifles.

"I'm pretty sure it's them," Ellie said in that same

mumbling voice, eyeing the two armed men who were approaching the car. "This isn't exactly a well-traveled road. But they were obviously expecting us."

"Some welcome," McCall muttered back. "Nice people you do business with."

"It's understandable. They don't want us to know exactly where their camp is. They'll probably blindfold us before they take us there. Just do what they say...."

"No problemo." As if he was planning to argue with men pointing machine guns at him?

The man on his side of the VW was gesturing emphatically with his weapon, indicating that McCall was to get out of the car. The man on Ellie's side was doing the same. A short distance away, other armed men stood with weapons at the ready.

"Just remember to shut up and let me do the talking," he said in a grating undertone as he pushed open his door. And, he prayed, *Please, God,* please *don't let her even think of trying anything with that gun.*

He stepped from the car with his hands in the air and was instantly grabbed and jerked around, slammed against the car and thoroughly patted down, to the accompaniment of terse commands delivered in tones that resembled whip-cracks. Through it all he remained silent and stoic, steeling himself, concentrating on controlling a perfectly natural male-aggression response to such violations of his person and pride.

And at the same time he was bracing himself, preparing for the violent action he was certain was going to be required of him when these people—whoever they were—discovered Ellie's gun. And they would discover it, of that he was certain. She was being subjected to the same thorough search he was—how could they not find it? He watched from the corner of his eye, holding himself in rigid anticipation, tense as wire, feeling every rough, rude touch she experienced as if it were a violation of his own body, frustrated beyond bearing at being unable to help her, expecting every second to hear the cries of triumph or outrage....

Which, mystifyingly, never came.

Apparently—and incomprehensibly—satisfied, the man who'd been searching Ellie then straightened up and pulled a black scarf out of his pocket. While McCall was giving himself permission to breathe again, a second man jerked her around and pulled off her sun visor while the man with the scarf wrapped it roughly across her eyes and tied it behind her head.

"Please," McCall heard her say in a quavering voice, "can I have my visor back? My skin...I burn easily... please let me keep it."

The sun visor. Whatever it was in there, McCall thought, it was obviously important. He called out to her captors in a croaking voice he barely recognized, translating the request, and was relieved when one of the men said something and then laughed as he shoved the visor back on Ellie's head. He saw her lift her hands and resettle it, murmuring thanks in clumsy Spanish.

While this was going on, he was aware that yet another man had snatched the canvas beach bag out of the car and was pawing hurriedly through it. He saw the man remove the manila envelope full of money and thrust it inside his shirt, then toss the bag away into the jungle undergrowth. So much for brunch, he thought. And then his world went dark as a scarf was pulled tight across his eyes.

"Can I have my cigarettes?" he asked, and was surprised at how mild and calm he sounded. "Both packs," he added as he felt the half-empty pack that had been taken from his pocket along with his lighter come into his hand. A moment later, with a laughing comment in Spanish, the unopened pack that had been tucked behind the VW's sun visor was thrust into his shirt pocket.

"Gracias..." McCall tapped out a cigarette and put it to his lips, then held out the lighter. *"¿Por favor...?"* There was a comradely chuckle as someone took the lighter, clicked it on and held it to the end of McCall's cigarette. He felt the heat, heard the crackle...inhaled smoke and murmured again, *"Gracias."*

There was another chuckle and a careless *"De nada,"* as the lighter was pressed back into his hand.

Making friends? he thought as he dropped it into his pocket. Or the condemned man's last cigarette?

Then hands gripped his arms and he was pushed and shoved and guided until he was walking—stumbling— down what he was certain must be the grass and gravel track they'd been driving on only moments—it seemed like hours—before. There was no conversation among the troops now—no sound except for the muffled tramping of feet, a few bird calls, the screech of a monkey and the whine of a jillion insects.

And a moment later, a burst of automatic weapons fire.

For one interminable instant, McCall thought it was *he* who'd been shot. Shock lanced through all his vital organs; his knees turned to water. The world stopped.

Then he was pretty sure *he* hadn't been shot. And that was much, much worse.

"Ellie!" Her name ripped through his throat. The images in his mind were an agony he was certain he could never survive.

"It's all right. I'm here." Relief shook him like a strong gust of wind. Her voice was unexpectedly near...bumpy and frightened but obviously unharmed. "I think they sh-shot the car."

"The car!" Still quivering and numb with relief, McCall tried to digest that. It made no sense to him, so he ran it through again. "They shot my *car*?" It didn't sound any better.

"I think so." Ellie's voice was still hushed and shaky. "I heard glass breaking."

"I see," said McCall. And after a moment... "I don't like the sound of that."

Ellie didn't like it much, either. She could think of only one reason why their captors would have done such a thing. Fear trickled coldly down her spine. She said with a grim confidence she didn't come close to feeling, "I had a feeling they might do something like this. That's why I took out a little insurance."

There was a grunt and some muffled swearing from McCall. He must have stumbled, she thought, or gotten slapped in the face by a branch; the trail had gotten narrower and considerably more overgrown. She was relieved to hear a surly undertone, "What the hell do you mean, insurance?"

It was on the tip of her tongue to tell him—anyway, the part about leaving half the money behind in their hotel room, buried in her overnight bag and stuffed under the bed. She even thought about telling him about her weapon, and the last-minute premonition that had made her take the ankle-holster off this morning and hide it behind the dashboard of the VW. To the best of her knowledge the smugglers hadn't found it...thank God. Thank God she still had her visor, too, and her watch and earrings. She should tell him about those, too, she thought. Just in case....

But before she'd made up her mind to do that, one of her captors gave her arm a jerk and rapped out a warning in Spanish, reminding her that they were surrounded by a dozen armed men, any of whom might know more English than they pretended. And she only had time for a hissed, ''Trust me,'' as she threw up her arms to protect her face from vegetation she couldn't see.

McCall didn't answer, but she thought she heard him laugh.

And why shouldn't he laugh? she thought, once again lapsing dangerously into gloom and self-blame. I'm not sure I'd trust me, either. All I've done so far is get us into a mess.

Keep your wits about you, Rose Ellen.

And don't lose confidence, either, she scolded herself.

Things really weren't that bad. And so far, not her fault. She really couldn't see how things would have been any different even if Ken had been with her. After all, they'd expected something like this might happen. Talked about and prepared for just such a double cross. Okay, shooting the car had been a bit unexpected, but so what? The important thing was that she was being taken to the smugglers' camp, according to plan, presumably to meet with the head honcho. To whom she—or more probably McCall—would explain that if he wanted the other half of his money he was going to have to return them to their hotel unharmed. As McCall might have said, *no problemo.*

And if things didn't go according to plan, well…they would just have to find a way to escape, that's all.

''McCall,'' she called softly, ''are you there?''

''Yeah.'' He sounded, Ellie thought, rather like a bad-tempered camel.

''How much damage do you think they did?''

''To the car?'' There was a pause, and then a grudging, ''Hard to say. Those Beetles are pretty hard to kill.''

''Think you can fix it?''

"Assuming we make it back there, you mean? Don't know, depends on what they hit. How many tires we have...." His voice trailed away, but not before she heard the hopelessness in it. *Assuming we make it back there...*

Remorse and regret settled around her again like a cold mist, making her feel chilled in spite of the heat. Poor McCall. She should have told him everything. She should have trusted him. Of course he was thinking that even if they did manage to escape from the smugglers' camp, they were in the middle of a jungle with no way of knowing which way to go in order to find their way back to their car. And she had no chance to let him know that that scenario, too, had been anticipated and prepared for.

"Too bad they threw away our lunch," she said, acutely conscious of the guard beside her...of alert and listening ears. "I guess we could have used some bread crumbs right about now..."

McCall's only reply was another grunt. Oddly, though, this one wasn't nearly as surly as before. In fact, it sounded almost...surprised.

A moment later she heard him call out to his captors, asking in Spanish for a cigarette break. The request was passed up the line and responses came back, good-natured and relaxed, most of them. The column halted, and Ellie heard the rustle of cigarette packs, the scritch of matches, the click of lighters. Some laughter and low-voiced conversation. She smelled tobacco smoke...a hint of a cigar. It seemed an interminable time, waiting in blindfolded isolation, until they started moving again.

They stopped for a smoke-break several more times after that. And each time, her sense of remorse eroded in indirect proportion to her own physical discomfort. As she waited, slapping at the insects that whined in her ears and flew into her nose in spite of the high-powered repellent she'd all but bathed in that morning, she tried to keep her mind sharp and her impatience in check. But it was a losing battle. What, she wondered, was the matter with these people? With McCall? Dammit, didn't it occur to anyone that she was miserable and uncomfortable, itchy, hungry, thirsty and in need of a bathroom? What was McCall hoping to do? she wondered. It was almost as though he was trying to postpone their arrival at the smugglers' camp—assuming that was their intended destination. If so, to what purpose? As far as Ellie was concerned, the sooner they got there the better—at least then they'd probably let her go to the bathroom.

She had no way of knowing how long they'd been walking, or how far from the road they'd gone—for all she knew they might have been walking around in circles—when she began to feel a difference in her surroundings. The air felt cooler, though no less humid. She had a sense of open spaces where branches and vines no longer grabbed at her legs or slapped her in the face. Underfoot, the soft mushy vegetation now seemed to be broken with flat mossy stones. Sunlight that burned hot on the top of her head alternated with patches of deep shade.

In the near distance she could hear the raucous calls of birds—lots of birds—macaws, parrots, toucans and cockatoos, by the sound of it. Too many in one place to be natural. Her heart quickened and excitement prickled through her scalp and shivered her skin with goose bumps. This was it—she was sure of it—the smugglers' camp. She was here—she'd made it. At last.

Hands gripped her arms, pulling her to a halt. She felt fingers fumbling with the knot of her blindfold. Impatiently, she reached up to take off first her sun visor—carefully—then snatched off the blindfold. She replaced the sun visor, blinking in the suddenness of light, slightly disoriented by the mottled patterns of sunlight and shadow. Then her eyes focused. She uttered a sharp, shuddering gasp.

Staring back at her from out of a thicket of jungle growth, wrapped around with vines and festooned with bromeliads and wild orchids, was a gigantic stone face. As imposing as it was, taller than she was by at least a foot or two, after that first shock her first thought was that there was a kind of sweetness about it, with its blank, sleepy eyes and babyish roundness, like a doll dropped there by some Titan's child and forgotten.

"Olmec," McCall said from close beside her.

She glanced up at him...and was utterly unprepared for the fierce stab of joy she felt at the sight of his beard-stubbled, scowling face. Even the scowl seemed wonderfully comforting to her, and the stubble as familiar to her as if she'd known him all her life. And at the same time she felt as if she were seeing him for the first time, or after a long absence. She just wanted to stare at him, drink him in, stamp the image of every line, every pore and whisker indelibly on her memory...on her soul.

I should have told him. I should have trusted him.

She *should* have—she *could* have. She knew that now. Now that it was too late. Oh, but why hadn't she recognized the honesty and intelligence in those keen blue eyes? Why hadn't she known about the strength and character, courage and honor that lay behind the beard and the don't-give-a-damn attitude?

But, of course, she *had* seen. Her instincts had known, and that was why she'd turned to him in the first place. She just hadn't trusted her instincts far enough.

"What?" He was staring down at her, his eyes narrowed and wary.

"Nothing—I didn't..." She shook her head and peeled

her gaze away from his. Inside she felt fragile and shaken, trembly with the urge to touch him, to reach for his hand, to find reassurance in his strength. She grabbed a desperate breath. "I—what did you say?"

"I said they're Olmec—the heads. I've seen—"

"That is correct. I see you know your ruins." The new voice came from close behind them—a familiar voice, speaking Spanish.

Forewarned by the odor of cigars, McCall gave no indication of surprise at the intrusion. He merely nodded a cool acknowledgment as the smoker from the cantina moved up beside him, keeping just beyond arm's reach.

"The heads are Olmec—the largest yet discovered, I believe. Larger even than the ones found at Chacan Bacan. These ruins have only recently been discovered, you understand. They are not yet open to tourists."

"Ah," said McCall. "Interesting."

The smoker chuckled—obviously feeling more relaxed and hospitable here on his home turf than the last time they'd met. "Yes, yes—but you did not come here to see ruins. Forgive me—you must be hungry and thirsty after your…journey. I hope it was not too long and unpleasant? Perhaps you would like to…how do you say it in America? 'Freshen up'?" He removed the cigar from his mouth as he looked past McCall, displaying his large, tobacco-stained teeth in a smile. "Your wife is very quiet today, *señor*. Perhaps you have followed my advice, eh?" That was accompanied by the same unmistakably descriptive gesture he'd used in the cantina.

Close beside him, McCall felt Ellie's body tighten and silently prayed, *willed* her to silence. Aloud he said mildly, ignoring the last comment, "That would be appreciated. And we would gladly accept your gracious of-

fer of refreshment...since your men did not allow us to
bring our own.''

''Ah—my men.'' The smoker gave a shrug, an elabo-
rate gesture of regret. Then he continued as he turned
away, indicating that McCall and Ellie were to accompany
him, ''Sometimes they can be a little, shall we say, over-
zealous?''

''Yeah?'' McCall lit a cigarette as he moved to the
smoker's side, thereby establishing himself on a socially
equal footing. He could only hope Ellie would catch and
understand—not to mention obey—his hand-signal that
she was to follow along behind. He kept his tone
mild...conversational. ''Does that include disabling my
car?''

''They harmed your car?'' The smoker took his cigar
from his mouth and favored McCall with a look of sharp
dismay. ''Señor Burnside, please accept my sincere apol-
ogies. Let me assure you that when you are returned to
your car, any necessary repairs will be attended to.''

''*Gracias,*'' said McCall dryly. The ambiguity in that
sentence made his skin crawl; the words *when* and *necessary* spoke volumes.

He could feel Ellie's impatience like a sub-audible hum
in his own bones. She'd be champing at the bit, he knew,
eager to get down to business, anxious to see the animals
she'd come to buy, demanding to speak to the man in
charge. She wouldn't understand the Mexican way of doing things. Understand that here the conventions must be
adhered to first, polite greetings made, concern for health
and well-being expressed, hospitality offered. Even if,
McCall reflected wryly, the party you were doing business
with was planning to kill you.

''Our amenities are few here, as you can see,'' the
smoker went on, with an expansive wave of his arm. He

pointed toward a pyramid-shaped pile of great stone blocks half-buried in jungle foliage. "I would suggest you go in that direction for privacy." He halted and turned to look at McCall, sharp black eyes narrowed against the smoke of his cigar. "You may have five minutes—each—one at a time. In case one of you might be tempted to wander off...exploring. You understand—the jungle can be very dangerous..."

"My wife and I appreciate your concern," McCall said without inflection. He turned to relay the instructions to Ellie, adding a low-voiced, "You go first," as his eyes gripped hers in desperate communication, sending messages he'd no reason to expect she'd understand.

"Ask him—" she began, breathlessly.

"Not now." And he was silently pleading with her, asking as she'd once asked of him: *Play along with me...please.*

A moment...a heartbeat...and then she nodded and turned away.

"Be careful," he called after her as he watched her pick her way through undergrowth and disappear into the jungle.

Beside him, he heard a soft chuckle. He turned to find the smoker watching him, and there was both amusement and satisfaction in those hard eyes. *"¿Perdoneme?"* he asked coldly.

The smoker smiled around the stump of his cigar. "I understand now, *señor,* why it is you do not take my advice regarding your wife. I think...you care for her...very much. *¿Es verdad?"* He waited for McCall's reply, and after a moment of stony silence, gave a small shrug. "I see it in your eyes when you look at her. Ah well...perhaps the little one is more woman than she appears. A little tiger, eh?" He laughed, and his eyes glinted like black water. "Be careful, *señor*...even very small tigers have claws."

"*Es verdad,*" said McCall, with a shrug of his own.

He hoped so, anyway. In fact, he was counting on it.

Ellie had been fighting the fear for so long.... Much as she hated to admit it, she was beginning to think the fear might be winning.

It was the roller-coaster ride that was wearing her down—periods of cautious optimism alternating with episodes of self-doubt, spiced with moments of utter terror. When they'd shot the car, for instance—that had been the worst, of course, those few seconds when she'd thought—she'd been so *sure*—they'd killed McCall. Probably the most terrible moment of her life—so far. And she devoutly hoped and prayed she never had to experience a worse one. Then—a moment later, the almost equally terrifying explosion of relief and joy when she'd heard him cry out her name.

Looking back, she realized that together those two events had been a major milestone in her life...one of those turning points by which everything else is measured. Henceforth, Ellie thought, her life would forever be divided into two parts: *Before* that moment, and *after*.

Since that moment, it seemed that all her perceptions, her perspective had been influenced by one thing: McCall. The bad times—the moments of fear and doubt and despair—were when he wasn't with her. As long as he was at her side, as long as she could see his face, hear his voice...touch him, she felt certain that somehow, some way, everything would be all right.

There. She'd faced it. Admitted it. That, in itself, was a kind of relief, though it certainly wasn't the way she wanted to feel, and acknowledging the feelings gave her no joy. It was rather like accepting the diagnosis of a debilitating though probably not fatal illness, she thought. It simply *was,* and there was nothing she could do about it now except make the best of it.

Though that was hard to do right now, when he'd been taken off somewhere, God knew where, presumably to talk business with the cigar-smoking smuggler. To do *her* job, the job she'd been trained for, while she was left here under armed guard to worry and wonder. Up to now she'd been treated well enough—she supposed she should be grateful for that, at least. After a surprisingly delicious meal of pit-roasted pork wrapped in banana leaves, she and McCall had been given a tour of the ruins, and at last shown the animals they'd supposedly come to buy. That had been hard, seeing those cages filled with so many beautiful birds and animals, many of them endangered in the wild, knowing most of them wouldn't survive the journey that was planned for them. Hard to contain her rage, to ask only the questions that were expected of her, the interested buyer, to remember to keep the camera in her sun visor focused on the evidence before her....

After that, they'd been brought to this palm-thatched shelter, a large lanai backed up against a wall of the ruins and furnished with camp chairs and string hammocks. Ellie had been told to wait there, with guards posted on all three open sides, while McCall went off with the cigar-smoker, laughing and joking in Spanish like longtime buddies.

He'd been gone a long time. She'd tried not to worry. She'd told herself to trust McCall. She tried not to imagine what might be happening...wherever he was. He was good at thinking on his feet. He wouldn't let her down.

But...she'd let *him* down, hadn't she? The truth was, she'd sent him off to negotiate with armed and dangerous men…unprepared. Lacking one vital piece of information. Why? Because she hadn't trusted him enough.

She hadn't had a chance to tell him about the money.

But they hadn't been left alone together, not for a minute, since they'd arrived in the camp. And now, all she could do was hope and pray he'd remember what she'd said to him back there on the trail about *insurance.* Hope and pray…and vow that she'd tell him everything… *everything*…the minute she got the chance.

If she got the chance…

There. He was coming back. Her heart gave the little leap of joy she'd come to expect at the sight of him, the sound of his voice, though the voices were still some ways off, the speakers screened behind a stone wall festooned with vines and broken with moss-covered carvings. She would know his voice anywhere now.

Then the guards posted outside the lanai were tossing away cigarettes and straightening up alertly as two more guards rounded the end of the wall and came toward them with McCall between them. And they were laughing and talking together in Spanish like old compadres, Ellie noted jealously, having gone weak in the knees with relief.

And now, of course, seeing that he was not only unharmed but had obviously been enjoying himself immensely while she'd been worried sick, fear and concern morphed instantaneously into anger. Already seething with resentment at being excluded from the business discussions solely on the basis of her gender, and now on top of that being forced to accept her new and terrifying— and uniquely feminine—vulnerability concerning McCall, she was tense and riled and, as Aunt Gwen would have said, spoiling for a fight.

"Well?" she snapped the instant he ducked under the overhanging thatch. Her arms were folded beligerently across her chest. Yes, and all she needed, she thought, were the rolling pin and the furiously tapping toe and she'd be the image of the classic shrewish wife. He couldn't—mustn't—know the folded arms and snappish tone were meant to hide trembling weakness and a wildly beating heart.

He straightened beside her, swaggering a little, and gave her a lazily superior look. "Well, what?"

Ellie sucked in air and took a step back, all at once overwhelmed by his nearness. "You stink," she said accusingly, to cover it. "Of cigars and—" she sniffed delicately "—tequila."

McCall lifted the cigar he was holding and smiled smugly at it. "Cuban, if I'm not mistaken." He gave a cackle of half-inebriated laughter, and then, snaking an arm around her waist, caught her hard against him and kissed her—loudly and with gusto.

For several moments Ellie was too surprised to respond at all. Surprised? No...*stunned* would be more like it. She went rigid, forgot to breathe, absolutely could not move. The shock of his body against hers was like an instantaneous paralyzing drug...his mouth—sensitive lips tasting sharply of tobacco, prickle of beard stubble, warm breath laced with tequila—a straight shot of whiskey. Her world rocked; her head swam.

Over the thunderous pounding of her own pulse she could hear the guards laughing as they watched. Incensed, humiliated, she hauled in one burning, outraged breath...and as she held it, cocked and primed, she heard McCall's urgent whisper.

"This is the only way I can talk to you. Play along..." His arms gentled around her. Tipsy laughter gusted past her ear.

Dazed and oxygen-high, Ellie felt him walking her

clumsily toward the back of the lanai, as far from the listening guards as they could get. As he walked, interspersed with laughter and nuzzling kisses along the side of her neck, he was whispering, "Pretend you're glad to see me, dammit...."

Shaking and jerky, she managed to lift her hands to his shoulders, then laced them together at the back of his neck. "Like this?" Her whisper was like sand in her throat.

"That's better. Maybe you could laugh a little...."

Laugh? Dear God... She tried, but it was a high, nervous giggle, nothing at all like her own husky chortle.

"Our friend the smoker..." and his hands were moving on her back...touching her everywhere—her waist, the ticklish sides of her ribs, the flats of her shoulder blades, the nape of her neck.

"Yes?" It was an airless gasp; she dared not breathe. Her pulse fluttered like a frightened bird's wings against the taut muscles of her belly.

"His name's Israel, by the way. Israel Gavilan..." He seemed so short of breath...and was that *his* heart she felt, beating so fast and hard against her chest? "Okay—" and wasn't his voice growing hoarser, too? "—pull away from me a little bit. Pretend you're mad at me..."

No problemo. "I *am* mad at you." But it was breathless, unconvincing.

"Not too much. Just a little. Tell me I'm drunk."

"Aren't you?"

"*No.* Dammit, it's an act. Come on—"

She swayed back against his embrace, flattening her palms against his chest as she aimed her very best glare at his chin. "You're *drunk*," she said in a quavering voice.

And, oh, how her fingers wanted to rub against the

warm, damp roughness of his shirt, to learn the hidden, forbidden textures of skin and hair and flesh that lay beneath. Tears sprang to her eyes; her fingers trembled. In desperation she snatched her hand away from his chest and would have slapped his cheek with it, except that he caught it in time and, laughing, carried it to his lips instead.

"Only a little, my dear...only a little," he said with jovial overconfidence. And then, in a low growl that resonated through her body, bowing his head close to hers, "Good girl..."

She could only stare at him, utterly at a loss now; her head was spinning. His eyes burned back at her with a desperate urgency as he whispered across her curled-up fingers. "I have to talk fast. I'll whisper in your ear. Act like I'm talking..." a corner of his mouth lifted "...you know, talking sexy to you."

She gave a high, whimpering laugh and ducked her head, hiding her face from him as heat flooded into her cheeks. Then his lips brushed her ear and shivers showered her like a hard cold rain.

"Israel was *not* happy about the money...especially when I told him we'd left it behind as insurance." She started violently, but he held her tightly...held her still. "It's a good thing you did that. I have a feeling we'd both be dead right now...." His suggestive chuckle was incongruous...horrifying. Ellie just did remember to giggle and squirm seductively in his embrace. "As it is, they've got a call in to the head honcho. I guess they're going to let him decide what to do with us."

Ellie jerked back, forgetting her role for just an instant. "How—" But he struck like a hawk, swooping down to capture the rest of the question in his mouth.

Once again she was caught unprepared. His mouth was

hard, urgent, angry…hers was soft, open…defenseless. She gave a single whimper…her eyes closed. She felt herself melting…going sweet and soft as chocolate Kisses left out in the sun. Deep in his mouth she felt the quiverings of his response, and knew a strange burgeoning joy. And then…

"Listen." It was a grating, guttural sound, and so was the laughter that followed. At the same time he caught her arms with barely controlled violence and spun her around so that her back was against him, so that he was between her and the avidly watching, listening guards. He held her pinioned that way, with his arms crisscrossing her breasts and her buttocks pressed tightly, intimately against him, and his body arched over her, taut and tenuous as a drawn bow. She could feel him trembling. "And for God's sake, *laugh.*"

She hardly knew whether she obeyed him or not. More than anything else in the world, what she wanted to do was cry. Once again his lips were at her ear, blowing gusts of terrifying sensation through her already oversensitized body.

"They've got a satellite hookup—up there, on top of the pyramid. This head honcho—I gather he's somebody on the inside. Somebody high up in the Mexican government. They call him the general."

Ellie felt herself go still. It was so strange…a moment ago her senses had been dangerously overloaded, maybe one caress away from complete meltdown…and now she felt nothing. Nothing at all. It was as if she existed in a vacuum, a little bubble of perfect calm. From somewhere outside the bubble she heard a voice asking, "General what? Did they happen to mention his name?"

And another voice, McCall's voice, replied, "Yeah…I think it was Reyes. General…Reyes."

Chapter 10

MᶜCall felt her body go slack and heavy, as if her knees had buckled. For one terrible moment he thought she'd fainted.

He tightened his arms around her, and forgetting that he was supposed to be happily, drunkenly amorous, said in a voice gone hoarse with concern, "Ellie—what is it? What's wrong? Do you know him?"

"Yes." It was barely a whisper, airless and urgent. Her hands were gripping his forearms as if she were dangling over a precipice and they were all that was keeping her from falling. "McCall—I have to tell you some—"

He cut her off with a finger pressed against her lips. They stood silently together, frozen in that intimate embrace, listening to the whap-whap-whap of a helicopter's rotors, rapidly growing louder. A moment later they braced against buffeting winds as it passed directly over their heads.

"That's probably him now," McCall said as he let go

of her and they both turned to watch the chopper, painted drab military green, swoop by just above treetop level.

The guards muttered amongst themselves, then four of them went jogging off, following the chopper. The one left behind walked after them a few paces, then reluctantly halted and stood at parade rest with his rifle cradled in his arms like a baby and watched his compadres disappear into the jungle.

McCall caught Ellie's arm and spun her around to face him. "Quick—before he comes back—what was it you wanted to tell me?"

She swallowed, and it made a tiny sticking sound. "Are you sure he doesn't speak English?"

"One way to find out," Making his voice loud enough for the guard to hear it, McCall sang out, "By the way, my brother, there is a great big poisonous snake right behind you, just about to crawl up your leg."

Showing no signs of alarm, the guard turned to look inquiringly over his shoulder. McCall waved at him, showing all his teeth in a friendly smile. "I heard your mother is having an affair with a donkey." The guard smiled back, shrugging his shoulders.

"Oops, sorry," said McCall, returning to Spanish. "I was just asking what's going on."

"What, you mean who is in the chopper? Ah—that is the general." The guard grinned and gestured meaningfully with his rifle. "He will tell us what to do with you two. So you'd better have your fun now, huh? While you still can." Laughing at his own little joke, he went to lean against a Mayan carving of a fierce-looking animal with open mouth and big teeth, in the long, late-afternoon shadow cast by the section of ruined wall.

McCall whipped his attention back to Ellie. "Okay. Tell me what?" She stared up at him, and her face was pale and still, her eyes flat and lifeless as stones. Without their golden shimmer and her natural vivid coloring she looked like a faded and washed-out copy of herself. Alarmed, he gave her a wake-up shake. "Come on—we don't have much time."

She licked her lips. "He said...that was the general, didn't he?" Her voice was as flat as her eyes.

He considered briefly whether he ought to slap her, but since he knew he didn't have it in him to do that, gave her another shake instead. "Yeah, he did. What do you know about him? *Come on.*"

"I know he's going to kill us." Her lashes settled onto her cheeks, dark crescents against cinnamon-dusted ivory. He heard her take a breath and release it in a small, uneven sigh. "Oh McCall...I got you into this. I'm sorry. I'm so sorry..."

"Into *what*, dammit?" His throat felt raw. *"Tell me."*

She nodded, and once more gazing into his eyes, took in air like a diver preparing to jump. "First I have to know something. How did you know—about the money? How did you know I'd left half of it behind? I only mentioned insurance. I didn't—"

"I saw you." His hands fell away from her arms, and he let out a breath he didn't know he'd been holding. He didn't want to go on looking at her, but for some reason couldn't tear his eyes from her face. "Last night." The emptiness of his hands distressed him, so he tucked them into his armpits. "Through the window."

"Oh...God." She closed her eyes again, briefly, but when she opened them he thought he caught a hopeful glimpse of that golden fire. "Then...you know about—"

"The gun. Yeah. I saw it. What happened to it, by the way? What the hell did you do with it?" His voice sounded harsh...angry. And yet the feeling inside him wasn't anger. Not exactly. Damned if he knew what it was.

"I changed my mind. I was afraid we might be searched. I was afraid of what might happen if they found a weapon on me, so I...hid it."

"For God's sake, where?"

"In the car—behind the dash."

He clapped a hand to his forehead and swore in utter exasperation. "Fat lot of good it's doing us there!"

"Would you rather *they* had it?" Her eyes glared into his, and now there was no mistaking that golden fire. Color was coming back into her cheeks, too. He felt suddenly as though his heart was bumping around loose inside his chest, ricocheting in dangerous, unpredictable ways.

"Lady," he said slowly...softly...because he was in a dangerous and unpredictable mood, "who in the hell *are* you?"

Her eyes clung to his; she moistened her lips and whispered as if it was the most important thing she'd ever say, "Not Mrs. Burnside."

"Not...Mrs. Burnside." He repeated the words without really grasping them, because they were so far from anything he'd expected. He stared at her and she stared steadily back, her eyes more like beacons now than flames, and he felt his consciousness shrinking, narrowing, laser-like, until his entire being seemed focused only on her face. He forgot about the guard. "Then...who—" His surroundings...the circumstances...the danger...had all ceased to exist.

Which was why he was caught unprepared when an amused voice—not Ellie's—replied in only slightly accented English, "May I, *señor*? May I have the honor to introduce to you Special Agent Rose Ellen Lanagan, of the United States Fish and Wildlife Service.''

At the first words McCall had started violently and spun toward the voice, tilted like an off-balance top. Now he jerked an incredulous look back at Ellie. Her face was pale but composed. She gazed past him, her eyes riveted on the speaker much the way McCall might have kept his eye on a coiled-up snake.

''General Reyes,'' she said in her dry and raspy voice, ''I presume.''

The general laughed, pausing in the process of lighting up a cigar to mumble, ''Unfortunately for you…yes.''

He was tall for a Mexican, with native Indian coloring and European features and build—a good-looking man, and aware of it, McCall thought, and obviously proud of his luxuriant black mustache. He was dressed in the same jungle camouflage as the men with him, the only difference being that, instead of an automatic rifle slung over a shoulder or held ready across his chest, he had a big black pistol snapped into a leather holster at his hip. That, and his pant legs were tucked into the tops of a nice pair of well-cared-for lace-up leather boots. The only indication of military rank McCall could see was some indecipherable insignia on his cap.

The general strolled toward them, tossing his match carelessly aside. He removed the cigar from his mouth and jabbed it at McCall as he said to Ellie, ''Perhaps you would return the favor. Please be so kind as to introduce me to your friend—'' his eyes narrowed as he paused to puff delicately on the cigar ''—who I can only say for certain is *not* your partner, Ken Burnside—who is at this very moment, I am happy to say, recovering from his emergency appendectomy in a Florida hospital. Fate is funny, is it not?'' His fine mustache tilted as he made a soft ironic sound. "It appears his so painful and untimely illness has saved his life."

"He's nobody—just a guy I hired to bring me here," Ellie said breathlessly, pushing in front of McCall. "He doesn't know anything."

"That is too bad...." The general moved with a relaxed and easy swagger into the shade of the lanai, leaving his contingent of armed soldiers outside. McCall felt those hackles rising again when he halted in front of Ellie, but the general was looking over her head at McCall. "No man should have to die without knowing why, eh?"

McCall felt a shock wave of rejection shake Ellie's body...and when had his hands come to be holding her upper arms? He'd no recollection of having put them there.

"Is that not true? So, Mr...?"

"It's McCall." He ground out the words between his teeth.

"Ah. So, Mr. McCall, if you like I will tell you what this foolish woman has so carelessly involved you in that is going to cost you your life."

"Why not?" Badly in need of calming, McCall patted the pocket where he normally kept his cigarettes and found a half-smoked cigar there instead. He took it out and put it in his mouth, and instantly heard the scritch and flare of a match. "Damned nice of you," he muttered as he bent his head to accept the general's light, then watched the match, still trailing a tiny plume of smoke, drop into crushed and trampled grass.

The general chuckled. "I admire a man who can keep his sense of humor under such circumstances. It really is too bad that I must kill you. But...unfortunately it is necessary to discourage the United States and Mexican governments once and for all from any further interference in my…shall we say, my private business enterprises. The United States, you see, has a very low tolerance for war casualties. To have two of their agents killed—''

''One,'' Ellie said sharply. ''One agent—me. I told you—he's nobody. He doesn't know anything. If you just let him go—turn him loose—by the time he finds his way out of the jungle—if he does—you'll be long gone, as usual. What harm can he do?''

''Interesting…. You seem to care a great deal what happens to this man.'' There was a long pause while the general squinted at her through smoke, smiling slightly. McCall didn't much like the looks of that smile. He could feel his blood pressure soaring…adrenaline squirting into his system…ancient male-female protective instincts rampaging.

Then he heard Ellie snort a wholly unconvincing denial, and the significance of that finally penetrated the red fog of rage that had enveloped him. He felt a new and strange sensation…a growing, spreading, tingling warmth inside his chest that felt incongruously… *impossibly* like joy.

''Well.'' The general gave a thoughtful shrug. ''That may be most useful to me later on. You see,'' he said, bringing his attention back to McCall, ''for years the combined resources of our two governments have tried—unsuccessfully—to halt the lucrative and growing business of trafficking in rare and endangered species.''

''And *drugs,''* Ellie bit out in a contemptuous tone.

The general waved that impatiently aside. ''Only a small sideline. Why waste the cargo space, eh? However, time after time, the government has attempted to raid these traffickers' camps, only to find an empty nest, the birds flown—pardon a little joke. Why?'' He paused, arching his eyebrows, enjoying himself. ''Because there is no camp. The smugglers operate here in the jungle much like what you call in the States a floating crap game. Here one day, gone the next, without a trace—you see?"

"Of course they were gone," Ellie said bitterly. "With you telling them when we were coming."

The general acknowledged that with a complacent chuckle. "However, Mr. McCall..." once again he paused directly in front of Ellie, and this time McCall could feel the menace radiating like heat from his narrowed black eyes, "...even advance warning would not prevent government forces from finding these traffickers, if someone were to gain access to their camp and plant tracking devices.... Ah yes, I see you understand. That was to have been the task of Agents Lanagan and Burnside. First, establishing themselves as buyers—a young married couple who own a pet shop—they then express dissatisfaction with the condition of the merchandise and suggest that they might be able to use their superior knowledge of wildlife—Miss Lanagan has an advanced degree in biology, did she tell you that?—to the advantage of all concerned, by increasing the survival rate of the merchandise and the profits as well. To do this, they naturally would have to visit the source of the merchandise— yes...clever, eh? Once in the traffickers' camp, the agents would plant tracking devices in, say, something that must always travel with the personnel—communications equipment, perhaps. Or the men's clothing...their shoes. There are a thousand possibilities. And the devices these days can be so small as to be almost undetectable.

"So you see, Mr. McCall..." his lashes dropped almost seductively, and he blew a gentle stream of cigar smoke directly into Ellie's face "...before I kill Agent Lanagan, here, it is most important that I learn exactly where and how many of these devices she has managed to distribute."

"None!" It burst from her throat, a sound like ripping cloth. Tense with his own self-restraint, McCall could feel her arm muscles quiver in his hands. "I didn't have a chance—I don't even have any with me. They were in my bag. Your men threw it into the jungle."

"Hmm…perhaps." Smoke floated away from the general's smile as he gazed down at her, his eyes resting, heavy-lidded and thoughtful, on her sun visor. "We will see. I think your friend Mr. McCall will be very useful in determining whether or not you are telling the truth.

"However—" and he was brisk again, all upright and military "—I will leave you two to think about that while I attend to a few things. There is a storm coming in—did you know that?" Now he sounded almost conversational, as he dismissed that with a casual wave of his hand. "Not a hurricane, they tell us—only a little tropical storm. Nothing to worry about, but there are some things that must be taken care of. You will be comfortable enough here…for now. But I think the two of you will have a lot to talk about, eh?" He chuckled, and his eyes touched Ellie first, then McCall…gleaming with promises and anticipation.

"You're hurting me," Ellie finally said. She had no way of knowing how much time had passed since the general had left them. How long they'd been standing there in that frozen pas de deux.

"Sorry," muttered McCall. He peeled his fingers away from her arms, then stood frowning at his hands as he flexed them, as if they'd gone numb.

Moving stiffly herself, she turned away from him and lifted her hands to her sun visor and carefully removed it. She hesitated, reluctant to let it out of her hands even for a moment, before finally setting it down on one of the moss-covered Mayan carvings nearby. Then she stood and rubbed slowly at the marks his fingers had left…feeling, for the first time in her life, utterly and completely lost. She didn't know what to do…what to say. She wished *he'd* say something. Wished she could just turn back into the safe, warm shelter of his arms.

"Are you mad at me?" she idiotically whispered. She couldn't look at him.

He gave a light, soft laugh, one she'd never heard before. "*Mad* at you? Sister, that's what Ricky gets when Lucy's just tried to slip one of her crazy little schemes past him."

With her back to him she lowered fragile eyelids over simmering tears. "I am sorry. I can't imagine what you must think of me."

"Not…as bad as I did, actually." His tone was wry, and strangely gentle. "Back when I thought you were one of the bad guys."

She slid her eyes sideways in order to steal a look at him, and it seemed like the riskiest thing she'd ever done. His features were almost lost in the deepening shadows, sandy brown hair hanging across his forehead, beard-stubble dark on his cheeks and jaws. His eyes seemed the only light in all that darkness, like beacons on the shore…and she thought, if she could only find her way past the reefs and shoals to that promised harbor….

Her heart pounded with terrifying force, jarring her body, shaking her voice. "You must have a jillion questions."

"Well, no, actually, I think the general 'bout covered it." He gave his nose a quizzical scratch with a forefinger, then lifted his head and aimed a look straight into her eyes. "Except for one thing."

She held her breath. "What's that?" There was something about his eyes....

"Why you felt you couldn't tell me."

She hung there, quivering like a water droplet at the edge of a faucet, utterly helpless. Knowing there was nothing she could do to prevent what was about to happen, but desperately afraid to let it go. Trying not to speak or to breathe, just to postpone the inevitable for one…more…moment. And yet, bravely facing it, refusing to turn away or hide behind handkerchief or hands.

"At first, I didn't know if I could trust you," she whispered at last, lifting her drenched and defiant eyes to his pain-filled ones. "You weren't exactly the most sterling-looking character, you know. And I was on my own…I didn't know who was supposed to contact me. For all I knew, you could have been one of *them*."

"And later?" The pain in his eyes had leaked into his voice. "You must have known, after I turned down the money you offered. After I tried to talk you out of going through with it." He was squinting at her in spite of the growing dusk, as if she were a light too bright for his eyes. "You couldn't have told me then?"

"I wanted to. I thought…I was protecting you."

He flinched from her, suddenly wary as a wild animal circling a tempting morsel. "Protecting *me?* Protecting yourself, you mean."

"Yes! That, too. I'm sorry…"

"You didn't trust me."

"I didn't *know* you! I wanted to." She lifted her chin, riled and defensive. "But you wouldn't…talk to me. You wouldn't tell me anything about yourself. How was I supposed to know I could trust you?"

"I guess," he said wryly, "I thought my 'sterling character' would shine through all by itself." He paused, then in a different, huskier voice, said, "Words don't mean anything, you know. I could have told you a dozen different lies about who I was...where I came from. How would you know what the truth was?"

She gave a high, desperate laugh and futilely touched the back of her hand to her streaming nose. "How *do* I know? How do I know *now?*"

And yet she did know. Long before he said it.

"Actions—that's the only thing that matters. I'm here, aren't I?" And he was scowling at her, his face as fierce as an embattled warrior's behind the barricade of his folded arms.

She stared back at him for what must have been an eternity, listening to the echoes of his words inside her head...the accompanying beat of her heart, weighing risks, contemplating terrifying uncertainties. Then, with what she felt certain must be her whole world, her entire existence on the line, she closed her eyes and took one step forward.

And...a miracle happened. At least it felt that way to her, just as it had that day in the plaza, the first time he'd saved her from disaster. Instead of the unyielding barrier reef of those folded arms, she met enveloping warmth... heard the whisper of an exhalation...the thunder of a pounding heart. Then the arms came around her and with a glad little sob she went sailing into their harbor.

He held her at first like a just-rescued survivor, dazed, not yet willing to believe the miracle was real. But the woman in his arms was vibrant flesh and bone, no doubt about that, and the warm tears soaking into his shirtfront were real, too. Cautiously, he brushed his lips across the top of her head. Then, with an easing in his muscles and in his heart, he buried his face in her hair and tried with all his being to drink in the scent, the very essence of her.

His senses told him she smelled of the jungle…of sweat and dust and bug repellent. His heart said orange blossoms and sunshine.

For a long time he simply held her, buffeted by emotions and a rising wind neither of them noticed or cared about, rocked by their two hearts bumping against each other like out-of-sync dancers. Then, dazed and still disbelieving, he eased one arm from around her, tipped her chin up and kissed her.

Her lips were cool and wet and salty with her tears…his senses insisted that was so. How was it, then, that they tasted so warm and soft and sweet to him? Sweet…and with just a touch of cinnamon….

Long-dormant emotions and desires swelled and surged to life within him; laughter and sobs fought it out inside his chest. Some of each found their way into his mouth and joined happily, giddily with hers. He felt her fingers touching his face, shakily, wonderingly, as if she thought *he* were the miracle. *Crazy woman…*

He took her face gently in his hands and held it still so he could look at her…convince himself that she was real. And…was that shimmering golden glow in her eyes really for *him?* He touched her mouth with his, lightly, yearningly, asking her that question. And felt her lips form a smile as her eyelids came down on a welling flood and drenched them all over again. He laughed as he sipped her salty-sweet tears; he could only laugh, because he had no words…. Miracles, he supposed, did that to a man.

We have to get out of here.

Oh, he hadn't forgotten about that. *Those* words had been hopping around in his mind for a while, now, trying to get his attention. He held them at bay a moment longer, just for one last hungry kiss before he said them out loud, in a growling whisper against her mouth.

Her head moved quickly, urgently with her whispered, "Yes..."

He took her by the shoulders and put her a little distance from him—it was the only way he could think clearly. "The guard," he said, breathing like a long-distance runner.

"There's only one..."

"He has an automatic rifle—how many bullets do you think he'd need? No—what we need is some kind of distraction...."

A distraction. Ellie stared at him through a blur. Then she shook her head and furiously brushed away the last of her tears. *Keep your wits about you, Rose Ellen.* Oh, but it was hard, hard, when her wits and her world had been shaken and turned upside-down.

She sniffed—and smelled... "That cigar you were smoking," she whispered urgently, clutching at McCall's arms. "Where is it?"

Startled, he looked at his hands. "I don't know—"

"I can smell it. You must have dropped it. Never mind—" she caught again at his arms as he turned, looking at the ground around him. "Why were you smoking a cigar anyway? What happened to your cigarettes?"

He made a wry face, then looked mysteriously smug. "All out. Actually, I—"

"Never mind that. What about your lighter? Do you still have your lighter?" It was growing darker—too dark in the sheltered lanai to see her face clearly—but he could hear the excitement in her voice.

Her excitement, her urgency were contagious. McCall's heart knocked against his ribs as he drew the lighter from his pocket. "Right here." His hand shook a little as he held it out to her; he was pretty sure he knew where she was headed with this. And it was a crazy idea. Completely crazy...

"You're going to think I'm nuts...."

"Sister, I don't think, I *know* you are." But he was smiling when he said it, and let her hear it in his voice.

"No, listen—" and he felt her hands again, tightly gripping his arms. "There's this legend in my family. It goes all the way back to my great-great...I don't know how many greats...grandmother. Her name was Lucinda Rosewood—my mom's named after her. Anyway, the story is, she saved herself and her baby from a Sioux raiding party when she set fire to her house and barn and fields and then tied her baby up in her apron and climbed down the well and hid there while the fire burned all the way to the river."

"But that's—" McCall began. But she cut him off with a hand pressed across his mouth.

"No, wait—that's not all. See, my mother remembered that when she was kidnapped and held hostage by the mobsters who were after my father—remember, I told you about that? She was being held in this high-rise office building that was still under construction, and she remembered Great-great-grandmother Lucinda, and so what she did was, she took off her clothes and used them to start a fire, and then she hid behind the ceiling panels while the alarms brought the police and fire fighters to the rescue."

She waited, holding her breath. McCall seemed to be holding his, too. Cautiously, she took her hand away from his mouth. He still didn't say anything.

"Don't you see?" she hissed. "It's almost like fate. Or Providence or something." She paused, then added thoughtfully, "My Aunt Gwen was always a great believer in Providence...." She tilted her head back and looked at the thatched roof over their heads. "That would do the trick. If we could get it going good..."

"Aren't you forgetting something?"

"Like what?" She caught her breath as a wind gust shook the lanai. "You mean, the storm? The wind—"

"No," said McCall, "I mean, a place to hide. We haven't got a well or a ceiling to crawl into."

Ellie was gazing thoughtfully at the guard, who had apparently tired of standing against the wall and had found himself a seat out of the wind. He was now sitting in the wide-open mouth of the snarling stone beast, with one booted foot propped against an upthrust fang.

"How about that?" she whispered, jerking her head toward the guard.

"Looks to me like it's taken."

"No, no—there's another one here, here on this side— see it? It's under all those vines."

"There's only room for one of us," McCall said after a moment. "You take it. I think I can get over the wall. If I can get it between me and the guard, I'd have a good chance to make it to the jungle before he gets a clear shot. You wait for your chance when he goes after me, then you do the same."

"I don't like the idea of us splitting up," Ellie said, chewing on her lip. "What if we can't find each other again?"

He'd already thought of that—and had vowed to himself that in the future there was only one thing that was going to separate him from this crazy woman, and that was a possibility he refused to contemplate. "We'll meet," he said. "What about the cages? Think you can find your way back there?

"Oh, yeah." There was a curious purposefulness in her

voice. And no fear at all, just a breathless excitement. "Okay then. You distract the guard. I'll light the fire."

"You sure you know how?"

"Hey—" she said, bristling, "I'll have you know—"

"Oh, wait—let me guess." Goody Two-Shoes—he should have known. "You were a Girl Scout, right?"

"Well, no, 4-H, actually, but—"

"I thought 4-H was more about raising cows than building campfires."

"Well, what, then?" She had her hands on her hips, and reminded him more than anything just then of a riled-up hen. "You want *me* to go chat up the guard?"

"Okay, okay, you're right. Are you sure you can reach it, though?"

"I can if I climb up on those carved thingies. Just try to keep the guard from looking this way while I'm doing it."

"Right," said McCall.

"Okay, then…ready?"

"Give me a minute. I'm thinking—okay, got it." He caught her by the arms, and before she had time to think about it or prepare herself, his mouth swooped down and caught hers in a swift, hard kiss. And then he left her.

A strange—under the circumstances—little shiver of joy rippled through her, followed by an equally strange sense of calm. She waited, like a veteran runner in the starting blocks—primed, prepared, but without nervousness—and watched McCall stroll to the edge of the lanai, close to where the guard was lounging, bored and smoking a cigarette. He got up, of course, when he saw McCall, and came unhurriedly to meet him, his rifle held at an angle across his chest.

McCall spoke to the guard—evidently something reassuring—and made a jerking motion toward Ellie with his head. The guard laughed and said something to McCall, then made an exaggerated point of turning his back to Ellie. A moment later she heard the tiny but unmistakable screech of a zipper.

Reigning in an impulse to giggle, she picked up her "cue" and stepped into the shadows between the back of the lanai and the Mayan wall, supposedly to answer her own "call of nature." With McCall's cigarette lighter clutched tightly in her hand, she felt for hand- and footholds that would lift her high enough to reach the palm-thatched roof of the shelter, at the same time keeping one ear tuned to what was happening with McCall and the guard. What she could hear above the noise of the wind sounded friendly and relaxed enough, punctuated by soft, snickering laughter; masculine camaraderie sounded about the same in any language. The wind shook the lanai and rustled in the palm thatch, masking perfectly any sounds she might have made as she climbed.

There—she was in position. By holding on to the vines with one hand and stretching with the other, she could just reach the edges of the tinder-dry thatch. The time was now. But...what would happen when she clicked the lighter? What if the guard heard it, and caught on to their plan before the roof had a chance to ignite?

Then, as if he'd heard her thoughts, she heard McCall asking in a raised voice for a cigarette and a light.

Braced and balanced with the lighter at the ready, she waited in suspenseful agony, praying she'd be able to hear the sound of a match or lighter above the thumping of her heart, eyes straining against the darkness for the telltale flicker. *There. Now.* In perfect sync with McCall, she clicked the lighter and held her breath as a tiny flame blossomed...nibbled tentatively at a feather of palm thatch...and encouraged by the wind, grew larger. And hungrier. She touched the flame to another spot...and another...

Enough, Ellie! In order for this crazy idea to work, she had to get into her hiding place *now,* quickly, before the guard noticed the flames. Half jumping, half sliding, she made her way down the ancient broken tumble of wall. The flames were making quite a bit of noise now—surely any minute the guard would hear it....

No. Not the flames. Not the wind, either. Rain!

Just as she felt solid ground under her feet again, the sky opened up. Rain came in sheets, driven almost horizontally by the wind. Instantly drenched, Ellie was already groping and clawing her way into the thicket of vines that curtained the snarling mouth of the stone Mayan beast. Crouched there, she watched in despair while the rain drowned her infant flames—and her hope with them.

Chapter 11

So much for Providence.

Her heart felt so heavy she doubted whether her body could even carry it. Might as well just crawl into the mouth of the beast and die there, she thought. And with any luck, a poisonous snake or scorpion would kill her before General Reyes did.

But then, what would happen to McCall? She couldn't let him die because of her. She had to think of *something,* do something to convince the general—

It was then that she heard the shouts. Then gunshots.

And in that instant Ellie knew that Providence hadn't deserted her after all. She'd just had her own ideas.

The lanai was leaning ominously, its thatched roof disintegrating, blowing away branch by branch in the wind. Through billowing curtains of rain Ellie could catch glimpses of the guard as he scrambled up the ruined wall, his rifle slung now across his back. There was no sign whatsoever of McCall.

Clawing her way back through the jungle growth, she ducked under the leaning, creaking remains of the shelter, groped for and found her sun visor—couldn't leave without that!—and jammed it any-which-way onto her head. Then she took off running, bare feet splashing through infant lakes and rivers, barely able to see or breathe through the clinging curtains of rain.

McCall had known the second the skies opened up that that was the end of Ellie's plan—plan A. As he was kicking the guard's legs out from under him he was confident, hopeful—praying—that his crazy Cinnamon Girl, as quick a thinker as she was, would have no trouble at all slipping along with him into plan B.

He heard the gunshots as he was hauling himself up the last few feet of wall. It was a very strange feeling, being shot at for the first time in his life. Almost surreal. Almost as if part of his mind had shut down—the part, anyway, that knew fear, or had any real awareness that he might actually be hit. That he might die.

He felt utterly detached as he listened to the strange sounds...whines and zings and thunks...and then felt the sting of something hitting his arm. Just a tiny sting—a bit of rock or gravel thrown up by a bullet, he thought. No problemo.

Then he was on top of the wall...scrambling, falling, tumbling down the other side. And running, pounding through the rain as if the hounds of hell were snapping at his heels, not looking back, not looking anywhere, focusing only on his destination—the dark and wind-whipped jungle. No matter how sinister it looked, he knew instinctively that the jungle meant safety—at least for a moment.

Behind him he could hear the guard scraping and scrambling over the wall, yelling at McCall to stop or be shot. And a great exhilaration exploded through him, lifting him on a new wave of adrenaline into the sheltering trees. *Yes.* The guard had followed *him*. That meant Ellie would have her chance to escape.

Now, all he had to do was lose the guard and get to the designated meeting place. The cages—crude wooden structures built to temporarily house the hundreds of birds and animals now awaiting shipment—were off to the right, he was sure of that. Somewhere just beyond the giant Olmec heads, he remembered, he should come to a raised causeway leading off into the jungle to the left. Flanked by remnants of ruined columns, it had probably once been a magnificent promenade ending in an open court at the base of a smallish pyramid that was now no more than a steep-sided mound rising out of the jungle floor. The cages had been assembled in that courtyard, under a canopy of palm thatch and camouflage netting. He'd figured it should be easy enough to find, even in the twilight and pouring rain, which was why he'd suggested it—that, and he'd known it had made a big impression on Ellie, so she'd be unlikely to forget it, either.

So. The way McCall saw it, all he had to do was stay in the jungle, follow the perimeter of the ruins until he came to the causeway and then hang a left, meanwhile avoiding the other guards and not getting himself caught—or shot. And then hope and pray Ellie could do the same.

He didn't think about what he'd do if she didn't make it. His mind just refused to let him.

Not in a million years would he have imagined she'd get to the rendezvous point before him. Which was why, when she jumped out at him from behind a ruined pillar, he attempted to knock her into next week. And found himself flat on his back with the wind knocked out of him instead, and a rock that looked about the size of Iowa ready to smash down on his head.

"McCall!" Ellie let go of the rock—actually a broken chunk of Mayan sculpture—and dropped to her knees in the sodden grass beside him. "Oh God—McCall, I'm so sorry. I didn't realize—I thought—are you all right?" She didn't hear anything but some strangled gasping noises. Leaping to her feet, she straddled his hips, got her fingers inside the waistband of his jeans and heaved upward. Lowered...then lifted again...lowered...lifted...and was finally rewarded with some really beautiful wheezing croaking coughs.

"Dammit...enough...already!"

She dropped to her knees, still astride him, weak with relief. "Oh...God..." And a moment later, furious and shaking, "Don't *scare* me like that! I almost...I could have—"

His arms came around her, and she was lying on his chest, their bellies bumping together with—of all things— laughter. "I guess—" and his whisper was scratchy in her ear "—I know now how you took care of those two guys the other night at José's Cantina."

"That was the first time, actually—except for in class. You're the second."

"Lucky me. Help me up and let's get the hell out of here. The general's men are going to be swarming all over this place in a minute. Wait a minute—" He paused in a half-crouch to haul in great gulps of air. Swiping a hand over his face in a futile attempt to get rid of the water, he lifted his head to glare at her. "How'd you get here ahead of me? I was running like a bat outa hell, and you were behind me."

Face-to-face with him in a similar crouch, she gave a breathless, exhilarated laugh. "Simple—you went around the perimeter of the ruin. I went straight across—took a shortcut.''

"This place is a maze. How'd you know—''

"Never mind that now. Like you said—we've got to get out of here before they figure out which way we've gone.''

"Speaking of that...'' McCall said morosely. He straightened up and made another swipe at the water in his eyes as he looked around him. "I have no clue which way the car is. I thought I had us covered there, but...I guess the rain's taken care of that.''

"Had us covered? What do you mean?''

Even in the near-darkness she could see his look of chagrin. "Ah, hell,'' he said with an embarrassed little throwaway gesture, "it was probably stupid anyway. I was just...you know, thinking about that 'trail of bread crumbs' thing. Seemed like it was worth a try....''

"You left...a trail of bread crumbs?'' She said it on a yeasty bubble of laughter, full of a strange lightness, warm and cozy as the smell of Aunt Gwen's fresh-rising bread in the farmhouse kitchen of her childhood. "What on earth did you use?''

He hesitated, trying again to wipe rain from his face. "Cigarettes.''

Still laughing, she said incredulously, "*Cigarettes?* You used your *cigarettes?* So that's what happened to them. I wondered.''

"But,'' he muttered gloomily, "I don't imagine there'd be much left of 'em, not after this.''

Ellie fought to straighten her face and failed miserably.

"I'd think you'd be taking this a *little* more seriously,'' McCall said in a crochety tone as he watched her double over with mirth, "considering we're lost in a jungle in a tropical storm, Lord knows how many miles from anywhere, not to mention surrounded by cutthroat killers.''

"You're right," she managed to mumble, winding down through a series of chortles, "except for the part about being lost. I can get us back to the car—at least, close enough. But first—"

"You can get us—*how?*"

"Remember those tracking devices the general mentioned? What I told him was the truth—they *were* in my bag, and his men did throw it into the jungle. Except for one." She tapped her ear, and McCall noticed that it was missing its earring. "This one I planted in one of the cages, when we were here earlier. That's so government forces—" she paused for an ironic snort "—can find them later. But—" and she tapped the stud in her other ear and smiled broadly, radiantly "—this one's a receiver, and it's set to the frequency of the ones in my bag. All we have to do is follow the pings. But—" her smile disappeared and was replaced by a look of grim purpose "—there's something I have to do first." She looked around, squinting against the pummeling rain, then darted into the maze of cages with a breathless, "Come on—help me. It'll be quicker...."

Funny, how he'd already known what she meant to do. And even funnier was the fact that, as crazy a thing as it was to be doing under the circumstances, he didn't even think of trying to talk her out of it. He didn't say anything at all, just took one row while she took another, and together they ran from cage to cage, struggling to pull apart makeshift latches and untie sodden twine, throwing wide the rickety wooden doors. Behind them they could hear squeals and squawks and caws, a few confused flappings...and then the air seemed to fill with beating wings, brilliantly colored wings—all painted in primary colors, like the crayons in a small child's toy box, but muted and blurred, now, by rain and twilight into a misty rainbow swirl.

"Ellie," McCall panted, "we have to go. Come on— leave the rest." In the distance he could hear shouts... gunshots. Coming closer. "We can't—"

"I can't leave them," she gasped. "There's just a few more..."

Crazy woman. She was going to get them both killed yet. And, as much as he was beginning to love her crazy ways, enough was enough. Intercepting her in a narrow aisle and blocking her way, he caught her by the arms and gave her a little shake and shouted down at her through the wild storm-sound, "We can't save them all. They're coming—can't you hear? You want to die for those birds? Because *I* sure as hell don't." He paused while she glared at him, charged-up and furious, spitting fire and water at the same time. Then he ducked his head down and kissed her cold, drenched mouth—kissed it hard, kissed it deep and with unmistakable intent, while the storm raged around him and the sounds of deadly pursuit got louder. He pulled away finally, breathing hard, and in a guttural growl he didn't recognize, said, "I want to *live,* dammit! Those birds mean more to you than your life? My life? Our lives?"

She stared at him with wide, dazed eyes. Her lips moved, but he couldn't hear what she said. Then she shook her head and caught haphazardly at his hand and they were both running, heads down, as a half-dozen shadowy figures burst out of the jungle and into the court-yard and gunshots crackled through the storm like ex-ploding firecrackers.

"Which way?" McCall gasped as they ran.

"Doesn't matter," she sputtered back. "Just...quickest way to cover."

Cover. Cover of jungle or of darkness? Neither one seemed very friendly to McCall. Either could be their salvation or their doom. Still, considering the alternative... "This way," he hissed, grabbing her hand and tugging her toward a jumble of stone blocks and fallen pillars half-buried in vines. While there was still enough light to see by, he reasoned, the ruins would afford them more substantial cover than vegetation. Leaves couldn't stop bullets. Stone would.

The jumble of blocks turned out to be a collapsed section of wall. They scaled it together, pulling and pushing each other over the hard parts, scurrying like lizards over the easier stretches, using vines for handholds and praying they wouldn't turn out to be snakes, and all the time listening for the crack of automatic rifles and the whine and zing of bullets, and bracing for the *thunk* of impact.

McCall's heart was a red-hot hammer in his chest by the time he boosted Ellie over the topmost block of the wall. He hoisted himself the last two feet and crouched there, listening to the scraping sounds she made going down the other side, then the definite but controlled *thump* of her landing. Darkness was almost upon them now; he couldn't see a thing beyond the ruined wall but rain...and more rain.

"Ellie?" he said hoarsely—a muted shout in all that noise. Hearing no response, he dropped over the side of the wall and after a bumping, scraping but thankfully short descent, felt the reasuring smoothness of stone under his feet. And Ellie touching him, one hand reaching for him, clutching at the leg of his jeans. "You okay?" he croaked, feeling oddly lightheaded—with relief, he imagined.

"Hey—let's get the hell out of here. Looks like it's clear—" He took a step.

With a strangled cry, Ellie wrapped her arms around his knees. He gave a startled yelp of his own and pitched forward, face first, into darkness. He put out his arms to break his fall, expecting to break one of them in the process, or a wrist, at least. Instead—and even more horrifying—his hands met…nothing. Just emptiness. Thin air.

"McCall—" He could hear Ellie's sobbing breaths. Her arms felt like a vise around his legs. "Hold on," she was whimpering. "Please…hold on."

"I'm holding, I'm holding," he managed, grinding sounds into words through clenched teeth as, using muscles he hadn't even known about, he fought to bring his upper body back onto solid ground. When he caught a handhold—a vine? A root?—pain shot through his arm and shoulder and down into his back and ribs, taking his breath. Ignoring it—after all, what was one more pulled muscle, more or less?—he gritted his teeth and pulled himself onto the stone ledge where Ellie was lying flat on her belly, arms still wrapped in a death-grip around his knees.

"Hey, you can let go now," he said gently as he rolled over and lay back, propped on his elbows, breathing hard. And after a moment, looking around him at the darkness and rain. "What the hell *is* this? Some kind of well?" How calm he sounded, denying his hammering pulse and the chilling residue of adrenaline.

"I think it's a *cenote*," Ellie said in a cracked, unsteady voice, shifting around so that she was facing him, on her knees. "I've read about them. That's a collapsed cave— collapsed, then flooded. There are a lot of them around here. They must have used it as a cistern."

"I know what they are." There was less rain and wind

here, in the shelter of the wall. He could feel her reach for him…feel her touch his face. His heart surged frighteningly as he caught her hand and pressed it to his lips. "Thanks," he growled against her palm.

She gave an odd little hiccupping laugh. "No problemo."

Then they both went still as the sounds of momentarily forgotten pursuit grew suddenly loud and triumphant on the other side of the wall.

"We're trapped," Ellie whispered. "Unless we jump. And I don't know if there's even any water in there, or how deep, or how far down it is."

McCall craned stiffly to peer into the void. "It's too dark to see. We'd probably kill—"

"Wait!" It was an excited breath against his cheek. "I have an idea. Quick—find a rock. The biggest one you can lift. *Hurry!*"

He heard scrapes and bumps and some quick, urgent breathing. There were bumps and scrapes from the other side of the wall, too, and someone barked, *"Cuidado, estupido!"* Reaching, searching with his hands, McCall found a stone, something roughly round and oblong-shaped. His fingers located ridges and indentations that could only have been made by human hands. "Got it," he grunted.

"Get ready," she gasped back at him, from only a foot or two away. "Follow me—do what I do. Okay?"

Crazy woman…what's she up to now? Yeah, but she was *his* crazy woman. And he was about to trust her with his life. Why didn't that worry him? Why, instead, did he feel a strange, wild exhilaration, and more alive than he could remember feeling in…Lord, so many years?

"Okay," he breathed.

He felt her hand on his arm, one fierce little squeeze. "When I scream, throw your rock into the pit..."

"Gotcha. Ready when you are..."

The pursuit sounds had reached the top of the wall, and had grown stealthy...cautious...listening. Even the storm seemed to pause. And in that brief respite, Ellie yelled, *"Now!"* and then cut loose with a scream like a dying banshee. McCall let go with a milder bellow himself, though she hadn't asked him to, and at the same time heaved his chunk of rock into the void. A moment later he heard two distinct splashes, one right after the other.

Shouts came from the top of the wall, changing rapidly in tone from triumph to dismay. McCall grabbed Ellie and pulled her down into the scrabble of vines and broken pillars at the base of the wall. With his arms wrapped tightly around her he crouched, holding them both as still as statues, praying with pounding heart for miracles, for invisibility, at least, while flashlight beams stabbed evilly through the rain curtains and arguments and questions in shouted Spanish flew back and forth in the darkness.

It came to him there, in those moments of utter terror and despair, that he would protect the woman in his arms, if necessary, to the death. His head felt clear and calm while he made his plan. He would make a stand here, he decided; hold them off, keep them busy while she made her escape back over the wall of the cistern. She had the receiver—she could make it to the car by herself. And most likely she could get the VW running by herself, too—he was beginning to believe there wasn't much his crazy Cinnamon couldn't do, if push came to shove.

Even as his heart swelled within him, though, his sense of nobility and purpose were tempered with irony. Funny, he thought, that he'd spent so many years trying to hide from his White Knight tendencies, only to finally die because of them. No regrets, though; no use trying to outrun destiny. He began to feel pumped-up and ready...charged with passion. So must Sir Galahad have felt, riding out to face the dragons.

It was about then he realized the shouts were becoming fainter and more distant.

Ellie stirred against him. He felt rather than heard her croak, "They're going."

"Yeah..." He felt odd, suddenly. Cold and clammy, hollow inside. His voice seemed to echo as he added, "They've gone to tell the general."

"I can't believe it." Her voice was shaking, incredulous. "It worked. They think we jumped. I don't believe it."

"'Course it worked," he mumbled. His wonderful, incredible, quick-thinking Cinnamon Girl.... "C'mon, let's get out of here...." The general might not be so easily fooled. McCall rose to his feet. And realized, to his utter horror, that he was about to pass out.

He sat down again, much more abruptly than he'd intended to.

"McCall? Are you all right? What's wrong? McCall—" And she was touching him in the darkness, her fingers cold on his rain-wet face. Her hands slipped to his shoulders...his arms...clutched him—hard.

Pain knifed through him. Breath hissed between his teeth and nausea threatened.

"McCall! Oh God—McCall, you're bleeding. Why didn't you tell me you were hurt?"

"First I knew of it," he muttered, trying *very* hard not to throw up while her fingers were exploring his upper arm.

She said in an appalled tone, "I think you've been *shot*."

"Just a scratch." He felt quite pleased with himself at that. He thought it seemed like something Clint Eastwood would have said.

"There's an awful lot of blood for 'just a scratch,'" she said accusingly. He heard rustling sounds as she straightened, then nothing as she thought it over. Then she bent down close to him again and shouted, as if he'd suddenly gone hard-of-hearing, "Are you okay? Can you make it to the jungle?"

"I'm *fine*," he barked back at her, and was gratified to discover that it was more or less true. At least the nausea had passed, along with most of the dizziness, now that his heart rate was returning to normal. *Suck it up, McCall. If you don't make it, neither will she. There's not a chance in hell she'll leave you here....*

He stood up again, more carefully this time, and announced that he was ready to get the hell outa there. It was pretty much the last thing he remembered with any degree of clarity about that night.

By her watch, it took less time than Ellie had expected to find the car; the smugglers' path through the jungle apparently hadn't followed a straight line. But just as on that blindfolded trek, the walk out seemed much farther and longer than it really was. Mostly because she was just so worried about McCall. He was hurt—she had no idea how badly. He'd lost blood—she had no way of knowing how much. Oh God, she thought, what if he's bleeding to death, right now? She didn't know what she'd do if he collapsed on her—he was too big to carry, and there was just no way in the world she was going to leave him. Not now. Not after...after what? The way he'd saved her life? That didn't seem all that big a deal right now.

So...what? After she'd gone and fallen in love with him?

Okay, that was a *very* big deal. And the biggest of a whole series of shocks and confusing turnabouts that had left her reeling and not really sure about anything at the moment.

"I'm *fine*. Quit fussing over me," he growled at her, the fourth or fifth time she asked him how he was feeling, sounding reassuringly like his old cranky McCall self. "You make it awful damn hard for a man to be manly and intrepid."

"You don't have to be, for me," Ellie said, amused and tender.

"I do for *me*," he snapped back at her, now sounding more than anything like a grumpy child. "I do still have some ego, you know."

Ellie was thankful for the darkness that hid her smile.

It was only a few moments later, when the electronic signal in her ear was approaching pain level, that she felt him grab her arm as he said in a hoarse whisper, "There—I think I see it. I can see the car."

She halted, trying to see through the impenetreble sheets of rain. "Where? I can't see a thing."

"There—wait. Okay...now, see it?" As if on his command the curtain lifted for just an instant, and there it was...the Beetle's pale, rounded shape, like some great animal, huddled and miserable in the deluge.

"What about a guard? Can you see anyone?"

"Don't think so," McCall muttered. "Looks deserted to me."

"This thing is going bananas," Ellie said, listening to the pings in her ear. "My bag should be right around here somewhere, but I can't...find it. If I just had a flashlight— there's one in the bag, but—"

"I've got one in my toolbox. Wait...right here." And before she could stop him, he was gone.

It seemed an eternity, waiting isolated and lonely in the darkness and rain, before she saw the slashes of silvery shimmer...the gleam of light on wet metal. And another lifetime before he was back beside her. And it took all her willpower not to hurl herself upon him, trembling and sobbing with relief and gladness. Where was her strength and common sense now?

"No guards," he panted, his face ghoulish in the flashlight's shadow. "And only one tire gone, far as I could tell."

Her teeth were chattering; she clenched them together and asked, "The engine?"

She could see the shine of his teeth when he smiled. "Blew the air filter to kingdom come. Told you those Beetles are hard to kill. She might run a little hot, but she'll run."

"What about the tire? Have you got a spare? I can change it if—"

"Never mind the damn tire. She'll run on the rim if she has to—no need to worry about speed in this mess. We can change it later. Right now let's find that bag of yours and get the hell out of here."

Between the flashlight and the pings, that didn't take long. And miracle of miracles, though sodden and limp on the outside, thanks to its plastic liner, the bag and its contents seemed more or less intact. Ellie gathered it up and held it clutched against her chest as they ran for the car, hands clasped and laughing giddily, like lovers caught out in a summer shower.

"Man, I never thought this little car could look so good," McCall said, shaking water from his hair as he squeezed himself behind the wheel and slammed the door after him. With the storm suddenly shut outside like an unwelcome stranger, the inside of the car seemed unbelievably still and warm and safe.

"Sorry I insulted her." Laughing and breathless, Ellie patted the dash—then remembered. Holding her breath, she felt underneath....

"Is it—?"

"Yes—it's here." Oh, so carefully, she pulled the gun from its hiding place—her nice little nine-millimeter double-action Beretta Cougar, less than thirty-six ounces unloaded, ten rounds in the clip. She'd hated and feared the thing when Ken had first gotten it for her and insisted she learn to use it in addition to the firearms training the agency had provided. Now, her hands were steady as she checked it over, and her feelings toward it were downright tender. "It's okay. It's ready," she said on an exhalation as she leaned over and placed it on the floor between her dripping feet.

The bag on her lap squelched softly as she opened it. Her searching hands found the flashlight first. She placed it on the floor beside the gun and went back to pawing through the bag.

"What're you looking for?" McCall's voice was soft and sputtery as he wiped away rain.

"S-something…" Her hands had begun to tremble. Suddenly, *she* was trembling—all over. She couldn't seem to control it. She dug more frantically into the contents of the bag—desperately almost.

There was a tiny click and pale light washed the inside of the Volkswagen. "Here," McCall said in a gravelly voice, "let me." Gentle hands lifted the sodden bag from her lap. A moment later he held up a bar of chocolate. "This what you're looking for?"

She made a small affirming sound that was somewhere

between a laugh and a whimper and reached for it. Holding her off like an eager puppy, he peeled the wrapping off and broke it in half, then held one part out to her. She felt her throat swell as she bit into it, her eyes clinging to his through a shimmer of tears as he did the same. And all the while she trembled and ached inside with a strange, fearful happiness. What was this? *What is this?* Such a small thing, she thought. Such a simple little gesture...and yet she'd never felt so *cared for.* So *loved.*

"Don't suppose you'd have any cigarettes in that bag?" His voice was raspy and seemed unnaturally loud.

"Sorry," she murmured on a gulp of shaken laughter, hurriedly swallowing tears and chocolate.

"Bread crumbs..." He muttered that under his breath as he searched for the car keys. He seemed surprised to find them still in the ignition, right where he'd left them. "Damned stupid idea," he said, glowering at the keys but making no move to turn them. He sounded angry, but somehow Ellie knew he wasn't.

"It wasn't," she whispered. "It was a great idea. You just forgot one thing."

He transferred the glare to her, eyes fierce and bright in a shadowed face. "Yeah, what's that?"

"You've forgotten the story. Hansel and Gretel?" She leaned toward him, urgent and shaking. "Don't you remember? Bread crumbs don't work. The birds ate up the trail of bread crumbs. That's how they ended up lost. That's how they wound up in the witch's—"

And suddenly his arms were around her and his hard, cold face was pressing against hers, his beard stubble a soft wet prickle on her skin. She could feel that he was shaking, like she was, and that some of the wet on *his* face wasn't rain, either. His breath smelled of chocolate, as hers did. It bathed her face in warm, sweet puffs as he kissed her quickly, urgently—her forehead, her eyelids, her cheeks and nose, her lips—as if he feared he might never get another chance.

"We have to go..." Who said it? Who cared?

"Yes—yes...I know..."

"They could be after us any minute—"

"We have to get to someplace safe—"

"Just hope the damn car starts...."

"Well, try it and see!"

Ellie sent up a prayer while McCall pumped the gas pedal, then turned the key in the ignition. For the second time in recent memory, the VW's engine fired on the first try.

Chapter 12

"We can't go back to the hotel," said McCall. "That's the first place they'll look for us."

"I know. I know."

He glanced over at Ellie. She was sitting upright in her seat, eyes riveted on the headlights' narrow path beyond the windshield, tense as a bird dog on point.

"Hey—we've got a good head start," he said gently. "They can't come after us in this. We've got some time."

She threw him a look, but didn't relax. "Not necessarily. Don't forget, General Reyes is a pretty big cheese in Mexican law enforcement. All he needs to do is make one phone call. There won't be anyplace in this country where we can hide."

McCall ducked his head to peer upward into the wind-driven rain. "With any luck this storm will have knocked out his satellite hookup. If we can make it to Chetumal we'll be okay. I've got a diving buddy there—he has a private plane. He can fly us to Merida. If we can get to the American consulate there we'll be safe.''

''With any luck,'' she muttered darkly. But she did sit back in her seat, at last, with an exhausted-sounding sigh.

They were on the main highway, heading east, according to Ellie's wristwatch, which had turned out to be a compass, too, as he'd suspected it might. They'd stopped to change the tire as soon as they hit paved road, Ellie doing her best to convince him that since he was injured, she ought to be the one to do the job.

Now...McCall was well aware that the world had changed a lot since the 1950s, and that he'd traveled a long road from his dad's garage in Bakersfield, California, and that women in this century were a whole lot different than his mother had been, with her soft white hands and red nail polish that had never so much as touched a dipstick. But in his book, there were just some things a decent man didn't do, and standing around holding a flashlight while a little tiny bit of a woman changed a tire for him was definitely one of them. Anyway, the wound in his arm had stopped bleeding, and even though it did still throb a bit, it was a long way from keeping him from being able to twirl a lug wrench.

Since then, the little VW had been churning slowly but steadily through the downpour, sending up wings of water on both sides of the car, occasionally sputtering a little, but otherwise hanging in there.

Which was about as much as could be said for her driver and passenger. Hangin' in there.

''Luck's been with us so far,'' he said softly, looking over at the woman beside him. Looking at the curling tips of her wet hair, dark and somehow childlike against her pale forehead, at her tense profile and slumping shoulders. Wishing she'd just put her head back and sleep. Wishing he could gather her into his arms and hold her while she slept.

Instead, unexpectedly, she straightened up and laughed. "Providence…" she murmured. "That's what my Aunt Gwen called it. And you know what? Knowing Gwen, I don't think she'd be surprised to find out Providence has such a sense of humor."

McCall snorted. "Sense of humor?" Personally, he was having a hard time finding much about the last couple of days that was funny.

She shifted in her seat, half facing him. "Ever since I got to this country I've been feeling kind of like Alice-in-Wonderland, you know? Everything flip-flopped, nothing like it was supposed to be. Now I'm thinking maybe all the time it was just Providence having this huge joke on me."

"Some joke—damn near getting us both killed."

"Yeah, but don't you think it's funny? I thought you couldn't be trusted, you thought I was totally bad news, and all the time, we're the good guys. Meanwhile, the head good guy, the man I'm *supposed* to trust, he turns out to be the head bad guy."

"Hilarious," he muttered under his breath. But he was beginning to see her point. He'd been wondering himself how his Goody Two-Shoes had turned into Indiana Jones.

"And then," she went on, really warming to it, "you go and sacrifice your cigarettes so we can find our way back to the car, and I try to follow my family tradition and start a fire as a distraction so we can escape, and the rain completely ruins both our plans. But as it turns out, the rain is what saves us. See what I mean? Providence."

McCall shook his head. "Uh-uh," he said with gravel in his voice. "*You* are what saved us, sister."

She stared at him. "I'm what got us into this mess."

"That may be true, but you're also what got us out of it." He cleared his throat and tried for a lighter tone. "You know, for a Goody Two-Shoes you're pretty damn good at this cops-and-robbers stuff."

There was a pause before she said, with a curious lilt in her voice, "For an artist-slash-beach bum, so are you...."

He looked at her and saw that she was smiling that glorious Cinnamon Girl smile. And when he remembered to look at the road again, he could see lights up ahead in the distance. They were coming into the outskirts of Chetumal.

Providence? He thought maybe that was as good a name for it as any.

Ellie sat shivering in the dark VW and watched McCall turn away from the pay phone, no longer even bothering to hunch up his shoulders when the deluge hit him, just letting it sluice down over him like a shower bath.

"Are the lines down?" she asked when he opened the door and she got a good look at his face.

"Nah." He pulled the door shut with a jerk, sending water droplets flying everywhere in a way that reminded Ellie of a big wet dog. "I actually got through to him— his answering machine, anyway. He's away on a dive. Says he'll be back on the second." His voice was strangely neutral, almost completely devoid of expression.

"That's tomorrow, isn't it? Or today—" she held her watch up close to her face and pressed the button to illuminate the numbers "—almost."

"The Day of the Dead..." They sat in silence, McCall staring through the windshield at the grocery-store windows behind the pay phone, all boarded up against the hurricane Paulette never had quite become, Ellie staring at him. "So," he said at last, glancing over at her with a look of apology. The fatigue in his face made her heart ache. She thought about his wounded arm, wondered again how bad it was and how much blood he'd lost. "That's it, I guess. No help there."

"Then let's just get a motel room for tonight. If he's going to be home tomorrow—"

"You're forgetting one thing."

"What's that?"

"What do we do for money? We left everything back in the hotel at Lago Bacalar."

"Not...everything." Ellie was already fishing around inside the beach bag. A moment later she gave a little grunt of triumph and held up the slender wallet containing her "cover" documents. "I still have Mrs. Burnside's credit card—U.S. Government issue."

He reached for her, took her face between his hands and gave her a swift hard kiss—an impulse born of joy he might have bestowed on just about anyone, but her heart gave a fiery little leap anyway. Already shaky with fatigue, she now felt a new kind of trembling, a strange pulsing vibration deep, deep inside.

"We're in business," he said huskily. "Now, if we can just find a hotel clerk awake at this hour...."

McCall knew Chetumal fairly well. Even in the darkness and pouring rain he didn't have much trouble finding the place he'd had in mind. It was well away from the modern Holiday Inn-type hotels in the center of town, down near the docks—a fairly scruffy area, but the hotel had rooms that opened onto a central courtyard so at least they wouldn't have to trek through a lighted lobby looking like drowned rats.

He parked the VW in a narrow side street and left Ellie there to wait for him while he went to try to rouse a hotel clerk. It took him a while, pounding on the door and the boarded-up windows of the lobby, but eventually, after he'd almost given up, a short stocky man came out of a door at the back of the office and shambled up to the night window, bleary-eyed and unshaven, scratching at the sleeveless white undershirt that covered his round belly. Though at first obviously not pleased to see a customer so late, especially one who must have looked as though he'd just come out second-best in a back-alley brawl, he perked up considerably when McCall showed him the credit card and offered to pay him double the going rate for what was left of the night.

With the room key in his pocket, he splashed his way back to the Volkswagen to find Ellie crouched down like a frightened rabbit with her head between the steering wheel and the back of the driver's seat.

"I saw a car go by...out there, on the main street," she explained in a croaking, slightly embarrassed whisper. "I thought...you know, just in case it might be—"

"Wouldn't do *you* much good to hide," he said mildly as he edged in behind the wheel. "It's the car they're going to be looking for." She made a small, rueful sound and put a hand over her eyes. He threw her a glance. "If it makes you feel better, we can park it in the back, out of sight. But I don't think they'd be after us yet. Not in this."

She nodded but didn't say anything. She hadn't had much to say for a while now—stress and fatigue wearing on her, he supposed. Only natural she'd be coming to the end of her rope, after everything she'd been through.

Except that there was something vibrant, almost electric about her silence, a strange kind of subaudible humming that seemed to reach out and touch him in the darkness and make his skin tingle and his heartbeat accelerate in response. In response to what, exactly, he didn't know. Fear, he thought—uneasiness at being still in danger, still so vulnerable—that would make sense. Except that his own responses didn't feel like fear. He wasn't an adrenaline junkie and never had found fear a particularly enjoyable sensation, but right now what he felt like more than anything was a kid waiting in line to get on a really wild and scary roller-coaster ride.

He started the VW, rolled it slowly, almost silently down the narrow street and turned into the even narrower alley that ran behind the hotel. He parked, not bothering to lock it up. There was one more dash through the downpour, through water that ran ankle-deep in places, a brief struggle with a balky lock and an old key, and then they were inside, surrounded by walls and darkness and silence and, for the moment at least, safety.

It was humid and musty in the little hotel room, as it usually was in the tropics, with or without air conditioning. Without much hope, McCall flipped a switch near the door. Miraculously, light flooded the room and a ceiling fan reluctantly began circling.

"Power's on, at least," he muttered; it was by no means a given in that part of the Yucatan, even without a tropical storm.

He carefully avoided looking at the single bed in the room, which looked even smaller than the one in the "honeymoon suite" at Lago Bacalar in which he'd spent a mostly sleepless night—had it only been *last* night, twenty-four hours ago? It seemed like a month. He thought about how they'd discussed it then, who would sleep where, just as a matter of course. Why was it that now he couldn't think of anything to say that didn't seem fraught with pitfalls, with infinite possibilities for misunderstanding?

He looked instead at Ellie, who had lowered the beach bag to the floor beside the dresser and was slowly taking off her sun visor.

"We should be safe here, for the time being, anyway," he said gruffly. "At least until the storm moves on. Even with all his resources, there's not much the general can do while it's raining like this."

Ellie nodded. She took off her wristwatch and placed it beside the sun visor. And still she hadn't spoken.

"You can have first crack at the shower, if you want…"

Her body gave a little jerk, face turned away from him, and he heard a soft, ironic laugh. "Right now what I'd give almost anything for is just to be *dry.*"

He'd have liked to have laughed with her, but all he could come up with was a snort. "Best we can do is rinse our clothes out in the shower, wring 'em out good and hang 'em up for what's left of the night—don't think they'll do much drying in all this humidity, but in the meantime we can share—I mean, each take part of the bedclothes…." Damn.

It didn't help matters, the way she was looking at him now, arms raised, fingers combing her wet hair back from her face. The room light, under a parchment shade, gave her skin a warm, buttery glow. The freckles scattered across her nose and cheeks looked like a sprinkle of cinnamon. His mouth began to water. Then he happened to glance down, and it went dry instead. Under the clinging T-shirt, her small round breasts stood out in perfectly defined relief, nipples dark and—there was that word again—*pert.*

"Yeah," she said softly, "we could do that." She gave her head a little shake, then went on looking at him…her face so open, so honest, he wondered how he could ever have been so stupid as to believe her capable of committing a crime...or an infidelity. Even lying, he remembered, had made her blush. He remembered that he'd called her Goody Two-Shoes and wondered if that was why.

"McCall," she said, tilting her head slightly to one side, "Can I ask you a personal question?"

"Shoot," he said, a sound raspy as a snarl.

Her chin came up a notch, the only sign she gave of nervousness or that she might not be quite as confident as she seemed. "I know you don't like personal questions, but I thought, since we're about to make love, it would be really nice if I knew your name."

It was a moment or two before he could speak at all, and in those moments he watched a blush creep across her face—not the bright hot lying flush he'd come to know, but the sweet shy pink of wild roses.

"Are we? Going to make love?" he asked gently.

She nodded. "Yeah, we are. Now that you know I'm not married, and I've proven I'm not too young for you, and after...everything we've been through, I think it's high time. Though I realize that I'm probably going to have to seduce you. With your exalted sense of honor, you'll probably say I'm not thinking rationally, or I'm too tired or too upset after everything that's happened, and refuse to take advantage." She gave an exasperated little sigh. "And you call *me* Goody Two-Shoes?"

Again for a few moments he could only gaze at her. He felt as though his body had been plugged into a powerful electrical circuit, temporarily shorting out his brain. Only for a moment, but apparently long enough for her to lose the tenuous grip she'd had on her self-confidence. As he watched, her face seemed to blur around the edges.

She suddenly seemed almost unbearably young…achingly vulnerable.

"Unless, of course," she said, her voice gone thick and ratchety and much deeper than usual, "you really don't want to. If your arm hurts too much or if you're too tired. I wouldn't—"

He was across the room in less time than it took her to draw a breath in preparation, and took her face between his hands and stopped her words with his mouth. Stopped them right there. And while he was kissing her he thought of all the ways he'd kissed her before—or she'd kissed him. The first, desperate make-believe-wife's kiss, then the little thank-you peck on the cheek, standing on tippy toes like a little child, that had made his sleeping heart stir and awaken to remembered pain. Then his own charade back there in the jungle, holding her close in his arms and nuzzling her ear, pretending to be drunk so he could tell her what he needed her to know. And the one after that…like water in the desert, like manna for the wandering pilgrim, the one that had made him believe in miracles again.

He wanted to erase them all. He wished with all his heart for *this* to be the first, their very first moment together…ground zero, the birthday of a brand-new life. But since he'd never been in on a birth before, anyway not one he remembered, he tried to make light of the awe he felt, did his best to deny the overwhelming joy.

Drawing back from her only a little, he said in his customary growl, "My arm doesn't hurt and I'm not too tired. Quit fussing over me, woman." Then he gave her a Snidely Whiplash smile, all the while quivering inside with a giddiness that was more like Little Nell. "Have to say, though, I rather like the notion of you seducing me. What did you have in mind?"

"Well, for starters—" and he could feel her body trembling, too "—I thought we could share the shower. Save hot water—"

"Overkill," he rasped. And her laughter sang across his lips and danced on his tongue.

He tasted rain and orange blossoms. She smelled of hot cinnamon and brown earth. Her warm body was the Sunday-morning kitchens of his childhood, and the ache inside him the wistful yearnings he remembered from back then, hearing his parents laughing and whispering together behind the closed door of their bedroom. Longing overtook him, so intense he felt a chill of panic, like a gusty little wind through his soul.

He withdrew from her mouth again and stared down into her face, holding it between his two hands like a treasure he'd found, brushing his thumbs across the sprinkle of freckles on her cheeks. Her eyes gazed back at him, shimmering with a soft golden light. "So, seduce me," he said in a ragged, breaking whisper. "Give it your best shot."

The only reply she could manage was a tiny whimpering laugh; her lips were hot and swollen, useless for forming words, though ideally suited, she supposed, for seduction. *Give it your best shot....* If only she knew what that might be! She wasn't a virgin—she'd ceased to be one much earlier and more foolishly than she'd intended, and hadn't *always* been Miss Goody Two-Shoes in the years since—but...*seduction?* In spite of the brashness of her opening gambit, she wasn't at all sure how she should proceed. Would it be better to take off his shirt first, she wondered, or her own?

His hands were on her neck, now, so warm and rough...callused and gentle. She wanted to lean and round herself into them, like a kitten; she could feel herself vibrating inside with a deep inner current, like purring. Her eyelids wanted to close.

"I'm not sure..." she licked her lips and felt his lips, his tongue...their moisture blend with hers "...what I should do."

"Silly girl...you don't have to do anything, don't you know that? Just *be*."

She looked at him then, really *looked* at him, her passion-fogged eyes struggling to focus on his familiar beard-stubbly face. And all at once, as if the fog had suddenly lifted, she felt as if she were seeing him for the first time. Oh yes, there was the openness and honesty she'd seen there before, the character and strength and compassion. But now, for the first time she saw loneliness and longing, and realized that they'd been there all the time. And something else, now, too, lurking like a wild thing behind the challenge in his eyes...a hunger so intense and so agonizing, her loving, giving soul cried out in instinctive rejection of it—though all she let him hear of that was a tiny sound that might easily have been mistaken for a laugh.

Confidence flooded her. Her heart felt certain and strong—in bewildering contradiction to the trembling weakness in other parts of her. "Take my shirt off," she ordered in a shaking whisper.

She heard a low growl of warning that seemed to come from deep inside his chest, and then his hands were on her shoulders, clutching, pulling...gathering the cold clinging material of her T-shirt and peeling it up and off her like an old skin. The growl deepened in intensity when she reached for him, meaning to return the favor, and he put his hands up like a barricade, holding hers at bay while he looked. Just...looked. Her heart flip-flopped. A great shiver tore through her.

Instantly, he reached for her, offering her his warmth, a sigh of compassion on his lips. But now it was she who held him off, with a scolding cluck and a murmured, "Uh-uh—*me*…"

Then she divested him of his shirt, though not nearly as quickly and cleanly as he had hers. Her fingers fumbled on the buttons, and she had to fight a childish urge to rip them apart. She was whimpering, barely realizing it, by the time she'd managed to pull the two halves of the shirt apart; her breathing ceased…her heart hammered as she pushed them back over his shoulders and down.

And just like that the game of seduction they'd been playing collapsed. A shudder rocked her. She gave a horrified cry and dropped the shirt to the floor. "Oh God—McCall, your arm," she cried as she reached instinctively toward the ugly, dark-crusted slash across the fleshy part of his shoulder. "Oh Lord—I forgot—we should have—here, let me—"

Again, the sound he made was much like a growl. "Sister," he warned, "don't you dare stop now."

His arms came around her, and she gasped when his cold skin met hers. He trapped her gasp with his mouth and gave it back to her, and then her hungry little cries and deep rasping breaths and thundering heartbeats were blending with his in a duet as old as passion and compelling as drums on a hot and sultry night. She no longer heard the rain…forgot she'd ever been chased through a jungle and shot at in a Mayan ruin. Forgot about the fact that there were men who wanted to kill her, and McCall, too. Only one thing mattered, and that was the man in her arms…and the fact that she was in his arms…and the fact that she loved him.

There was no more talking, no more playing at seduction; the rest of their clothing came off…somehow; neither of them remembered how, exactly, or cared. Then he was bearing her down onto a hasty tumble of bedclothes, and his careless and sensitive fingers were urging her body into quivering compliance, molding it to his wishes like a master sculptor. Sighing, she closed her eyes and let his touch paint her world with the colors of joy…primary colors…sunshine colors…like a child's box of crayons. Then, with the warmth and generosity of spirit that was her nature, she gave the joy back to him.

Poised on the brink of accepting what she so eagerly offered him, he pulled back, his weight braced on his arms. She gave a soft, inquiring cry; she could feel him trembling, all his muscles taut with self-control. And when he spoke, his voice was guttural with strain.

"It's Quinn," he said.

A smile broke like a sunrise across her face. "Quinn…" she softly sighed, and wrapped him in that warmth and brought him home.

Exhausted, McCall lay awake, listening to the rhythms of wind and rain and watching the ceiling fan stir sluggishly in the sultry air. Just below his chin and near enough to brush with his lips if he only tilted his head the slightest bit, Ellie's cinnamon head rose and fell gently, like a boat riding a swell.

He didn't wonder about the ache of sadness deep inside his own chest, just beneath that tender weight, when such a short time ago he'd known happiness more intense than anything he'd ever imagined. The course of his life so far had taught him that the flip side of such happiness could only be despair.

What had he been thinking of? How had he fallen so short of his own moral code? Not, "Live and let live," but the code that had dogged him so quietly and insistently all his life, in spite of all his efforts on certain occasions to drown its implacable voice. He'd never been one to act so precipitously, without considering the far-reaching consequences of his actions.

Very short-term, the woman sleeping in his arms was pleasure, the most incredible pleasure he'd ever known. Long-term, she was pain, pain such as he'd promised himself he'd never allow himself to know again. She was that ultimate cruelty—a glimpse of the heaven he couldn't have. He thought he knew, now, how Moses must have felt, gazing across at that Promised Land.

Short-term, she was sugar and spice, warmth and generosity and laughter and common sense—all the woman a man could ever dream of, wrapped up in one pert and sexy little package. Long-term…there was no way in hell she'd ever want to stay with him. No way in hell.

His heart gave a lurch as the tender weight on his chest lifted. He propped his head on his uninjured arm so he could meet the eyes that gazed sleepily at him, luminous in the lamplight and wondering as a baby's.

"Hi," he said, and waited for the miracle of her smile.

"Hi, yourself." Her voice was rusty with the after-effects of sex, stimulating recently awakened responses in him. Pain twisted in his belly as he watched the smile break across her face. It's beginning, he thought. Already.

"Quinn…" she said, testing its sound like a child learning a new word. *"Quinn."* She said it again, liking the crisp, clean sound of it. How like him it is, she thought. A little unusual, but simple…uncomplicated. Honest. She stretched to kiss him. "Nice to know you. Nice to know…who I'm kissing."

"You *don't* know me." His voice was harsh, and she froze in wary surprise, watching him. "You don't know anything about me, remember?"

She said nothing for several heartbeats, her gaze relentless, so searching, so intent he couldn't bear it, finally, and looked away. When he felt her small hands on his jaw, firmly pulling him back to her, his chest contracted with the pain of a strange guilty happiness.

"I know enough," she said softly...stubbornly. "I know everything I need to know."

Enough for what? he wanted to know. Enough for *this?* For a few hours of pleasure snatched from a nightmare day? For a few days or weeks out of the rest of his life? He was dismayed to discover that "this" wasn't enough for him anymore—if indeed it ever had been. That after tonight the "live and let live" *numero uno solamente* existance he'd nurtured and guarded so carefully for so many years wasn't ever going to be enough for him again.

He made a wordless sound of denial, of rejection, not of her but of the pain that overwhelmed him when he looked at her, trying to pull himself away, turn away from that piercing golden glare.

"You don't—" he began.

She stretched up and pressed her lips against his, stopping him there. *"I do,"* she insisted in her funny, raspy little growl. "I know who you *are,* Quinn McCall. I know *what* you are. It took me a while to realize it, I know, but I do. You're kind—" embarrassed, he made a sound of denial, which she silenced in her usual way "—and decent and honorable. *Honest.* And caring. You're brave and clever and resourceful..." She paused, finally, eyes glowing, her lips bringing her smile close enough for him to taste it. "And...you're one damn fine kisser, McCall."

He laughed with her, then, but reluctantly, opening the purse strings that held his happiness and letting a small measure trickle into his heart like a miser relinquishing his gold. Let *this* be enough, he thought, filling his arms and hands and senses with her, trying to drink in the very essence of her the way he once had the orange blossoms of his childhood.

Thinking that maybe, if he could somehow make her a part of himself, he wouldn't have to let her go.

Ellie dreamed that she and McCall were riding horseback on her parents' farm back in Iowa. She was riding Belle, her first gentle mare, and McCall was riding Rocky, Belle's far more rambunctious colt. They were happy, carefree, laughing like children as they galloped down the dirt lane between lush green fields, with the sunshine hot on their shoulders and a sweet summer wind lifting their hair and rustling through the leaves and stalks of corn.

Then suddenly, in her dream the world darkened. The wind turned fierce and gusty, and carried with it a strange, evil smell. Looking over her shoulder, Ellie saw the sky had turned that terrible color all midwesterners know and dread—the thick yellowish-purple of old bruises. The very air around her felt heavy and menacing.

"Tornado!" she screamed. She couldn't see it in the gathering darkness, but she could *feel* it, feel it like a massive and evil presence, coming deliberately and with purpose, straight for them. *"Run!"*

Then somehow the horses were gone and she and McCall were running, running hand-in-hand through the cornfields, chests straining and breath like fire in their lungs, afraid to look back, but knowing the tornado was there, coming after them, gaining on them, that strange, evil smell growing stronger and stronger, the aura of menace becoming thicker and heavier, suffocating her....

She woke up in cold vibrating terror. The strange evil smell was still with her, only now she knew what it was. *Cigars.* And she knew, too, that the menace was real, and that it was there in the room with her.

Chapter 13

"Do not move. Do not make a sound..." So close to Ellie's ear, General Reyes's whisper seemed tender, almost like a lover's. Which made his next words seem all the more obscene. "...if you do not wish to feel your lover's blood and brains splattered all over your pretty face."

She was lying on her stomach with the pillow bunched in her arms, and it was the general's weight that was bearing down on her. She could feel his knee pressing into the small of her back, his hand between her shoulder blades, compressing her chest so it was hard to breathe. Without moving her head, in the soft light of the lamp they'd left burning above the bed, she could see the blurred shape of McCall's head on the pillow beside her, and just beyond that the slender dark shape of a rifle barrel. She didn't have to look further to recognize the man who held it—the general's lieutenant, the smuggler they'd nicknamed Smoker—she couldn't recall his name. Behind him and toward the foot of the bed, a third form hovered, a faceless backup presence.

"Understand?" The pressure on her spine increased until she feared it would break.

"I...understand," she gasped. Her mind was racing at lightning speed. She stalled desperately for time, knowing she hadn't much. "I won't...make a sound. Please—I can't...breathe."

There was a soft chuckle. "I'm glad we understand each other." The weight on her back lifted, first from her shoulders, then her lower back. She felt rather than saw General Reyes straighten up beside the bed.

"Can I...turn over now?" She could hear McCall's breathing, raspy and strained. Please be still, she telegraphed silently, desperately. *Don't try anything!*

"Go ahead." The general took one step back. On the outer edges of her peripheral vision she could see him make an impatient motion with his hand. Was there a gun in it? She couldn't tell. *"Slowly."*

Slowly, Ellie raised herself up on her elbows, keeping her head bowed and one hand still hidden under the pillow. She coughed, hard and convulsively, to cover any movement when the searching hand found and closed around the hard, cold shape of the Beretta. She coughed again to cover the sounds she might have made when she thumbed the safety. She counted slowly to three, rehearsing the sequence of her next actions in her mind. Visualizing...preparing.

Then, in a single swift motion she rolled to her side, drew the pistol from under the pillow and fired.

The Smoker dropped backward without a sound; his rifle fell across McCall's chest. Ellie was dimly aware that McCall had snatched it up and was on his feet, swinging it by the barrel like a club at the other thug, but long before that she had already turned her own gun on the general. Still only half upright, braced on one elbow, she fired once. The general gave a terrible snarl, like a wounded tiger, and lunged. She fired again, just as he fell heavily across her, pinning her to the mattress. Helpless under the deadweight of his body, she could only listen to the sounds of desperate struggle. Grunts...scuffles...a sickening *thud*. And then silence.

It seemed an eternity—an eternity during which she dared not hope, or think, or feel—before she heard harsh and labored breathing. The suffocating weight on top of her was dragged roughly aside and McCall was staring down at her, teeth bared, his hair sticking out like a wild man's, eyes burning in his gaunt and ravaged face. She thought she'd never beheld a face so terrible before. Or so beautiful.

"Ellie—oh God, Ellie..." And now his face was a mask of sheer horror as his gaze swept down over her body.

She followed his gaze and found herself fighting an urge to throw up. She caught at his hand as he reached for her. "It's not mine. *It's not mine.* McCall—he didn't shoot me. I'm okay—I'm okay, I swear. But we have to get out of here. There might be more—McCall, do you hear me? *McCall?*"

He was staring at her, like a man frozen in mid-scream. She squeezed his hand, shook it urgently, and he finally gave himself a single violent shake and wheezed, "You're okay...you're not—"

"I'm fine. It's the general's blood." McCall heard her quivering voice as the roaring in his own ears faded away. He saw her throat convulse as she swallowed hard. "I sh-shot him. What about the other one? Is he d-dead?" She kept staring at him, as though she couldn't bring herself to look at the three men lying helter-skelter on the hotel-room floor. Reaction was setting in, he realized; in another minute she'd be shaking too hard to walk. And he didn't think he was in any shape to carry her.

"Don't know," McCall said. "And I don't think we ought to waste time finding out, do you?" He was pretty sure the guy he'd clobbered with the rifle butt was only out cold—no way of telling for how long. No way of telling how many more of the general's men might be waiting for them outside, either. Or who else might have heard the gunshots, and how long it would take for someone to decide to call the cops—or get brave enough and come to investigate themselves. "Like you said—we'd best get the hell out of here."

He was already pulling on his pants, barely aware of how cold and stiff and wet they were. He glanced at Ellie, who was still standing motionless, staring down at the general's body. He started to say something, then realized it was her clothes she was looking at, and that the general was sprawled on top of them. He tossed her his shirt. "Here—put this on. Forget the rest."

If we make it to the Volkswagen we'll be okay, he thought. It wasn't far to his friend's place. Al might be home by now, and if he wasn't, well…under the circumstances, McCall didn't think his old diving buddy would mind a little breaking and entering.

His shirt hit Ellie about mid-thigh. He watched her struggle with the buttons for a second or two, then abandon the job and just wrap the two halves of the shirt across herself, ignoring the blood that was smeared over the upper half of her body. He felt the tension in his chest ease a little bit when she did that; it had been a hard thing to look at, even knowing the blood wasn't hers.

"Let's go," she said breathlessly.

He nodded; the VW's keys were already in his hand. Flattening himself against the wall, he fingered the curtain back from the window and took a cautious peek. Tropical Storm Paulette had moved on; the darkness was thinning, leaving only the brightest stars to wink in and out among the remnants of storm clouds. He couldn't see anyone moving around in the courtyard, or hear any shouts or running footsteps. But when he stuck his head out the door he could hear hushed and excited voices farther down the way, and see the pale rectangles of opened doors.

"Coast is clear," he whispered. "For the moment. Hurry—"

"Wait—" One second she was there, pressed against his side, and the next she was gone.

"What the hell are you—" That was all he had time for before she was back.

"Couldn't very well leave without my chocolate," she said breathlessly, holding up the beach bag. "Or *this*," she added, as with the last word she jammed it onto her head—the hot-pink sun visor with the word *Acapulco* embroidered across the band in rainbow colors.

He rolled his eyes skyward as he caught a glimpse of her smile—or a feeble memory of it. Then they were running, splashing through puddles, running together through the gray dawn as the Day of the Dead awoke with slamming doors, and cautious whispers rose to shouts behind them.

"I just want to know one thing," McCall panted when they were in the car and he'd coaxed the VW's engine to grudging, wheezing life. Hunched over the wheel and still breathing hard, he tore his eyes from the alley's potholes and puddles long enough to throw her a look. "What in the hell have you got in that thing that's worth risking your life for?"

Ellie was concentrating on breaking apart the chocolate bar she'd just unwrapped. "Video camera," she said as he took the half she offered him. She paused to lick her fingers. "I've got it all on tape—the whole operation…the general's part in it." The look she gave him was bleak and frightened, and he knew suddenly that even though the blood on her body wasn't hers, she had wounds on her soul. "It's the only proof we've got that I didn't just kill a Mexican government official in cold blood. If we can just get it to someone…. Someone we can trust."

"I'll get you there," McCall said. It felt like a vow to him.

Fifteen minutes later he was wishing with all his heart that the video camera in Ellie's sun visor was still operational. He'd have given just about anything to have been able to record the look on his diving buddy Al Loman's face when he opened his front door, just as dawn was breaking in all its rosy tropical splendor, to find the two of them half-naked and bloody on his doorstep.

McCall was avoiding her. Ellie was certain of that, just as certain as she was that he'd deny it if she accused him of such a thing. And it was true that she had no proof at all, other than an uncharacteristic heaviness in her spirit…a deep and mystifying sense of loss.

It had been more than twenty-four hours since they'd arrived at the American consulate in Merida, late in the evening in the midst of the eerie and uniquely Mexican celebration of death known as *Dia de los Muertos*. Postponed by Tropical Storm Paulette, the annual festival had been in full swing, with church bells tolling, streets and shops decorated with papier-mâché skeletons and grinning skulls, and candlelight processions winding their way to local cemeteries for all-night vigils of respect and remembering. For some, the ancient ritual was a solemn occasion; for others—including most of the tourists—it was simply an excuse for a party.

It had seemed odd to Ellie—almost surreal—to be riding in a taxi through streets awash in a magnificent redgold sunset and filled with carefree people, all singing and dancing and calling out to one another and consuming enormous quantities of *pulque*. Death had come too close to her—not the papier-mâché make-believe kind, but the real thing. She could feel it still—warm blood no shower could ever wash away…cold terror and yawning black emptiness. She had shuddered and shuddered, gazing at the chanting celebrants and dancing skeletons through the windows of the taxi, and had longed for McCall to notice and put his arms around her and comfort her. But he'd been lost in his own reflections and hadn't seemed to notice, and for some reason she hadn't been able to bring herself to tell him how much she needed him.

It's been a long and stressful day, she'd thought. *We're both exhausted…probably a little in shock.* She realized now that his withdrawal from her had begun long before that, almost from the moment they'd arrived on his friend Al's doorstep, bloody and barely clothed.

Things had happened so fast after that. She and McCall had been whisked into showers and borrowed clothes and then off to the airstrip and onto a private plane for the long flight across the Yucatan to Merida. During all of that time they'd had no chance whatsoever to talk, no time to be alone together. McCall, of course, had been in constant and friendly company with his friend Al, leaving Ellie with plenty of time to reflect on the fact that she'd just shot two people.

The blur of activity had continued after their arrival at the consulate. There'd been a party in progress there, too, and the sudden appearance of two American citizens in desperate need of assistance hadn't exactly been a welcome interruption. Once Ellie's status and the full urgency of their situation had been made clear, she and McCall had been hustled up back stairways and installed in separate rooms and told to "get some rest," while an endless series of phone calls was begun and the machinery of government agency interaction set in motion.

Morning had brought the news that General Reyes wasn't dead after all. He and his two lieutenants were said to be in a local hospital, the two gunshot victims in critical condition, the third man suffering from a concussion. Ellie had mixed feelings about that. Based on the videotaped evidence she had provided, the three had been placed under arrest pending further investigation.

Ellie had spoken on the phone with her supervisor and with her partner Ken Burnside, still in Miami and recovering nicely from his emergency surgery. McCall had spoken with some acquaintances who would check in on Inky. They'd been questioned intensively, together and separately, by both American and Mexican government officials. Arrangements had been made to fetch Ellie's overnighter from the hotel at Lago Bacalar; there was no word, yet, as to whether it or the money she'd hidden in it had been recovered.

It was evening, now, and Ellie hadn't seen much of McCall since the midday meal, which had been served around two o'clock, according to Mexican custom. She found that she missed him with an intensity that astonished her. She felt depressed and restless, and filled with a strange, indefinable fear. She wanted desperately—needed—to be alone with him, to talk with him. She knew that something had happened to her in the course of the past few days, something that would change her and affect her life forever. Like a child waking up in strange surroundings, she needed to be held and soothed and told that everything was going to be all right.

But before she could allow herself to go in search of him, there was one more thing she had to do. She told herself she'd waited so long to call her parents because she wanted to be sure they were home, all the farm chores finished and both of them snug in the house. It could be cold in Iowa, this late in the fall. She wondered if they'd had snow.

She couldn't explain why her palms were slippery with sweat when she picked up the phone, or why her fingers shook when she dialed.

"Mom?"

"Ellie? My goodness…" Why did her mom always sound so surprised to hear her voice? "Wait—let me go get your dad…" and she could hear Lucy calling in the distance, "Mike! It's Ellie—pick up the cordless." A moment later, breathlessly, "Oh, honey, I'm so glad you called. How did—"

At the same time there was a click, and her father's calm voice. "Hi, Punkin, how's it going?"

"Hi, Dad. Everything's fine. I just—"

"That job you said you had to do—that all taken care of now? How'd it go?"

"Fine, Dad. Everything's…okay. Uh…Mom, Dad, there's kind of a lot that's been happening—I can't really talk about it right now, but I just wanted you to know I'm okay, and…I'll tell you all about it later, okay?"

"Ellie?" That was her mom, sharp and alarmed. And then her dad's voice, quietly breaking in, "By the way, how'd that new partner of yours work out? What'd you say his name was? McNeill…McMurphy…"

"McCall," Ellie said on an exhalation. "Quinn Mc-

Call. Yeah…that worked out after all. Much…better than I expected. Really well, in fact.'' She paused, not wanting to give away too much…and became aware of a strange breathless silence on the other end of the line. ''Uh…Mom? Dad? You still there?''

''Quinn McCall…you don't say,'' said her father. His voice was as calm and quiet as always, but she heard something else in it—an unmistakable note of excitement.

''That's right. Why? Dad, is something—''

''No, no—I used to know somebody named Quinn McCall, is all. Doubt if it's the same person, though. It was a good many years ago—seven or eight, at least. This partner of yours—can you tell us anything about him? Where he's from—''

''Oh, Mike,'' her mother broke in, exasperated, ''I'm sure it's not the same person. Wouldn't that be something—''

''I'm sure it's not,'' Ellie heard herself say. But her heart was suddenly beating fast and hard. *I don't know very much about him, actually. He could be anybody. Anybody at all.*

''Tell you what,'' said her dad, sounding *way* too casual. ''Uh, honey…is there somewhere I can send you a fax?''

Ten minutes later she was standing in the consular office, watching pieces of paper shiver one by one out of an antiquated fax machine. Her chest was beginning to ache from the bludgeoning it had been taking from her pounding heart. She drew a deep, shuddering breath as the machine's beep signaled the end of the transmission and the last page trembled into the basket. Her fingers shook as she reached to pick it up…blinked it into focus and began to read.

The breath she'd been holding whooshed from her

lungs in a single shocked gust. ''Oh…God,'' she whispered, ignoring the curious looks she was getting from the consulate's receptionist. She snatched up another page—then another, and another. ''Oh, God—Quinn…''

McCall had spent most of the evening in his consulate guest room, trying to decide what to do with the rest of his life. There were several good reasons why he didn't think it was going to be feasible for him to go back and pick up where he'd left off; the trouble was, he hadn't been able to figure out a good alternative.

That's what comes, he thought, of getting involved in other people's business. Twice in his life, now, he'd set foot on that slippery slope. And twice, now, it had cost him everything he'd worked for. Everything he'd held dear.

Funny, though, how different this felt from the last time. Before, he'd felt great loss, it was true, but he'd also felt angry…bitter…betrayed. He'd come down here to Mexico knowing in his heart he'd done the right thing, the only thing he could have done under the circumstances, and determined to cut himself off from the world that had rejected him for that. This time…this time he *still* knew he'd done the right thing, and the only thing he could have done under the circumstances, and once again it had cost him dearly. But now instead of bitterness and anger he just felt…empty. And sad. And awfully damn lonely.

Last night he'd tried to sleep—should have slept like the dead, exhausted as he was. But the big comfortable bed had felt cold to him. Every muscle in his body had ached to feel the warmth of one neat, tidy little body snugged up against his. All his senses were primed and alert, searching for the sweet orange-blossom scent of her…listening for her funny, scratchy voice…watching for the sunlight of her smile. He'd tried to make her part of himself, and he'd succeeded, it seemed. Too well. Now, how was he going to live with that for the rest of his life?

Of course, he'd thought about going to her, knowing it would be the selfish thing to do. Unforgiveably selfish. Then, tense and wakeful, he'd waited for her to come to him, half of him hoping she would, the other half terrified she would. He'd never be able to turn her away if she did, he knew that. And to stay with her any longer would only make the inevitable separation that much worse. He was already wondering how he was going to manage that, and trying his best to justify slipping away like a thief first thing in the morning, without saying goodbye... taking the coward's way out.

When the knock came that evening, he knew instantly who it was, even before he heard her soft and breathless, "McCall? Are you awake? It's Ellie."

He thought about not answering her...feigning sleep. And discovered that, when it came to his Cinnamon Girl, he had no willpower at all.

He went to the door and opened it, and then just stood and looked at her while his heart tried its best to leap out of his chest. She looked like a girl, fresh and clean as new grass in some sort of greenish-blue Oriental-style silky lounging outfit the consul's Chinese-American wife had lent her, and for a few treasured moments he feasted his hungry soul on the warm earth and sunshine colors of her. Then his eyes fell on the untidy sheaf of papers she held in her hands. His heart seemed to plummet through the floor of his chest and into his belly. The colors of his world turned gray.

"Aren't you going to invite me in?" she asked huskily.

He stood aside without a word, and she walked past him. He shut the door carefully, then turned to face her.

She didn't have it in her to be dramatic. She was simply…Ellie, straightforward and inexorable as rain, standing in the middle of his room with the papers in her hands, looking at him. Just…looking at him. Then at last, in a cracking voice, she said, "Why, McCall?"

He gave a deep sigh. Defeated and heavy, he nodded at the papers in her hands. "Your father's articles, I suppose. He did a whole series on me, back then. I gave Mike Lanagan the story because he was the only one I trusted to tell it right." He felt his face stretch unevenly with his smile. "Just thought you'd like to know that…."

She nodded, taking the compliment for granted, and then said it again, this time in a whisper. "Why, McCall? Why couldn't you just have told me?"

"That I'm the notorious whistle-blower, you mean? The man who single-handedly destroyed one of the oldest and largest auto makers in the world, sent the U.S. economy into a tailspin and put thousands of people out of work?" He spoke the exaggeration sardonically, and watched her eyes glaze suddenly with tears.

"But you were a *hero.*"

He gave a mild snort. "Not everybody saw it that way. I think it was Mike Wallace on *60 Minutes* who first called me 'The Most Hated Man in America.'"

"But thousands of people would have died if you hadn't done what you did!"

His smile was gentle as he shrugged. "Nevertheless. I broke the rules. Betrayed the code of honor. Became a snitch. Ratted on my bosses…my co-workers."

She held out the papers, and they rattled faintly in her shaking hands. "It says here you lost everything—your job…your home…your wife. I just find that…so hard to believe."

"Believe it," he said softly. "It happened."

"But why did you leave?" she cried. "It would have blown over—those things always do."

He made an angry gesture with his hand, then corraled it, pressing it between his injured arm and his tense and quaking body. "For the rest of the country maybe—not for me. Maybe I was a coward, I don't know. But I didn't want ever to go back—not to that life. Not to the business world. Not ever."

"I'd never ask you to—" Her voice broke. Then, for a long time there was silence, except for labored breathing and charging heartbeats.

McCall listened to the echoes of her words, considered all their possible implications, and finally said in a gentle voice he could barely hear above the rushing, pounding rhythms of his own pulse, "I don't think you know what you're saying."

"Don't patronize me," she snapped. Her chin jerked upward, and he felt a sudden guilty jolt of joy. "I may be small, but I'm not a child, McCall. And I meant what I said the other night—I know all I need to know about you. I didn't need these—" disdainfully, she hurled the sheets of paper from her, and they drifted across the floor like wind-blown leaves "—to tell me who you are. I already know what kind of man you are. I know—" She stopped, suddenly looking trapped and scared.

"What do you know?" He stepped closer to her, holding himself together with tightly folded arms.

"I—uh…" She closed her eyes, but even so he could see her woman's heart doing battle with her proud and competitive nature. "I know I…um."

"I don't have anything to offer you," he said quietly, taking pity on her. "You know, I'm basically a beach bum. I have a house and a kinkajou. I paint pictures for tourists…"

"What's that got to do with anything?" She was angry now, and her eyes were shooting out red-hot cinnamon sparks. "Who you *are's* got nothing to do with what you *do,* or how much you *have,* McCall, don't you know that? It's because of who you are that I..." And again she stopped, closing panic-stricken eyes.

He gave her a moment, then said gently, "One of us has to say it first—" just as she was finishing it in a sighing, "—love...you."

Her eyes popped open. She blinked and whispered, "You mean you—"

"Yeah," he breathed, trying hard to smile and getting cramps in his jaws instead. "Me, too. Actually, I think it must have been love at first sight. You know, there had to be some reason I kept feeling a need to save your—" She did have the most appealing way of shutting him up.

Sometime later, when he was able to think and breathe again, he mumbled into her soft, cinnamon hair, "I meant what I said, you know. I haven't got a thing—except my pride, and I've got way too much of that to let the woman I love support me. But I sure don't see myself going back to wearing a suit and tie, even if the suit-and-tie-world would have me back."

"I'd never want you to go back," Ellie declared, leaning back a little in order to look into his tired, honest eyes. "I meant that, too. As far as I'm concerned, you can go right on doing what you were doing before you met me— well, mostly..." She tried to tease him with a smile, but he was shaking his head. His eyes held a hint of sadness that tore at her heart.

"Don't think that's a good idea," he said wryly. "From what I've heard, in jail or not, seems like our old buddy the general still has some pretty powerful friends in this part of the world. Somehow, I don't think Mexico's going to be a very healthy place for me from now on.''

"So? There are lots of other beaches...." But an idea was forming in the outer reaches of her mind...just a disturbance at first, but rapidly taking shape and gathering strength, soon to become the unstoppable force of nature her family and close friends had sometimes referred to as Hurricane Ellie. "Don't worry about that—we'll think of something." Her lashes lowered as she uncurled her fingers and slowly spread them across the muscles of his chest. Her voice turned soft and sultry. "Meanwhile..."

To her utter delight, he was way ahead of her. "Meanwhile—" looking stern, he drew himself up and folded his arms across his chest "—you and I have some unfinished business, sister."

"Oh yeah? What's that?" But her heart was already beating hard and fast, and warmth was pooling low in her body. She felt soft and sweet and gooey, like melted chocolate.

"Weren't you supposed to be seducing me? Before you chickened out...Miss Goody—"

"Hey—who're you calling Goody Two-Shoes?"

Her fingers dealt swiftly with the buttons of his borrowed jeans; her hands slipped inside the waistband and deftly shucked them down. At the same time she leaned hard against him, pushing him back...then down onto the bed. A sweet, uniquely feminine triumph filled her when she heard him gasp. And then, for quite a while, no one said anything. At least, not in words.

Until sometime later, when Ellie lifted her head and purred, "Now then...tell me the truth, McCall. Would Goody Two-Shoes do *that*?"

Epilogue

"A toast—to the newest undercover operative of the USFWS!"

Ellie lifted her bottle of *pulque*. With a lazy smile, her husband did the same. There was a tiny *clink* as the two bottles met, then a soft chuckle and a sigh. For a moment they were both silent, watching the sunlight play on the waters of the Gulf of Mexico, reveling in the feel of a warm autumn breeze.

Then McCall said, "And here's to our first assignment together. I can't believe they've agreed to let us be partners."

"Well," said Ellie a trifle smugly, "I do have a few connections, you know. One, anyway." She took a satisfying sip of *pulque*—she really had developed a taste for the stuff. "I must say, it was nice of Uncle Rhett to pull strings for us—especially considering he's only got a couple more months to be President of the United States." She gave a little shiver of anticipation. "I can't wait to get this new operation started. Malaysia—wow. I've always wanted to go to Malaysia. I can't wait to go after this ring—imagine killing Sumatran tigers, one of the most endangered animals on the planet—and selling the body parts for medicine!''

"Could be dangerous," McCall said, carefully not looking at her. He knew he was going to have to keep a lid on his protective instincts where she was concerned, to some extent, anyway. But he was learning to trust the instincts and resourcefulness of his Cinnamon Girl.

"Hey—" Ellie said, jumping to her feet and reaching for his hand, "I've got a surprise for you—well, for us, actually. Sort of a combination graduation and anniversary present. Close your eyes. And *no peeking*...

"...there, now. What do you think?"

McCall opened his eyes cautiously, one at a time. "A hammock," he said woodenly, after a moment or two of futilely hoping he was seeing things.

"Straight from the Yucatan," she said gleefully. "I had the consul's wife get it for me in Merida. Isn't it great?"

"Yeah, great," muttered McCall. "Reminds me of a giant spiderweb."

"I know you said you don't care for hammocks," his wife said, giving him a sideways look he'd come to respect—for its sheer stubbornness, if nothing else. Then her voice dropped to a new register, one that never failed to start his pulse hammering and make his blood heat up and all his objections melt away. "But I think that's just because you didn't have the *right* hammock."

"I see," he said huskily. "And what makes this one the *right* hammock, if I may ask?"

"It's got me," she said sweetly.

He snorted, knowing full well the effect his scepticism

always had on her contrary spirit. ''Big deal. You can't make love in a hammock.''

''Wanna bet? Come 'ere, Mr. Two-Shoes, and let me show you how it's done....''

He watched the smile he'd been waiting for break like a sunrise across her face. And taking a long deep breath, he drank in pure happiness...and the sweet scent of orange blossoms.

* * * * *

Feel like a star with Silhouette.

We will fly you and a guest to New York City for an exciting weekend stay at a glamorous 5-star hotel. Experience a refreshing day at one of New York's trendiest spas and have your photo taken by a professional. Plus, receive $1,000 U.S. spending money!

Flowers...long walks...dinner for two... how does Silhouette Books make romance come alive for you?

Send us a script, with 500 words or less, along with visuals (only drawings, magazine cutouts or photographs or combination thereof). Show us how Silhouette Makes Your Love Come Alive. Be creative and have fun. No purchase necessary. All entries must be clearly marked with your name, address and telephone number. All entries will become property of Silhouette and are not returnable. **Contest closes September 28, 2001.**

Please send your entry to: **Silhouette Makes You a Star!**

In U.S.A.
P.O. Box 9069
Buffalo, NY, 14269-9069

In Canada
P.O. Box 637
Fort Erie, ON, L2A 5X3

Look for contest details on the next page, by visiting www.eHarlequin.com or request a copy by sending a self-addressed envelope to the applicable address above. Contest open to Canadian and U.S. residents who are 18 or over. Void where prohibited.

Where love comes alive™

Our lucky winner's photo will appear in a Silhouette ad. Join the fun!

SRMYAS1

HARLEQUIN "SILHOUETTE MAKES YOU A STAR!" CONTEST 1308
OFFICIAL RULES
NO PURCHASE NECESSARY TO ENTER

1. To enter, follow directions published in the offer to which you are responding. Contest begins June 1, 2001, and ends on September 28, 2001. Entries must be postmarked by September 28, 2001, and received by October 5, 2001. Enter by hand-printing (or typing) on an 8 ½" x 11" piece of paper your name, address (including zip code), contest number/name and attaching a script containing 500 words or less, along with drawings, photographs or magazine cutouts, or combinations thereof (i.e., collage) on no larger than 9" x 12" piece of paper, describing how the Silhouette books make romance come alive for you. Mail via first-class mail to: Harlequin "Silhouette Makes You a Star!" Contest 1308, (in the U.S.) P.O. Box 9069, Buffalo, NY 14269-9069, (in Canada) P.O. Box 637, Fort Erie, Ontario, Canada L2A 5X3. Limit one entry per person, household or organization.

2. Contests will be judged by a panel of members of the Harlequin editorial, marketing and public relations staff. Fifty percent of criteria will be judged against script and fifty percent will be judged against drawing, photographs and/or magazine cutouts. Judging criteria will be based on the following:

   - Sincerity—25%
   - Originality and Creativity—50%
   - Emotionally Compelling—25%

   In the event of a tie, duplicate prizes will be awarded. Decisions of the judges are final.

3. All entries become the property of Torstar Corp. and may be used for future promotional purposes. Entries will not be returned. No responsibility is assumed for lost, late, illegible, incomplete, inaccurate, nondelivered or misdirected mail.

4. Contest open only to residents of the U.S. (except Puerto Rico) and Canada who are 18 years of age or older, and is void wherever prohibited by law; all applicable laws and regulations apply. Any litigation within the Province of Quebec respecting the conduct or organization of a publicity contest may be submitted to the Régie des alcools, des courses et des jeux for a ruling. Any litigation respecting the awarding of a prize may be submitted to the Régie des alcools, des courses et des jeux only for the purpose of helping the parties reach a settlement. Employees and immediate family members of Torstar Corp. and D. L. Blair, Inc., their affiliates, subsidiaries and all other agencies, entities and persons connected with the use, marketing or conduct of this contest are not eligible to enter. Taxes on prizes are the sole responsibility of the winner. Acceptance of any prize offered constitutes permission to use winner's name, photograph or other likeness for the purposes of advertising, trade and promotion on behalf of Torstar Corp., its affiliates and subsidiaries without further compensation to the winner, unless prohibited by law.

5. Winner will be determined no later than November 30, 2001, and will be notified by mail. Winner will be required to sign and return an Affidavit of Eligibility/Release of Liability/Publicity Release form within 15 days after winner notification. Noncompliance within that time period may result in disqualification and an alternative winner may be selected. All travelers must execute a Release of Liability prior to ticketing and must possess required travel documents (e.g., passport, photo ID) where applicable. Trip must be booked by December 31, 2001, and completed within one year of notification. No substitution of prize permitted by winner. Torstar Corp. and D. L. Blair, Inc., their parents, affiliates and subsidiaries are not responsible for errors in printing of contest, entries and/or game pieces. In the event of printing or other errors that may result in unintended prize values or duplication of prizes, all affected game pieces or entries shall be null and void. **Purchase or acceptance of a product offer does not improve your chances of winning.**

6. Prizes: (1) Grand Prize—A 2-night/3-day trip for two (2) to New York City, including round-trip coach air transportation nearest winner's home and hotel accommodations (double occupancy) at The Plaza Hotel, a glamorous afternoon makeover at a trendy New York spa, $1,000 in U.S. spending money and an opportunity to have a professional photo taken and appear in a Silhouette advertisement (approximate retail value: $7,000). (10) Ten Runner-Up Prizes of gift packages (retail value $50 ea.). Prizes consist of only those items listed as part of the prize. Limit one prize per person. Prize is valued in U.S. currency.

7. For the name of the winner (available after December 31, 2001) send a self-addressed, stamped envelope to: Harlequin "Silhouette Makes You a Star!" Contest 1197 Winners, P.O. Box 4200 Blair, NE 68009-4200 or you may access the www.eHarlequin.com Web site through February 28, 2002.

Contest sponsored by Torstar Corp., P.O Box 9042, Buffalo, NY 14269-9042.

SRMYAS2